ESCAPING THE DUKE

The Secret Crusaders, Book 1

Melanie Rose Clarke

Dragonblade Publishing, Inc. is an imprint of Kathryn Le Veque Novels, Inc.
P.O. Box 7968
La Verne CA 91750
ceo@dragonbladepublishing.com

Produced in the United States of America

First Edition June 2021
Mass Market Paperback Edition

ARE YOU SIGNED UP FOR DRAGONBLADE'S BLOG?

You'll get the latest news and information on exclusive giveaways, exclusive excerpts, coming releases, sales, free books, cover reveals and more.

Check out our complete list of authors, too!

No spam, no junk. That's a promise!

Sign Up Here

www.dragonbladepublishing.com

Dearest Reader;

Thank you for your support of a small press. At Dragonblade Publishing, we strive to bring you the highest quality Historical Romance from the some of the best authors in the business. Without your support, there is no 'us', so we sincerely hope you adore these stories and find some new favorite authors along the way.

Happy Reading!

CEO, Dragonblade Publishing

Additional Dragonblade books by Author Melanie Rose Clarke

The Secret Crusaders Series
Escaping the Duke (Book 1)
Captured by the Earl (Book 2)
The Untamed Duke (Book 3)

For Mom, Dad and Erika. Thank you for always believing in my dreams. I love you with all my heart.

PROLOGUE

1804

IT STARTED WITH a creak.

Low and brittle, like a thin branch breaking under her favorite garden bluebird. In the next moment, the carriage dipped, gently pressing her into the plush seat.

Then… the world plunged.

Priscilla slammed her eyes as the carriage pitched forward, thrusting her toward the inescapable hardness of the wooden wall. She braced for an impact that never came, as someone grabbed her, pulling her back against a softness she knew so well. Warmth and security blanketed her, even as the carriage tipped this way and that, straightening only to tilt once more. Yet no more fear surfaced. Grandmother would never let anything harm her.

Of course the world knew this, for just then

the carriage skidded to a halt, still erect if at a jaunty angle. A moment later, the door jerked open.

A blast of icy air blew into the carriage, swirling crystal snowflakes on its tendrils. A form loomed against a backdrop of shadows and danger. "Are you all right, Lady Susan, Lady Priscilla?"

Priscilla relaxed at the coachman's steady, if rushed, voice. Her grandmother gripped her, her usually merry blue eyes hard with concern. They softened only slightly as Priscilla returned the calm gaze. "Are you all right, child?"

Priscilla lifted her chin and said in a voice that wavered very little, "I am well."

A ghost of a smile graced her grandmother's lips before she returned her attention to the warmly garbed coachman. "And you, Dobbs?"

The coachman nodded, then glanced outside. Under the moon's dim light, his frozen breath swirled into tiny puffs. "One of the wheels shattered. Unfortunately, the carriage with your daughter and husband is far in the distance, and I doubt they realize we are no longer following. I know someone nearby who can replace it. Would you like to stay here, while I hurry to his home?"

Stay here? Priscilla just managed to hold in a gasp. Out the door, fluffs of white rode the blustery wind, a concoction of light against dark. There was little to see in the late night, yet what was visible gave little doubt as to the fortunes of the residents: broken down hobbles, garbage strewn about the streets, buildings a hearty breeze away from collapse. A group of children in ragged clothing peered from a windowless hole in a barely standing shack.

Something cold and sour settled in her stomach.

"Thank you, Dobbs." Her grandmother nodded. "Be careful."

"Of course." He nodded respectfully, then backed away, firmly closing the door behind him.

"Do not worry, my dear. He'll be back soon."

Priscilla sat up straight. "I'm not scared," she said in a voice that made her sound at least nine.

"Of course not." Her grandmother's lips quirked up. "It seems frightening, yet they are simply poor. I have visited here before."

Priscilla widened her eyes. "You have?" Her mother would never dare venture into such a world.

"I have friends of many circumstances." The older lady smiled. "Poor, rich, servants, lords, we are all people. Do not ever forget that, child."

Priscilla nodded, then jumped as the carriage shook in the wind, as the howling outside increased. Suddenly the door opened. Frozen air snapped at her, and she scooted back in fear of the monster who must surely be there. Yet only the frigid outside greeted her.

Her grandmother reached for the handle. "Do not worry, child. It was probably damaged in the–"

She stopped.

Peered outside, looked around.

Priscilla slowly moved forward. "Is all well?"

"I hear something," her grandmother murmured.

Priscilla listened closer, yet heard nothing save the trees blowing in the wind, the ramshackle buildings shuddering against the onslaught. The streets were deserted, no foolish soul willing to face nature's wrath. "I only hear the wind."

Her grandmother's gaze darted into the street, back to her, and then set. "I cannot leave you alone. Come along."

"We're going out there?" Priscilla rushed out in a hushed breath, even as she took her grandmother's proffered hand. "Surely it is dangerous."

"And well it is, for all creatures. Yet we haven't a choice." Her grandmother removed a shawl from her shoulders and placed it around Priscilla. "No one should be out in this."

Pricilla shivered at the nonsensical answer, sucking in a breath of cold as she stomped through the thick gray powder. Could one freeze from the inside out? If so, then how would–

A sudden cry pierced the silence. Was it some sort of animal? Her grandmother hastened her stride, still firmly holding her hand as she raced along a hedge of low bushes, covered in trash. As the cry came again, she moved almost frantically. Then, she froze. And Priscilla gasped.

The bundle was so tiny. Barely the length of Daddy's hand, and not much thicker. At first it seemed like a simple brown cloth, yet it was moving, squirming.

Her grandmother reached down, and slowly, carefully picked up the bundle. She swept aside the coarse fabric.

A scrunched up little face and a pink bow mouth. A tiny curl of hair and the most pathetic cry Priscilla had ever heard.

A baby.

"But how? Wh–" The words caught in Priscilla's throat. "No," she whispered.

"Come, dear. We must hurry." With a sturdy hand holding the baby to her chest, her grandmother stomped through the snow, in the direction *away* from the carriage.

The wind picked up, sending snowy pellets into her eyes, yet they continued on. Her grandmother clutched the baby closer. "We're almost there."

"Where are we going?" The wind swallowed Pricilla's words, yet it didn't matter as her grandmother released her to knock on the door of a wide two-floor building. It was plain and badly needed paint, yet further from collapse than most of its neighbors.

The door opened, sending a sliver of yellow candlelight into the night. A thin woman in a gray dress peered out, then opened it wider. A hushed voice betrayed clear surprise, "Lady Martha?"

"I'm sorry to bother you so late, Mrs. Henley." Her grandmother moved forward, bringing the baby into the warmth. "Our carriage broke down, and I found something in the bushes. I was hoping you may be able to help."

The young woman peered closer, then gasped, a hand to her lips, as she stared at the tiny bundle. "Alone?"

Her grandmother nodded solemnly. "I must have found her within minutes, though she is frightfully cold. I know you normally only take children with mothers, but I cannot bear to leave her at an orphanage and–"

"It's all right." Mrs. Henley reached out and carefully took the child. The baby cried, yet her voice was so weak. The woman held her close, gently shushing her. As the baby quieted, the woman called to someone behind her. "Elizabeth, fetch some warm blankets." She turned back. "I will ask around, of course. Make certain there was no mistake, no one missing her. I will also ask the authorities."

"And if no one should come forward?"

The woman gazed down at the baby, her expression softening. "I believe we have enough room for one more."

Priscilla released a breath of icy air. She stood taller, trying to see the little bundle.

"Thank you," her grandmother said quietly. "I will send extra this week."

The woman peered at her for a moment, then nodded.

Another gust of wind iced the world, and for just a moment, the two women stared at each other as if sharing some sort of secret communication. In the next moment, her grandmother stood taller and backed away. "I will leave you to warm the baby, and I will do the same for my granddaughter. Be well."

Her grandmother turned briskly around and took Priscilla's hand once more. Priscilla tried to get one last look, but the door closed with a soft click.

"We must return to the carriage."

They strode quickly as the snow started to thicken. Yet even the cold couldn't intrude on the thoughts tangled in Priscilla's mind. She squeezed her grandmother's hand. "Will she be all right?"

Her grandmother looked down, and her expression relaxed ever-so-slightly. "I believe so."

Priscilla breathed out.

"Do you realize what we did today?" her grandmother asked.

Biting her lip, she shook her head. Her grandmother smiled. "We saved a life today."

Saved a life?

Her grandmother stopped, bent down. Her eyes sparkled in the moonlight. "Some people will say you can't do amazing things, Priscilla, just because you are a female. Do not ever believe them. You can do whatever you wish to do. You *can* save the world."

Wonder bloomed in Priscilla, bright, beautiful and perfect, and she smiled so wide, her cheeks hurt. Yet she couldn't stop herself, not at the feeling that was better than a hundred of cook's tarts. A moment of absolute perfection in a world of darkness, changing someone's life. It was the best feeling in the world.

She never wanted it to end.

CHAPTER ONE

1817

Dear Lord P,

As usual, your tip was impeccable. I cannot fathom how you knew Lord Hamsford would be amenable to changing his vote when he had been so steadfast in his denials, but your suggestion of showing Lady Hamsford the factories worked perfectly. Within the hour, she convinced him to change his mind. Now he is fully supportive of our measure regarding worker conditions. Though you have denied my request already, I ask again for you to emerge from the shadows, for what we can accomplish will be even greater.

Yours,
Bradenton

"IT IS SO refreshing to see a lady who knows her

place."

Do not pick up the nearest vase.

"Serious matters are simply too much for gently-bred women."

Do not clobber him over the head with said vase.

"Leave the important decisions to men, who are far better equipped to handle such matters."

Do not start looking for another vase with which to clobber.

As if granted by the heavens above, the song ended, saving Lady Priscilla Livingston from the idiotic ramblings of the exalted earl and her hostess from the loss of a dozen priceless vases.

Only years of practice gave her the ability to maintain a serene expression. "Thank you for the dance, my lord. Your wisdom is always so…"

Preposterous. Absurd. So ridiculous a potted plant could best you in a game of wits.

"Enlightening," she choked out. "And now there is my next dance partner, right behind the potted plant. I'm afraid I must dash."

She turned before he had a chance to respond, a tad sharply yet not rude enough to blatantly insult. He was off the suitor list and onto the newly-created "I'm not nearly that desperate" list. Likely it would amass many, many suitors before the season's end.

She adjusted her ivory dress. The silky gown floated around her, an ethereal masterpiece glittering with delicate beadwork and intricate lace. Matching jewels sparkled upon the complicated creation of curls into which her maid had pulled, yanked and otherwise punished her hair. She felt confident, able to conduct both of her tasks:

Finding an appropriate suitor and…

Investigating.

She walked to the refreshment table and took a drink, sipping quietly as she observed the guests. They laughed and danced and mingled, reveling in frivolity. For them, life held no meaning beyond such trivialities. For others…

"You're being hunted."

Priscilla jumped at the whisper in her ear. She turned, relaxed at the sight of Lady Hannah Breckenridge. "May I ask who is hunting me?"

Hannah's gaze remained serious. She grasped Pricilla's arm and led her to a nearby corner, which afforded a slight measure of privacy. "I'm not joking," she hissed.

The inklings of unease churned in her stomach, yet Priscilla showed none of it. "I am certain you are mistaken. For what purpose would someone hunt me?"

"Someone has decided you would make a most eligible bride."

Priscilla released a breath, stood taller. "I am the daughter of a duke, with a handsome dowry, a good family and quite proper behavior." She smiled, lowered her voice. "The last may not be entirely true. I've had offers, but my father will not force me to–"

"It's Bradenton."

Priscilla froze. Tightened. Imagined the man who always got what he wanted.

An invisible cage rose on all sides.

"That's right," Hannah whispered. "The most powerful lord in the *ton* is interested in you."

"Impossible," Priscilla claimed, even as icy unease traced her spine. *Keep control. Breathe.* "Bradenton is not looking for a wife."

Hannah shook her head. "I overheard his sisters."

"You must be mistaken."

"I am not. Do you know what will happen if he discovers your secrets?"

All too well. Her friend had no idea the extent of the secrets she kept. The sewing guild that had nothing to do with sewing. The secret quests she undertook. The cause for which she fought.

If the duke uncovered the truth…

"I'm sure I can stop it." *That was a lie.* "It will be easy to convince him." *That was another lie.*

"I hope you're right," Hannah breathed out. "Because if he finds out – our *purpose* – he could threaten everything."

"I won't let that happen," Priscilla promised.

"It may be too late."

Priscilla turned… and stared.

There was no exact word to describe the moment the Duke of Bradenton entered a room. A distinct murmuring arose, passed from lord to lady, servant to servant, matron to debutante. Conversations changed from rowdy banter to hushed whispers as all turned towards a single target.

With a massive body defined by muscle and strikingly handsome features of coal black hair and sapphire eyes, Bradenton commanded attention. He stood well above six feet, with a presence that far transcended his title, one of power, control and unforgiving dominance. He made men cower with a mere look, affected women far more. And her?

They meant far more to each other than he could ever imagine.

Bradenton garnered attention wherever he went. The matchmaking mamas ran to him, trailed by giggling wide-eyed debutantes. The dignified lords moved only slightly slower, nodding regally, even as they surrounded him. Young pups and ladies of all ages joined what rapidly became a crowd.

Acknowledging people with a subtle nod, he seemed to know everyone there, and everyone certainly wanted to know him. The group around him grew as people stood on the outskirts of the rapidly forming mass, watching him as if he was the sole performer on a theater stage. A powerful middle-aged duchess approached, cutting through the crowd with her two eligible daughters. She stopped directly in front of Bradenton, pulling her daughters on either side.

Priscilla was too far to hear the words exchanged, yet a ripple came through the crowd. Bradenton reached out…

And signed a dance card.

Then another.

And another.

She froze.

The duke was indeed searching for a wife.

Something flashed through her, an emotion she couldn't even name, before she forced it aside. It was inconsequential if Bradenton was looking for a bride. No doubt he'd control every aspect of the wife he would legally own, not allowing her to interfere with his activities or manage her own.

It wouldn't change their relationship.

She needed to turn away before someone noticed her perusal. Of course that wasn't a substantial concern when half the ladies were watching him, and the other half endeavoring to throw their dance cards at him. Yet through it all, she stood frozen. Her heart skipped a beat, then thumped, as she sucked in a breath. The once cool room seemed hot as the summer sun. Then… he looked up.

Their eyes locked.

The musicians finished the song, and suddenly the moment was broken. She heaved in a breath of air fragrant with dozens of cloying perfumes, from people in excited conversations about the duke. She swallowed the feeling of suffocation, glanced back to where he was holding court.

Only he wasn't there.

She turned around. Taller than most, he wasn't hard to spot. He was no longer stationary, but moving straight towards her!

By instinct she took a step, yet a second later, she forced herself to stop. She would not let him chase her down like some small animal. She looked straight at him, raised an eyebrow and turned her head away.

It was a clear dismissal. She never would've dared from close up, not when it would have left tongues wagging all over London. But they were far enough no one but the two of them would notice.

She dared a look back. His eyes were narrowed, his gait slower. Yet even as he stopped, he looked no less determined. He turned.

Then pivoted directly towards her mother.

Priscilla silently recited every oath a lady should never know. Then did so again as Bradenton engaged her mother in conversation, as her mother's already ruddy cheeks turned even pinker with delight. Bradenton gestured towards her as her mother nodded eagerly.

This. Was. Not. Good.

Then suddenly they were in motion, walking towards her once more. Priscilla glanced around, searching for a means of escape. She was not running, merely making a strategic exit. It was crazy, of course, hiding from the most eligible lord in the *ton*, but Bradenton was everything she couldn't have in a match. Powerful. Authoritative. Domineering.

Her greatest secret.

She edged closer to a potted plant, a clearly useless exercise. Bradenton's tall stride ate up the ground, as he greeted but did not stop for the many people approaching him. Her mother's eager gait made up the distance her much shorter legs lost.

Then he was right in front of her.

A broad chest. Muscular arms. A tall, powerful body.

Perhaps if she had a conversation with his chest, there would be less chance of him reading the truth in his eyes.

"Priscilla, look up," her mother hissed, her tone a dizzying concoction of excitement, elation and exasperation. "You remember Bradenton."

She was being ridiculous. He couldn't possibly know the truth.

"It is a pleasure to see you again," he spoke, when it became clear she would not.

"The pleasure is mine, Your Grace."

"Is it?" He said it low enough to be out of earshot of her mother, who had edged back to provide them with a measure of intimacy. His lips quirked up at the sides.

Her mother, clearly sensing that things were not progressing as she'd hoped – since they were not yet betrothed, wedded and expecting her first grandchild – skirted forward. "The duke told me some exciting news. He is hunting for a duchess."

Priscilla cringed. Only her mother, a duchess herself, could speak so unsubtly without reproof. She forced a smile to her face. "I wish you success, Your Grace. I suspect it will not be a difficult endeavor."

"You flatter me." His voice was as smooth as finely aged wine. "And exaggerate."

They both knew she didn't. He had his choice of ladies, some of whom made an art out swooning into his arms. Forty-three had already done so this season.

Not that she noticed.

"Your mother said you are enjoying your season."

"Of course." It was far easier to investigate the lords who voted against her causes, gathering information that would change lives. Yet he mustn't know that. Every moment in his presence brought danger, only what would discourage him? Perhaps, she could be a little too excited. "I just love the season! Who wouldn't enjoy all the shopping? I always say, you never can have too many gowns. I'd spend all day at the modiste if I could. Oh wait, I do." She giggled merrily, looking at him from under hooded eyelids.

Her mother gave her the same look as when she'd been caught with fourteen of Cook's tarts hidden in her dress.

"Is that so?" he drawled.

She hesitated, then nodded.

"You are far from alone in that passion," he said graciously. "My sister regales me daily with tales of the latest fashions from Paris. Tell me, what is your favorite new style?"

New style? Despite her words, she spent as little time at the modiste as possible, usually only going when her mother commanded, begged or bribed (usually all three). She had no idea of the styles, old, new or otherwise.

But she had to say something. Her mind raced. "Sleeves!"

Um, what did she just say?

His lips twitched. "Sleeves?"

"Yes, exactly. The new sleeves are very fashionable. And the skirts. You know I wouldn't be surprised if hoop skirts came back."

The duchess choked. "My daughter is very accomplished," she blurted out. "She excels in all the skills of a lady. She is talented with a needle, speaks three languages and sings beautifully. Of course, she reads and writes and does math well enough to take charge of any size household."

Her mother was listing her attributes like a horse for sale. Soon she might gush about her straight teeth and invite the duke to take a look.

This had to end. Being in his presence usurped her discretion, and she couldn't risk slipping. "I have the skills of the average lady."

He cocked his head to the side. "There seems to be far more to you than you admit," he murmured.

Her face heated.

"What are you hiding?"

She bit back a gasp. "Hiding? What do you mean?"

"Don't play coy."

Did he know?

They stared at each other for a minute. "I assume you are an excellent dancer as well," he prodded.

She breathed out in pure relief.

"I would be honored if you would grace me with a dance."

Relief died.

Yet for just a moment, something akin to excitement flashed through her. She forced it aside. She was not some naïve girl just out of the schoolroom. She knew the consequences of giving herself to a man like Bradenton.

"What a gracious honor, Your Grace. How I wish I could say yes, but all my dances are taken."

Instead of disappointment, challenge lit his eyes. Focused. Unrelenting. Unstoppable.

"You appear to have several spots remaining." He pointed to her card, which was hanging at an angle to reveal empty lines.

"I left those blank on purpose. I have something to do."

"I see. If you don't mind my asking, what do you have planned?"

Investigating. "I get a little tired after dancing and need a rest." She batted her eyelashes. "Besides shopping, resting is my favorite thing to do."

The duke's eyes lit again. The schemes that worked so well with other men had little effect on the clever lord.

"That something you have to do is dance with the duke who was gracious enough to ask." Her mother snatched the card off her wrist, her lips stretched in a smile so wide, it looked as if her face might crack. She handed the card to the duke. "Take as many dances as you would like, Your Grace."

Priscilla fought not to grab the card back. Of course as a gentleman, he would just hand it back to her–

He scribbled his name across two lines.

Her mother's smile became twice as wide

and a thousand times more genuine. She clapped her hands.

Priscilla counted to ten. *One vase, two vases, three vases, four–* "You signed two."

He shrugged. "It gives us longer to converse. But don't worry, you still have plenty of time to rest. And perhaps you will even find the opportunity to shop."

Why, that sneaky– "But Your Grace, if we dance twice in a row, people may get the wrong idea."

Really?" He leaned closer. "And what idea might that be?"

Her heart slammed against her ribs. The scent of musk and oakmoss surrounded her.

"I don't see any problem at all!" her mother chirped, her eyes dancing with delight. "Priscilla is very pleased to enjoy your company. Aren't you, dear?"

Priscilla clenched her teeth. "Of course."

She hadn't a choice. She couldn't outright insult the duke. At least two dances would give her enough time to convince him to discontinue his pursuit.

She wouldn't think about the consequences if she couldn't.

"I look forward to it."

By now, several people had approached, more eager mamas with more eligible ladies. Bradenton nodded at Priscilla, "Until our dance."

With one last nod, he bid her goodbye.

He was stealing two dances, but she would not allow him to sabotage her investigation. Lord Roxbury, the ball's host, always voted against measures that aided the lower classes, convinced others to do the same. If she could find something that would change his mind, it might just be worth scandal. The risk to her person?

Still worth it.

But now Bradenton scheduled two dances in the span she'd allotted for sleuthing. Was there enough time before then? She couldn't be late, because he may start searching for her if she didn't show. Yet if she hurried…

She turned around. Roxbury was standing in a corner, arguing with his wife. Lady Roxbury's face flushed with anger, and with an angry gesture, she stomped off.

Priscilla stood up straighter.

Her last success with changing votes had been through a lady. With all their talk about how ladies were not their intellectual equals, men were often easily swayed by them. Perhaps if she could talk to Lady Roxbury, she might be able to convince her to influence her husband.

She took a deep breath. Her chance was now. With one last quick glance around the ballroom, she turned towards the door.

Time for Lord P to do some investigating.

CHAPTER TWO

Dear Your Grace,

Congratulations on yet another success. Respectfully, I must decline your request to share my identity. For reasons I cannot divulge, it is best I remain in the shadows. And if you are keeping count, you have in-quired 1,842,843 times.

I do wish to thank you for your earlier recommendation on visiting the new exhibit at the museum. It was as fascinating as you said it would be.

Yours,
Lord P

WHERE WAS SHE going?

Edmund narrowed his eyes as Lady Priscilla slunk from the ballroom, in the opposite direction of any room opened to guests. Her movements were casual, yet measured. Was she meeting someone?

The thought brought an unexpected surge of displeasure. She was on his list of potential duchesses, and her mysterious behavior during their brief interaction made him want to discover more. It would not do for her to find someone else before he had a chance to explore the possibilities. By her surreptitious movements, she wanted to be unnoticed. He stood up straighter…

And followed.

It took but a minute to realize she was following someone herself, trailing a person too far in the distance for him to recognize. His curiosity grew as they travelled through a cavernous hallway lit by few candles, creeping down the darkened interior, slipping past doors, descending deeper into the private areas of the home. Finally, she turned…

And slipped outside.

He frowned as he strode forward. Whomever she was chasing, she entered danger, for any woman alone could be subject to scandal, or worse, an event unsavory enough to cause it. He pushed the wide door open, wincing as it creaked. He hoped to wield an element of surprise, yet it didn't truly matter.

He wouldn't allow her to escape.

He entered a lush, emerald world lit by a brilliant full moon and twinkling lanterns. Lord Roxbury liked to spend money, and it showed in a garden rife with exotic plants. A thousand scents surrounded him, from roses, gardenias and an array of colorful flora. Rumors were Roxbury had a whole collection of towering statues, most depicting nude subjects, but none were visible here.

Lady Priscilla was nowhere to be seen.

But she was here. Hushed breathing broke the silence, low, shallow and fast. Had she heard him, realized she was being followed? He crept through towering vines and around hedges, following the sound of the breathing.

Her form became visible through a green screen of leaves. Victory surged as he blocked the exit to her hiding place, cutting off any and all escape.

"You've been captured."

A gasp sounded.

He walked around the wall of green. Lady Priscilla was folded against the leaves, her chest rising and falling, a look of almost panic on her face. Then she saw him, and clear relief transformed her expression.

"Were you expecting someone else?"

She tensed again.

Her discomfort bothered him, yet he wouldn't show it. He had to impart the danger of her ill-begotten wandering and ensure she never did it again. "What are you doing out here by yourself?"

Her eyes darted to the shrubs on either side of her. Was she looking for whomever she had followed? She notched up her chin. "I have an explanation."

His admiration for her rose, yet he kept his voice serious, firm. "I should hope so. Do you have any idea of the danger you are in? Lord Roxbury is not one to trifle with. If he caught you, he'd–" He stopped abruptly, his jaw tightening. "Let's just say it is fortunate I found you first. Why were you hiding from me?"

"I wasn't hiding."

"You were pressed against the hedge," he pointed out. "Hiding."

"No." She shook her head. "I was simply… relaxing."

He just managed to thwart the smile. It was an unusual feeling. "Relaxing?"

"That's right."

"Try again." He stood up taller, gave her the look that he usually reserved for political opponents.

"It's true." She nodded. "But obviously this was a mistake. I never meant to come here."

"Where did you intend to go?"

"I– I got lost on my way to the ladies' retiring room!"

He gave her an incredulous look. "You mistook the gardens for the ladies' retiring room?" He gestured to her hiding spot. "Was the entrance to the cloakroom behind that hedge?"

She blushed. "Of course not." She edged forward, accidentally brushed against him.

Attraction surged within him.

She felt it, too, as fire blazed in her emerald eyes. For one brief instant, the urge to push forward surged, but she was an innocent, and he was a gentleman. So he steeled himself and remained where he was. She tried to move forward again.

Again he stayed still.

As a gentleman, he should have moved aside and allowed her to leave. Yet she was clearly hiding something, and the thought of it involving danger compelled him to learn more.

She clenched her fists. "Obviously I did not believe this was the ladies' retiring room. I must have missed it in the hallway, and I thought the gardens would provide a quicker path back."

She was lying. Even if he didn't know she'd been following someone, it was obvious. Her expression was convincing, yet returning through the hallways would clearly have been the swiftest way back. "Then why did you enter the maze?"

"This is a maze?" She blinked. "I mean, of course it is." She smiled. "I thought it might be interesting. I enjoy gardens."

"Truly?" He folded his arms across his chest. "What do you like best about them?"

This time she had a reply ready. "The statues,

of course."

He raised an eyebrow. "You know about Roxbury's statues?"

"Of course." She looked around, stopped and pointed to a statue peeking through the leaves. "I particularly enjoyed that one. It was so realistic. I could just spend hours looking at every detail."

"Really?" If it was the type of statue Roxbury had, Edmund very much doubted she was telling the truth. He walked back to the edge of the hedges until the statue came into view, with her following close behind.

He froze.

And she whispered, "Oh, bollocks."

Literally.

It was a statue of the human form, only with the head and most of the limbs missing. What mainly remained was the torso and... what she said.

Their gazes met.

She opened her mouth.

Nothing came out.

His lips twitched.

"I think..." She took a step back.

"Your Grace..." She took another step.

"That it is quite..." She fluttered her eyelashes up and down.

"Something."

He coughed.

She squeezed her eyes shut. Opened them,

and rushed out, "Thank you for your concern. I better go!"

She took a step.

He matched it.

She moved to the side.

He blocked her.

"What are you doing?" she hissed.

"Discovering what you're doing." He straightened to his full height. The difference in their sizes was considerable, yet she held her petite form with strength. "We need to talk."

"We don't need to talk," she ground out. "I'm sorry for inconveniencing you, but I would like very much to leave right now. Please move aside."

He moved forward into the intoxicating scent of gardenias. "As a gentleman, I am required to help all ladies in need. If you are having a problem, I would like to help you."

"I appreciate the chivalry," she said tightly. "But it is completely unnecessary. As you can see, I was alone and not in any peril."

"I am more interested in your purpose." He edged closer, flexing his muscles. "Why are you really here, Lady Priscilla? Were you meeting someone?"

"Absolutely not!" Her vehemence took him by surprise. It seemed the obvious motivation since she had followed an unknown figure, yet she'd reacted quickly, and genuinely. For now, he would not reveal what he knew.

"I was hiding because I figured you were Roxbury and didn't want him getting the wrong idea. I was going to hide until he left."

That did make sense and explained the relief in her eyes. Roxbury was a brute, who would have no qualms about taking advantage of a vulnerable lady. The thought of him touching her sparked something inside him. "I may not know the truth – yet – but you were neither lost nor resting. No matter the reason, you will not do it again. You do not know Roxbury like I do. Do not wander again on his estate, or anyone else's."

She straightened, pure feminine power. "You're the one stopping me from returning to the party. For the final time, let me pass." She took a step forward. If he didn't retreat, she would crash directly into him.

"I will discover the truth."

She stopped, looked at him sharply. He allowed triumph to color his gaze. She had all but confirmed his suspicions.

"The only truth is I am leaving. Good–"

"Agnes, where are you?" A booming voice carried across the gardens. "Agnes!"

Edmund recognized the low and gravelly voice at once, and judging by Priscilla's response, so did she.

"Agnes!" The voice came once more, louder, closer.

"It's Roxbury," he whispered.

"He can't catch us here!" she hissed.

"On this, we agree."

If they were found together, scandal would occur. Then the inevitable:

Betrothal.

"We need to hide!" Her voice was low, yet frantic, and shattered any thought she had arranged any sort of entrapment.

He looked around, yet there was nowhere to go. Roxbury would see them if they tried to leave. Even if he revealed himself, the lord may still discover Priscilla. He would not take that chance.

He immediately took control, gently but firmly propelling her against the wall of leaves as far from the entrance as possible. He moved next to her, inadvertently brushing against her.

He could not miss her harsh intake of breath.

Roxbury stomped through the ground, louder, louder, louder. He was almost upon them…

"What are you doing out here?" Lady Roxbury's shrill voice pierced the air. "You should be at the party."

"I can't be at the party without you," Lord Roxbury growled. "Everyone will notice you missing. What should I tell them?"

"Tell them you had the audacity to invite your mistress to your ball!"

"I told you I didn't invite her. She just

showed up!"

"Do you think that makes it better?" she huffed. "I'm staying out here until the party is over."

The footsteps sounded again. They were coming closer!

He should have been furious, when after years of matchmaking attempts, he was inches away from the parson's noose. Yet the pungent suffocation of entrapment was shockingly absent. Moments from a forced betrothal, he was uncharacteristically calm, satisfied even.

Of course, it was simply because Priscilla was on his list, so he already knew she would make a perfectly suitable duchess.

And if it felt like something more, he would ignore it.

Flushed, visibly frightened, she clearly felt different. Yet she was fighting fate with weapons she didn't possess. If they were caught, she would not have a choice for her future. If they were not caught…

She may still not have a choice.

Priscilla paled. She spoke lowly, so only he would hear. "Do not announce a betrothal! We'll explain instead."

He stared at her. "You can't be serious."

"We'll tell them I got lost on the way to the retiring room, and you found me!"

He showed her the full force of his disapproval. "Do you think I'm the sort of man who would allow a lady to face ruin alone?"

Angry voices sounded again, closer this time.

Priscilla's breaths came quickly, shallow. "But you haven't compromised me. We haven't done anything wrong."

Edmund shook his head. "They're not going to believe that any more than they'll believe I just stumbled upon you."

She gaped at him. "You were following me?"

"I noticed you leaving the ball and wondered where you were going. If they discover us, they'll immediately assume we snuck off together. The outcome will be set."

"But nothing happened." She wrung her hands. "Once you claim we're together, there will be no turning back. Somehow I'll find a way to avoid ruination and betrothal. Let me handle it. Everything will be fine."

"It will be fine because I will control the situation."

"I will not be forced into a match when we didn't do anything!"

And he would not allow her to accept ruination alone.

She opened her mouth, yet no words emerged. Then it was too late.

The bottom of Lady Roxbury's dress became visible at the end of the green corridor. Priscilla gave a sharp intake of breath, thankfully at the same time Lord Roxbury spoke. Her chest rose and fell far too rapidly.

If she didn't calm down, she would give them away. Moving on instinct, he pulled her near, capturing her tight against him.

He leaned down to whisper in her ear. "All will be well. No matter what, I will take care of you."

Her eyes widened. If the Roxburys caught them, it wouldn't matter whether they were touching or not, the end would be the same.

The dress remained visible, but the Roxburys didn't move closer as they argued.

"That's it," Lady Roxbury screeched. "You go back to the party. I'll be looking at your disgusting statues!"

She started to move into the opening…

"Wait!" Lord Roxbury growled. "What about that ruby necklace you were eyeing at the jeweler?"

For a moment there was silence. "The one with all the diamonds?"

Lord Roxbury groaned. "Yes, the one with all the diamonds. Would that placate you enough to return to the party?"

Lady Roxbury sniffed. Yet a moment later, the edge of her dress disappeared from view. "Fine. But get rid of the whore."

"Do not worry. I will make sure she never bothers anyone again."

Edmund looked at Lady Priscilla. She looked sickened.

"Now let's get back. My friends must be frantic with worry over my absence."

Heavy footsteps reverberated through the air, then the door back to the home creaked open. A second later, it slammed shut.

An instant from ruin, they had been spared.

"We're safe." Priscilla whispered.

He said nothing. She didn't realize she wasn't quite safe from him.

"They didn't discover us, but we'll be missed if we don't return to the ball as soon as possible," he pointed out.

"Of course."

He gently grasped her arm as he brought her out of the hiding spot. She stared at him warily, yet a spark of defiance lit those beautiful eyes. The duke's daughter had far more fire than she let on.

He couldn't wait to uncover what else she hid.

"Are you all right?"

She smoothed down her dress, stood taller. "Yes, thank you."

He waited for more, but she stayed silent. If she wasn't going to mention the incident, neither would he, yet he would not forget about it. Just like he hadn't forgotten the mystery of her wanderings.

Despite her denials, the only logical explanation was she was meeting someone. But whom? A suitor? Annoyance raced through his blood. "Do you realize how dangerous it is to sneak off to meet a man?"

Her eyes flashed. "I told you before – I was not here to meet a man."

True, yet there was no other logical explanation.

"Suitors can be persuasive, yet hidden agendas often lurk beneath innocent facades. If another man had been here, the outcome might have been very different."

Likely the suitor had hoped to be discovered.

Priscilla looked like she had sucked on a lemon. It was strangely endearing. "You could not possibly be more wrong. As I said before, I thought–"

"This was the way to the ladies' retiring room." He leaned in. "We both know you are far smarter than that, Lady Priscilla."

She narrowed her eyes before straightening. "While I appreciate your discretion today, you have no right to dictate my actions. I am not one of your subjects. I will do as I wish with whomever I choose. Now I must return to the party."

"What do you think your father would say if he learned of this?"

She blanched. "You wouldn't."

"I take my role as a duke very seriously. If a lady is putting herself in danger, I have no choice but to take action."

"How dare you! After all the times we've–" She stopped abruptly.

He opened his mouth to retort, stopped. She no longer appeared angry – she seemed positively panicked. Her words indicated some sort of shared experience, *experiences*, yet except for the occasional greeting, they'd barely spoken a word. "After all the times we've…" he prompted.

She smiled. "You're right, Your Grace. I shouldn't have strayed so far from the party. I promise to be more careful next time. Now I really must get back. You don't want someone finding us here, of course."

He should've agreed immediately, yet instead he merely raised an eyebrow.

She licked plump lips. "Yes, well, let's just forget this ever happened, shall we? I am going to leave now. If you could wait a few moments before following, I would be eternally grateful."

He hesitated, but then gave a curt nod. He would not find answers now. But he would find them.

With one last look, she turned, then started to walk away. Yet he didn't miss the tint of regret as she glanced around the garden. His suspicion returned full force. Priscilla Livingston was definitely hiding something.

He wouldn't stop until he discovered what it was.

COULD THAT HAVE possibly gone worse?

Perhaps, if while they were in the maze, her parents had arrived.

Or the patronesses of Almack's.

Or her parents, the patronesses of Almack's and every single member of the *ton*.

Bradenton was suspicious. It was obvious by the distrust in his eyes, the questions she could not answer. Yet there was more to it than that. By the way he looked at her, he may indeed be interested in her, as Hannah had warned.

With the truth between them, any such notion was an impossibility.

The true problem was she could not get herself to dislike Bradenton. She couldn't even be apathetic to him. He was intelligent, kind and all things extraordinary. She admired him, for what he did for society, and for her.

For allowing her to change the world.

And now she not only changed the world, but helped others do so as well. Soon she would have to see him, but before she did, she had time for one last task. She walked to the corner, where a tall lady with green eyes, straight black hair and a light azure dress stood.

"Hello, Anne. It is a pleasure to see you

again."

Anne smiled. "A pleasure to see you as well, Priscilla."

"I have come to invite you to my group. Have you heard of the *Distinguished Ladies of Purpose?*"

Anne nodded, slight confusion tinting her features. "You're inviting me to your sewing guild?"

Priscilla did not blame the woman for her surprise. They were not much more than acquaintances, yet hopefully that would soon change. "You'd fit in perfectly."

Anne gave a slight cringe. "I appreciate it, but I'm afraid you are mistaken. I cannot sew very well."

"That's all right," Priscilla soothed. "Surely you have some experience. What was the last thing you sewed?"

Anne grimaced. "A donkey."

"How unusual." Priscilla smiled. "Yet donkeys are lovely subjects."

"It was supposed to be a likeness of my Aunt Agatha. Let's just say she was not pleased."

Priscilla bit back her laughter. Anne would do just fine in the Distinguished Ladies of Purpose. Of course, she already knew that from the research she conducted into all prospective members of the guild. "A sewing guild is the perfect place to hone your skills. Perhaps next time you can make Aunt Agatha look like a horse instead of a donkey."

The sides of Anne's lips twitched. She cocked her head to the side. "Is sewing the only purpose of your group?"

Not even a little.

"What else would we discuss?" Priscilla replied innocently. She looked around, ensured they were alone. "Certainly not anything unsuitable for ladies like social action or how to influence votes."

Anne's stared at her for a moment, as her lips stretched into a slow smile. "Perhaps I could stand to improve my sewing skills" she murmured.

"Excellent." Priscilla provided the information for their next meeting. "I look forward to seeing you there. You are welcome to share that you are attending my *sewing* guild."

"I can't wait."

Priscilla was smiling as she emerged from the corner, yet all good humor faded as she trudged to the dance floor. Images of Bradenton discovering the truth danced in her mind, set to the melody of her mother screeching in fury. Of course, he was the subject on everyone's lips.

A nasally voice next to her provided the evidence. "Isn't the Duke of Bradenton amazing?"

Priscilla kept walking. She would not say anything. Would not do anything. Would not betray they had any sort of connection.

The voice continued. "Soon he will be part of *my* family."

Well, she was simply not one to do nothing.

"What?" Priscilla's loud exclamation stopped the cacophony. She turned to Lady Lavinia, who made the comment that had every woman staring. The earl's wife possessed abundant money, substantial social influence and a striking deficit of kindness.

Priscilla kept her tone even. "I didn't know Bradenton was ready to make an offer."

Lavinia sighed loudly. "I just have a feeling. If only I weren't already married…"

Priscilla grimaced. Last season Lavinia had pursued the richest lord in the *ton*, despite his clear disinterest. They were caught together in a private room, prompting an immediate betrothal, and rumors swirled she had lured him there by unscrupulous means. Lavinia had a sister…

"Where is Lady Agatha?"

Lavinia gave an exaggerated shrug. "She's around here somewhere. I believe she was retrieving something that belonged to her."

Something that belonged to her? Something like Bradenton?

A thousand options swirled, without a single right one. How could she let the powerful man be caught by his own sense of justice? Yet if she intervened, everyone might notice. He certainly would. And if he did, what else might he notice about her?

But as before, inaction was simply never an option. She took a step back. "Excuse me, ladies, I just remembered somewhere I have to be." Without waiting for a response, she fled.

She threaded through the busy crowd, racing through ladies, lords and crisply attired servants. The home was substantial, with hallways upon hallways, each with numerous rooms. If Agatha was trying to entrap Bradenton, she would chose a location away from others, somewhere she could get him alone, but close enough they would be "discovered." Agatha's parents were probably in on the scheme. They had been the ones to find Lady Lavinia last season, with expressions far more resembling delight than dismay.

Priscilla searched room after room, with no success. Had she misunderstood Lady Lavinia's message? It seemed so obvious.

Suddenly Bradenton's unmistakable timbre rang through the hall. "Finally, we are alone."

She pivoted. All the nearby rooms were empty with their doors ajar, except one. She broke into a full out run, stopping short just as she reached the door. She flung it open. "Bradenton, you're about to be trapped into marriage!"

She froze, blinked.

Michael Colborne, the Duke of Crawford, and Philip Fitzgerald, the Earl of Peyton, gawked at her.

Crawford recovered first. He turned to Bradenton. "Say, good chap, I promise I have no intentions of trapping you into marriage."

"Neither have I." Peyton's expression remained utterly serious. "No offence intended, but we simply wouldn't match."

Bradenton simply stared.

"I… um… well… yes."

Bradenton's friends were trying not to laugh, yet he was staring at her like a specimen in a jar. Finally he spoke, "You were trying to save me?"

She swallowed. "Yes, well, obviously there's been a mistake. Crawford and Peyton aren't trying to trap you into marriage. Not that there's anything wrong if you were, well, you know." *What had she just said?* "I'm sure they would never resort to tricking you." *This was going from bad to worse.* "But obviously nothing is going on here except a normal, ordinary, perfectly fine discussion." *Clearly she had lost her mind.*

Peyton shook with silent laughter, while Crawford snorted a half/choke, half/laugh. And Bradenton? He never took his gaze off her.

She licked dry lips. "Well, obviously there is nothing going on, so I had better lea–"

"Wait."

The word was an order from a man accustomed to commanding others. He stalked towards her. "You thought someone was trying to trap me into marriage? Lady Agatha perhaps?"

Her gasp stole the chance to make a denial.

The other men moved away as Bradenton lowered his voice. "She did indeed try, yet I caught on to her scheme immediately. I have suffered enough attempts of entrapment to recognize the signs. Usually."

Heat crept up her neck. "Of course. I apologize. I heard something and…"

"Came to the rescue."

She cringed.

"I don't mean to embarrass you, Lady Priscilla. I am honored you would help me, especially since we barely know each other."

Actually…

He cocked his head to the side. "Perhaps that is something we should remedy."

"No!"

Bradenton's eyes narrowed, and she fought to keep her expression neutral. If he became suspicious, he may just investigate her. And if he looked in the right places, he may just discover the truth.

Definitely time to escape. She took a step back. "I meant to say it is unnecessary. I would have done the same for anyone. No one should be trapped into marriage."

He lifted an eyebrow. Said nothing.

"It was a pleasure to see you again." She turned and forced her legs forward. One foot after the next, not looking back, not even as she felt his eyes on her. Yet she could not ignore the clear consequences.

He would be watching her.

CHAPTER THREE

Dear Lord P,

I enjoyed your stories of childhood mischief. Although I never had such adventures, I have friends who partook in such foibles. I wonder if you are acquainted with any of them…

Your stories raised some concerns about your current strategies. While not aware of your exact methods, I can only assume you undertake some risk in your investigations. I urge you to take care. I do not need to warn you of the ruthlessness of many of our fellow "gentlemen." Do not allow the prize to blind you to the danger. If you are caught in a difficult position, come to me. I will do what I can to help.

Yours,
Bradenton

"THAT WAS UNUSUAL."

"Indeed," Edmund murmured. "A most unusual lady." He stared a moment more at the door through which the blond-haired, green-eyed beauty fled, turned to find his friends staring at *him*. "What is it?"

Crawford grinned. "Lady Priscilla was not the only one acting unusually. One might wonder if there is more afoot."

Usually when someone linked him with a lady, he immediately protested, yet no such urge hit.

Strange.

And especially vital, since tonight his search for a bride would commence. He had spent hours considering every eligible lady in the *ton* and finally secured a short list of half a dozen ladies. They were all of good position, poised and, most importantly, ladies he could imagine spending the rest of his life with.

Priscilla Livingston was on the top of that list.

Now she intrigued him even more. A woman who would risk her own reputation to save his. Who would burst into a room to stop a scandal. With anyone else he would assume she did it because she was interested in a match, yet her behavior afterwards indicated anything but. Yet now she didn't have a choice.

He would discover more about the woman who would save him.

For now, he had another mystery to unravel.

He had requested to talk to his friends about a far different matter: his suspicion one of them played the part of his informant.

He travelled to the sideboard and poured himself a generous splash of brandy. He swirled the amber liquid in the cut crystal glass. "I was actually wondering whether you had anything to tell me. Something about letters perhaps?"

Crawford cocked his head to the side, his lips quirked up, while Peyton watched with unsaid bemusement. "The Bradenton stare. I've seen grown men literally quake in their boots over it. Usually it's quite effective, but as we've known you since short pants, its efficacy is diminished. To what do we owe this pleasure?"

Crawford was right, in more than one way. He did tend to intimidate others. Yet Peyton, tall and dark with charm the ladies adored, and Crawford, whose angel-like face disguised a will of iron, held positions nearly as high as him.

Edmund stared at his friends a moment more, but nothing beyond patient amusement lurked behind their gazes. He pushed aside disappointment. It just seemed so logical.

"Then I suppose neither of you are my informant?"

"Your informant?" Peyton leaned forward. "This gets better and better. You have an informant?"

"Are you a spy?" Crawford cut in.

"Not at all." Although he had performed the occasional *favor* for the Home Office, it was certainly not enough to justify the moniker. Of course, that didn't mean he lived the wastrel life so many lords preferred, drinking and gambling and enjoying the pleasures their status afforded. He fought for justice every day, yet it was in the open, through life-changing votes and civil action. "Someone has been helping me secure votes for important causes."

"Helping?" Peyton's gaze sharpened. "In what way?"

"As in providing details that have altered the journey of several important votes."

Crawford frowned. "Nothing afoul of the law I assume."

"Of course not." Edmund shook his head. "I wouldn't risk the votes being retracted by utilizing less-than-scrupulous measures. No, my colleague discovers tidbits about various lords, details on how they may be susceptible to casting their votes in a more favorable way."

Peyton shrugged. "What's the problem? It sounds like a lucrative relationship."

Both Crawford and Peyton held sympathies towards Edmund's causes, helping when they could and casting their votes favorably.

"It is beneficial," Edmund agreed. "The problem is he hides his identity. We communicate through letters. With the amount of correspondence I receive, I've been unsuccessful in tracking them. He has me post my letters to a different person each time, but they never make it there. I assume someone who works with the mail diverts them for him."

"Why don't you just ask who he is?"

"I have, again and again, in subtle and not-so-subtle ways, and yet the answer remains the same, often with a bemused statement regarding the propensity of me asking." He grimaced, but couldn't stop a sliver of amusement. Even in the letters, his informant's clever wit shone.

Peyton gazed at him curiously. "So why bother? Why threaten your work by going against his wishes? He may have a good reason for the subterfuge."

"Or he may be in some sort of danger," Edmund countered. "Perhaps he's afraid to reveal his identity. Plus, with all we've accomplished anonymously, think of what we could do with our combined efforts."

"Perhaps. Or the relationship could be sabotaged, and you'd achieve nothing at all." Peyton cocked his head to the side. "Maybe the true reason for your curiosity is something else entirely. Are you frustrated because you do not control the situation?"

"That's ridiculous." Edmund straightened to his full six-foot-two height. "I have no desire to control him."

"Why not? You control everyone else."

Before Edmund could respond, Peyton held out his hand. "It's not an accusation. Holding a dukedom is a great responsibility, and you do it better than most. You're well aware of the power you wield."

Edmund relaxed slightly. As a duke, it was his responsibility to care for those around him. If he showed any weakness, others would take advantage.

Thus he never showed weakness.

"I do not wish for power over him," he said. "Merely to work with him."

Whether that was entirely true he would not ponder too deeply. Part of his quest for power was the ability to help people, even when they didn't realize they needed it. In addition to overseeing a dukedom, he was guardian to three younger sisters and several female cousins, a responsibility he took with utmost seriousness. Of course, he also made certain his mother had everything she needed.

Yet perhaps Peyton's words held a grain of truth. Did something else linger behind his desire to unmask his confidant? They had conversed for over a year, through dozens of letters, about matters far beyond politics. He considered the man a friend.

And if honesty ruled, perhaps he didn't like the loss of control.

"If I can help people, don't I have a responsibility to do so? By now he knows I would never betray his secret."

"Perhaps he doesn't want *you* to discover the truth." Crawford raised an eyebrow. "With your position, you know the vast majority of lords. Maybe your estimation of him in real life is different than in your correspondence."

"I considered, and discarded, that idea. From our long correspondence, I know more about Lord P than most of the *ton*. I simply can't imagine I misjudged his character so tremendously, especially when the man works so hard for social causes. It is all the more reason for us to meet in person. I want to know who I've been working with all this time."

Peyton studied him, his expression thoughtful. "I suppose I can aid you in your investigation, especially since this is the first time you've requested my help since an evil villain stole your favorite horse."

"I was four," Crawford protested, his sparkling eyes showing no remorse. "And the horse was wooden and three inches tall. But I suppose I owe you for that. Count me in to unmask your mysterious lord."

"Excellent." Edmund took another sip as he considered his two preys. One would be pleased to be caught – perhaps – the other most certainly not. Yet he would not stop until he had both of them.

Time for two hunts to begin.

Escaping a duke was an art.

One must be subtle, for anything blatant could cause scandal, retribution or both. One must show power, make clear she will do as she wishes when she wishes. When executed correctly, it was a beautiful thing.

Which was why Priscilla hid behind a huge potted plant when it was time for Bradenton's dance.

She hadn't planned it in advance. Yet as she walked toward the dance floor like a condemned man, she questioned why she was running to Bradenton simply because he decreed it. She'd made clear she hadn't wanted to dance with him, yet he took control. Why should she just blatantly give in to his demands?

From her vantage point behind emerald leaves, she could see him, yet he could not see her. Bradenton turned once and then twice, his expression remaining mild, not betraying any loss of control. Undoubtedly, the absence of a dance partner was a first for the popular lord. Then, his lips curved up ever-so-slightly.

He started to the potted plant.

Blasted! How had he seen her? No matter how, this was not good! Getting caught by a duke was far less enjoyable than escaping one. Perhaps she could thwart him yet.

She caught site of Viscount Dryson. The lord was rude, boorish and insufferable. He was also in the search for a wealthy wife to fund his gambling habit. If she chose him instead of Bradenton, it would send an inescapable message.

She walked as quickly as she could. Through the mirrors, she saw Bradenton following at a slower gait, his eyes narrowing as she stopped next to Dryson.

She sighed. "I do so enjoy this melody. How I wish I had someone to dance with."

Dryson looked up from the plate he had been piling with sweets. His face stretched in a greedy grin. "I shall be happy to dance with you, Lady Priscilla."

"Would you? Thank you."

With a lecherous wink, he dropped his plate right on top of the fresh food and led her out to the dance floor.

As she placed her hand in Dryson's, she peeked at Bradenton.

Power, and a promise for retribution, burned in his eyes.

"My dear, you are delightful. A true diamond of the first water. I do so admire you."

Priscilla turned her attention back Dryson. She should thank him, titter and bat her eyelashes.

Instead the question slipped out, "What do you admire about me?"

The lord stared.

It was not a polite question, and certainly not one a duke's daughter should be asking. Yet every suitor professed the same meaningless words on a quest to secure her wealth and familial connections. If all these men professed their undying devotion, surely they could name a single reason.

Unfortunately he stared at her like a suffocating fish.

Not much for one's confidence.

"You are lovely, of course," the lord hastened to reply. "And demure and proper and soft. And of course you have the utmost breeding, social standing and wealth."

So she was a wealthy, fluffy and popular bunny rabbit?

His eyes lit up as he mentioned her money. It was no surprise. Every time they met, he whispered sweet words of love to her dowry.

She snuck a look back at Bradenton. He raised an eyebrow.

And suddenly escape did not seem very certain at all.

HE DID NOT intervene when she danced with the insufferable Dryson. Nor when she danced with two ineligible lords clearly for his benefit. Likely she thought her little stunt would detract him.

Instead her efforts made him even more determined to learn more. She had piqued his interest, in more ways than one.

When she started walking toward a lord who was both charming and eligible, he stepped forward.

No longer would she avoid him. It was time for their dance, or rather, dances. When he signed the card, instincts had urged him to do something daring. He thought he'd regret signing up for two. He did not.

Now those instincts guided him as he approached her. She watched with wary eyes, her features undoubtedly more telling than she realized. Finding a bride had been a chore, a necessary evil of his position. For the first time, it induced a spark of excitement.

"Lady Priscilla, are you ready for our dance?"

She muttered something about a vase under her breath but it was too low to be certain. He hid his amusement as she gave an obviously strained smile. "Of course, Your Grace."

He took her arm. "You are aware you missed our dances?"

Amusement danced in her eyes. "You don't say?"

"Oh yes. A lesser man might have thought you were avoiding him."

"But of course a man like you is well aware of what it means."

"I assume it means you wanted three dances, and couldn't figure a way to ask."

She halted. "I assure you that is not what it meant."

If dancing twice sent a message, dancing three may as well count as a reading of the banns. He relented. "We will save three for another night."

She did not look relieved.

He had chosen a waltz, as he had seen her dancing one earlier, and wanted the opportunity to talk without interruption. He took her in his arms.

The music started. As expected, she swayed gracefully, never missing a step, yet something about her stance gave away tension she couldn't hide. He was accustomed to ladies being a little nervous around him, yet this was different. A softer man might have let her get away.

Not him.

In order to determine whether she would be a suitable bride, he had to uncover every layer behind his mysterious beauty.

"Do I make you uncomfortable?"

Her eyes flashed, even as she shook her head. "Of course not, Your Grace. I am at ease in every situation."

"Really?" They moved in perfect rhythm. "That sounds like a challenge."

Her eyes widened for the briefest of instances. "I can assure you it wasn't."

"Your mother tells me you will be accepting an offer this season."

"Isn't getting married the only suitable goal for a woman in my position?"

"Of course not."

She appeared startled, staring for a moment before responding, "I'm afraid you are alone in your beliefs."

"Not alone, but rare, I'll admit," he acknowledged. "Many think a match is a lady's primary role, but I see far more than that. For instance, when I take a bride I expect her to have her own pursuits."

Her expression remained neutral, yet somehow he could sense sadness in her. "Like sewing and music?"

"No."

She looked at him sharply.

"Well, yes," he amended, "if that is what the lady enjoys. However, I do not think a lady should be constrained to traditionally feminine pursuits."

She bit her bottom lip, her gaze softening.

He pressed on. "What do you truly like, Lady Priscilla? What interests you?"

"Nothing unusual," she quickly replied.

"Nothing?" he softly prodded. "No secret hobbies or undertakings?"

Unease once more passed through her eyes.

"I can tell there's something." He brought her closer. "You can tell me."

"I like…" She darted her eyes around as if searching for an answer. "I like… science!" Triumph, and relief, lit her expression. "That's the secret. I'm fascinated by the natural world. In fact, I can spend all day just learning about it."

"I find science fascinating as well. That wasn't too difficult, was it?"

Her smile faltered. Had she realized her quest of discouraging him was hopeless?

"I want a wife to do more than grace my side. I am looking for a partner."

For just a second, vulnerability passed through her eyes. "Your bride will be a fortunate woman." When he spun her, she attempted to pull back.

He tightened his grip.

Her gaze became steel. "Poetic words do not change the fact that a woman is at the whim of her husband. The law gives him the right to dictate what she can, and cannot, do. And there are many bad men out there, people who fight against your causes."

"My causes? What do you mean?"

A panicked look entered her eyes, reminiscent of the episode in the garden. She quickly continued, "Nothing of any importance. My father just mentioned you support humanitarian efforts."

He kept his expression neutral. She knew more about him than she admitted.

"Are you interested in the plight of the less fortunate?"

"Of course!" The response was swift, forceful and vehement. "As any lady would be."

That wasn't true. Most women, and men, cared little about the poor who suffered outside their golden homes. Was she worried about his reaction? For many men, interest in world affairs would be a negative aspect in a bride, but for him it was the opposite. Social action had been his passion ever since he was a child, when his father showed him the deplorable working conditions at the factories.

They had come from a *ton* party, filled with countless delights: showmen to induce belly-laughter, sweet ices from the ripest fruits, a gleaming ballroom alive with whimsical music. After an evening of careless frivolity, he clutched a sweet tart with one hand, his father with the other, as he left that world, to view an entirely new one.

In a nondescript carriage, they travelled from the glowing world of the ton to the darkest trenches of London's poor, where despite the late hour, the toilers' work continued. Men weathered into deep grooves worked next to children half his age, coated in dirt, their eyes as dull as the dust swirling around them.

Gray. He had come from a world of color, yet here life progressed only in shades of ash. The smells had been noxious, the odor burning his lungs, stinging his nostrils, its acidic taste on his tongue. The only music was the never-ending cadence of coughing, hacking rasps from beleaguered lungs. The world was dim, lit by tiny candles, so unlike the fat pillars gleaming from the *ton's* crystal chandeliers. On that day, a quest was born. One day, he would bring color to that gray world. Buying that factory and improving the worker's conditions was his first charitable project.

"I am pleased to hear it. Recognition is the first step to change."

She gave a curt nod, but didn't respond further.

"What is the main characteristic you desire in a suitor?"

The question was impertinent, but he simply couldn't help himself. She muttered something under her breath that almost sounded like "busy." In the next moment, she smiled widely, "Why, vast wealth, of course."

He couldn't stop a low chuckle, even as others turned their way. He didn't blame them. They must wonder what inspired a laugh from the duke. "I'm sorry, my dear, but something doesn't seem genuine about that."

"I care about a title, of course." She batted

her eyelashes.

His amusement flared. As an actress, she left something to be desired.

As a potential duchess, she was far more alluring.

"I won't ask if you're trying to scare me away."

She blinked. "Of course not, Your Grace."

"Instead I'm going to ask why you're trying to scare me away."

She stiffened. "I'm just being honest."

He leaned forward, whispered so only she could hear. "You haven't been honest since you claimed your dance card was full."

Her nostrils flared. First in discomfort, next in defiance. She *was* hiding something from him.

"You do realize this conversation is highly inappropriate."

"You do realize if we'd discussed the weather, we'd both be fast asleep by now."

The sides of her lips quirked up, replaced as quickly by another scowl. He enjoyed watching her try to hide from him. Soon, she would learn she couldn't.

"That's not true," she countered. "I can spend hours talking about the weather. In fact, after fashion and resting it is my favorite subject. Can I interest you in a two-hour discussion on weather patterns?"

The little minx was still trying to scare him. It

wouldn't work. "Of course. I would enjoy discussing anything with you. Tell me, what is your favorite type of cloud and why?"

She frowned before turning into a graceful swirl. Then she was back in his arms. And if he pulled her a little closer than he should have, she didn't complain.

"I'll be honest, Your Grace. While I am grateful for your attention, we simply would not match." They went through a few last motions as the waltz ended. "Thank you for the dance. If you wish to forgo the second, I understand."

"That will be unnecessary, Lady Priscilla. By now you have tried a variety of personas you believe I will find unappealing. Why don't you just ask what would turn me away?"

"It would help," she muttered.

He laughed lightly. There was something oddly familiar about her, an almost instinctual understanding. "I don't like ladies who are cruel or unkind. I would also prefer a bride with some intelligence, and a mind of her own."

She sniffed. "In that case, you should know I always do as others say, cannot count to twenty with my shoes on and kick dogs in my spare time."

He laughed again, once more drawing the attention of the room. The Duke of Bradenton never laughed like this.

It felt strange, different, *good*. "You do nothing of the sort. In fact, I'd wager you are quite the opposite of all those things."

"You flatter me, your Grace, but my intentions remain the same. We do not suit."

The words were set with steel and backed by courage. What was her game? If she hadn't wanted a match at all, her reluctance would have made sense. Yet if she had to choose a husband, either by her own desire, or most likely that of her parents, she should be pleased by his attention. As a duchess, she would have a title, wealth and power. Although those were probably not as important to her as she claimed.

The next song started, and they now danced without talking. He had learned more about Lady Priscilla, yet the mystery remained. One thing was certain: Despite her objections, they could very well match.

Finally, the song ended. He leaned in, staring straight into smoldering eyes. "Now I will make my intentions quite clear, my lady. I never back down from a challenge, especially when the stakes are so high." He took a bow, even as she stood speechless before him.

Soon he would discover every secret Priscilla Livingston possessed.

CHAPTER FOUR

Dear Your Grace,

I appreciate your concern for my well-being. Rest assured I take the utmost precautions. On my last investigation, I had an excellent plan in case trouble arose. Fortunately, I was able to extricate myself from the difficult situation, despite a large, oafish obstacle attempting to block my way. I am confident in my ability to best such hindrances. Too much is at stake for any other outcome.

Yours,
Lord P

"LADIES, I AM pleased to report the vote on factory working conditions was an unmitigated success. Thanks to your tireless work, thousands of children will see their situations improve. It was extremely close, and your efforts made the difference."

Light clapping filled the room, a modest response representing but a small portion of the true joy the news elicited. Eyes sparkling with tears betrayed sheer delight and pure relief, emotions kept closely guarded, the undeniable result of years of training.

"Our *Greatest Admirer* was also most helpful. The anonymous letter we received came just at the right time, with information that led to the favorable alteration of two votes."

More clapping sounded. Ironically, she engaged in not one but two conversations with anonymous writers. With Edmund, she was the enlightened one. Of course, he believed he was corresponding with a man, because the protective duke would never "allow" a woman to do something so dangerous as investigate. With the letters from her Greatest Admirer, she remained in the dark. The letters arrived at random times, with insightful knowledge regarding her current investigations. Perhaps it was someone she knew, someone right before her eyes, just like Bradenton.

Perhaps it was fate's way of getting even.

The letters had started not long after she started writing to Edmund. They were clearly written by a lady, and always signed Your Greatest Admirer. The print was generic and flawless, likely a deliberate attempt to hide the handwriting, something she wish she had considered when she started her correspondence with Edmund. They usually held several bits of valuable information, which she then passed along to Edmund with the fruits of her own investigations. They also conveyed some sort of advice, random and yet ironically pertinent to her chaotic life. Unlike with Edmund, she had no way to respond.

She turned her attention back to the crowd of kindred spirits. Adorned in pale dresses representing the latest fashions, the women looked like typical ladies of the *ton*: coiffed, primped and impeccably perfect. Yet underneath the glittering facade, they were a unique breed, a group of women with hearts to match their dowries, intelligence to complement their ladylike mannerisms. They had each been personally invited after displaying a generous nature so rarely seen in society. The world did not know the true intent of the Distinguished Ladies of Purpose: social action.

Now they sat in the gilded drawing room of the Sherring townhouse, surrounded by gaudy wine carpets, carved mahogany furniture and priceless paintings. Large windows showcased meticulously manicured gardens, while a crackling fire burned bright in a massive white marble fireplace.

"And of course your mysterious lord was quite influential." The clapping turned to giggles, as Eliza Sherman spoke her mind in a not-so-hushed whisper.

Priscilla pursed her lips at the mention of Bradenton. Only she knew the identity of her colleague. "My contact was useful, as always. He is an ally to us all."

"I have more news." Priscilla hesitated. The next announcement would be far less celebrated than the first. "I'm afraid the time has come." She breathed deeply. "I must succumb to my fate."

The mood in the room transformed from joyous celebration to the severity of a window's weeds in a moment. All mirth vanished, as to a woman they guessed the announcement's true meaning.

Eliza clutched her tight curls. "You can't m-mean..."

"Marriage."

Or more accurately, the practice of giving ludicrous sums of money to men so they could take ownership of a woman. "I'm afraid so."

"But I thought you weren't going to marry." Hannah looked at her in shock, no doubt remembering their conversation at the ball. "You said it would interfere with your work."

"I thought so as well," her other best friend, Emma Sinclair, said in a soft voice. The rest of the ladies chorused the sentiment.

Priscilla inclined her head, portraying calmness through the frustration and anger. "Like most women in our position, I have to wed. At least I have my choice of suitors."

"Will you disband the group when you take a husband?"

"Of course not." Clutching her skirt, Priscilla pushed back fears she would be forced to do exactly that. "I have no intention of abandoning the cause. I will simply find a husband who will allow me to continue my work."

"Have you considered your mysterious benefactor?" Eliza blurted out, her voice devoid of the earlier humor. The others nodded.

Her response was immediate. "He is not an option."

Yet it was another half-truth. For one senseless moment, she considered what her life could be like, *would* be like, if Bradenton offered. He was everything she claimed she didn't want in a man, and something about him called to her. Although they had never spent any time together before the Roxbury ball, he knew more about her than the men who'd professed their undying love. Of course, he still had no idea who she truly was.

She stood up taller, steeled herself. Too many people depended on her for impossible yearnings. "He's not suitable."

"Too old?" one woman guessed.

"Too ugly?" suggested another.

"Too cruel?" a third tried.

"Something like that." She forced a smile.

"Don't worry, ladies. I made a list of very suitable gentlemen. They are mild-mannered, accommodating and, most importantly, too busy with their own pursuits to bother with mine. Like me, they are only marrying out of necessity. After the obligatory celebrations, I expect life to continue like before."

Most of the women nodded in relief, but Hannah and Emma frowned. They knew it wasn't as simple as she proclaimed. It never was when a woman gave up the privilege of controlling her own life.

"We'll hold our next social action – I mean Distinguished Ladies of Purpose meeting – in two weeks. Until then, contact me if anything urgent arises."

The women nodded as they rose, gathering long forgotten embroidery. Most didn't sew during the meetings, instead bringing something for appearances' sake. As the daughter of a duke, Priscilla was skilled at the fabric arts, as well as singing, running a household and all the activities expected of women. She'd much rather conduct an investigation.

The women bid farewell with far more emotion than usual, gifting her with watery smiles and commiserating hugs. Hannah and Emma stayed behind while the others departed to their own matchmaking mamas.

When it was just the three of them, Hannah

grasped her shoulders. "I'm so sorry."

Priscilla breathed deeply. It was time to stop acting the swooning schoolgirl. She needed to be strong for the people who needed her. "Don't worry. With my plan, nothing will change. I have more than a dozen men on my list, many of whom have already shown interest."

"Tell us the truth." Emma gazed straight at her. "Was this your decision?"

She pursed her lips. "My father suggested I find a match and I agreed."

Only "suggested" wasn't the word he used, and "agreed" wasn't her response. George Livingston, the Duke of Sherring, had ordered it, under the threat of usurping her choice if she didn't accept one of the many offers already arriving, despite the current season's youth. She loved her father dearly, and he loved her, and likely considered this his duty. Still, she never thought she would walk the short journey that would change the path of a lifetime.

"As a woman, nothing really is our choice."

Her friends looked at her with pity.

"But there's hope. I may have to get married, but at least I have my choice of suitors. I have a plan. Instead of the most powerful, handsome or wealthy suitor, I have one requirement: He has to be busy."

Emma cocked her head to the side. "Busy?"

Priscilla smiled. "Too busy to notice when I

investigate. Too busy to care."

Neither woman looked convinced. "Can we see the list?" Emma asked.

"Of course." Priscilla walked over to a small writing desk and slid out a hidden drawer. She removed a crisply folded paper and handed it to them.

Their frowns deepened as they read it.

"They're not so bad." Priscilla took the paper. "They're titled, wealthy and scandal-free. Best of all, each and every one is far too busy with his own life to interfere in mine."

"And I can't imagine you being happy with a single one." Hannah took the sheet back and pointed. "This one barely says a word, this one spends all day discussing his rock collection and this one talks to horses."

"Exactly." Priscilla clapped her hands. "They all have a focus, something that leaves little time for marriage. They'll accept a match for duty, with no real wish for actual wedlock. Of course, this is just a preliminary list. I'll discuss the details of what I require before accepting an offer."

"I see," Emma said quietly. "And you think they'll just agree to whatever demands you request?"

She shrugged. "I don't see why not. Isn't a wife he can ignore every lord's dream? Plus, I didn't choose just anyone. They are all decent, upstanding men. None are excessive with drinking, gambling or dueling. They have good reputations and generally agreeable personalities."

"But what about you?"

Priscilla smiled. "I have a generally agreeable personality."

"That's not what I meant." Emma folded her arms across her chest. "Do you really think you could be happy with one of them? Haven't you ever wanted more?"

"No." The word was said with infinite conviction, but a little voice inside contradicted the claim. Once she had imagined a true match, a connection with kinship, meaning and something far stronger. A rarity in the *ton*, yet not an impossibility, a relationship that transcended mere friendship. Something akin to… love.

Too agitated to stand still, Priscilla grasped her skirt and started pacing, the floor hard under the thin soles of her slippers. Men didn't have to put up with such nonfunctional clothing. "I simply want my freedom. I thought my father understood and agreed, especially since I have three brothers. Unfortunately, he decided I needed to be settled. His words." She spun, strode the other way. "The truth is, I've never been so unsettled in my life." She forced herself to stop, inhaled deeply. "But it's all right. I'll make a suitable match, and everything will be fine."

"Your parents may accept it, but will your suitors?"

Priscilla shrugged. "My suitors won't have a choice."

"I don't know about that." Emma pointed to the news sheet on the table. "Today's edition included an engagement announcement between Patience Forrester and Viscount Barrett."

Priscilla looked down at the sheet in surprise. "I knew Barrett was chasing Patience, but I thought she didn't want the match."

"She didn't," Emma confirmed, "until he went to her father with some sort of *offer*. Suddenly she changed her mind."

"Or her mind was changed for her."

Priscilla frowned. Even if a woman supposedly had the right to refuse, forced matches were common. "Her family is different than mine. My father won't force me." Yet was it true? She never thought he'd force her to marry at all.

"What about your mysterious lord? We know he's not old, ugly or cruel. A cruel man wouldn't fight for our causes, and no one ugly or old would elicit a blush every time you mention him."

"I don't blush."

Her face heated.

"I admit he isn't any of those things. He's one of the prime catches of the season."

Emma's eyes widened. "Then we know

him."

"He sounds like Bradenton."

It was all Priscilla could do to keep a straight face at Hannah's declaration. "I'm sorry?"

"He sounds like the duke. And we already know he is chasing you. Why did you dance with him at Roxbury's ball? Everyone noticed."

That she had no choice was not something she would mention. "It was nothing."

"Are you sure?" Hannah's astute eyes pierced her. "Apparently they're already wagering in the clubs."

Her breath hitched. "On whether we'll wed?"

"On *when* you will wed."

She should have gone for a vase when he signed two lines.

Priscilla stood tall. "Then every single person is going to lose. I have no intention of being with a man who is dictatorial, autocratic and domineering, no matter how handsome or powerful he is." She gave a curt nod.

Her friends just stared at her.

"You think he's handsome?"

"You think he's powerful?"

She closed her eyes, held up the paper. "I have my plan. I already danced with several lords who were most suitable."

"Suitable, were they?" Hannah said dryly. "Sounds exciting."

It wasn't. The potted plant was the most

interesting of the bunch. "Exciting is what I don't need. I have enough of that with my investigations."

"I almost forgot the investigation!" Hannah's eyes lit up. "Were you able to–"

"No." Priscilla glanced towards the door. Like all homes of the nobility, the walls had ears, or at least the servants who dusted right next to interesting conversations did. She lowered her voice. "I tried to follow Lady Roxbury, but was unable to speak with her."

Emma frowned. "You didn't get in trouble, did you?"

"I just ran into a very large and annoying obstacle."

Hannah looked at her suspiciously, but didn't ask for details. "What's our next move?"

Priscilla took a deep breath. "I have a list of lords to investigate."

"You're investigating more lords?" Emma wrung her hands. "Is that wise? You were almost caught last week, and I have a feeling you're not sharing everything about yesterday."

Only that Bradenton discovered her. Nearly found out her secret.

"Nothing substantial."

Emma frowned. "Deceiving them into revealing too much is harmless, but if you get caught alone with one of them..." Her voice trailed off, even as the unspoken word surrounded them.

Scandal.

"It's a risk, but a worthwhile one. Plus, even if I'm caught, no one is going to believe the Duke of Sherring's daughter would be involved in anything illicit. I could be knee deep in their bank accounts, and they wouldn't suspect a thing."

Emma grimaced. "I still think it's too dangerous."

"And I think she needs a cohort." Hannah pressed forward. "We could find much more with two of us looking."

"I'm sorry, but it's too risky." Hannah had wanted to join her since the beginning, but she couldn't risk her friend's reputation. "You already help so much by gathering information from unsuspecting nobles."

"Information I haven't been able to use," Hannah sniffed. "If only you'd let us blackmail them."

Emma gasped. "Hannah, no!"

"Don't worry." Priscilla put her hand on Emma's arm. "On this, I agree with you. There's little risk in passing along information, but blackmail is something else entirely. I won't truly risk ruination."

Emma looked relieved and Hannah frustrated, but both accepted her decision.

Priscilla rubbed her hands together. "I'll continue our work at the theater. And while I'm there, I'll find a lord who is nice, calm and above all, very, very busy."

And no matter how tempting, that lord would not be the Duke of Bradenton.

THERE WERE ADVANTAGES to being a duke.

People listened to you, respected your opinions and accepted your decisions. They treated you with consideration and admiration. You could break social customs, such as visiting unannounced, and be immediately admitted. Which was exactly what happened when Edmund knocked on the door at the Duke of Sherring's townhouse.

Peyton and Crawford accompanied him, partly because he asked and partly out of curiosity. The official story was Peyton was returning a book his mother borrowed, a purely social exercise since the book had been loaned four years ago. Yet it provided a convenient excuse for visiting the household without an appointment.

His friends would not stay long. A few minutes perhaps, for appearances' sake, giving him the chance to learn more about the mysterious Lady Priscilla. He hoped to convince her, or more likely her parents, to allow him to take her on a turn around Hyde Park. A ride would give him the opportunity to learn more about her.

And discover the secrets she kept hidden.

The footman was exactly what one would expect in a ducal household: impeccable, poised and meticulously groomed. "Yes, Your Grace, of course they are home. Please do come in."

Edmund was led to a well-appointed drawing room with gilded highlights and overstuffed settees. He did not sit, but stood next to the crackling marble fireplace, Crawford and Peyton beside him. Less than a minute later, the duchess arrived, her cheeks pink, slightly out of breath. All the enthusiasm her daughter lacked, she displayed in hearty amounts.

"What a pleasant surprise!" The duchess made no effort to hide her delight as she feasted on the sight of them like Christmas fruit cakes. "I am honored for your visit. Lady Priscilla was inordinately pleased as well, and is just freshening up. She will be down soon."

He hid a smile. *Pleased* was undoubtedly a metaphor for angry, petulant and defiant. Yes, she didn't have a choice. She couldn't refuse him without infuriating her parents.

He nodded. "Thank you. We beg your forgiveness for not announcing our visit beforehand."

Crawford stepped forward. "I came to return the book my mother borrowed."

The duchess turned a critical eye towards

Crawford. She took the book he offered. "Just under five years. What impeccable timing."

Crawford grinned. "Just so. Again, we do apologize for our lack of notice."

"You are more than welcome anytime. I'm only dismayed the duke is not here to receive you. He is at his club."

"Of course."

She looked out the door. "I'm sure Lady Priscilla will be here any minute."

Only contrary to his hostesses' prediction, Lady Priscilla did not arrive "any minute." A minute passed, then five, then ten. The duchess' smile grew more and more stretched, her voice higher pitched, even as he reassured her he didn't mind waiting. It was true. He saw Priscilla's actions for what they were. Another attempt to discourage him.

What would she say if she realized her clever antics had the opposite effect?

Finally, the duchess excused herself. *Many* minutes later, she returned, followed by Lady Priscilla. He straightened.

She was lovely.

Her cheeks were flushed pink, her lips full and red, her pale hair shimmering. Emerald eyes sparkled against creamy skin, their keen intelligence brilliant. An aqua dress skimmed over luscious curves, hinting at the bounty underneath. A flash of desire surged for the undeniable beauty, yet what lurked beneath was even more attractive.

She was accompanied by Lady Hannah and Lady Emma, two ladies of a similar age. Emma cast a genuine smile, Hannah a poorly hidden scowl.

Priscilla stared right at him. "I apologize for making you wait." The words were said graciously, yet defiance burned in her eyes.

He hid his amusement. "I do not mind waiting for such lovely ladies. It is always a pleasure."

Priscilla's cheeks tinged.

The duchess jumped in. "I believe the six of you have already been introduced?"

As the ladies nodded, Crawford smiled. "It is good to see you again, ladies."

Priscilla and Emma smiled in greeting, but Hannah only tightened her lips, gave a curt nod.

Crawford's smile widened.

"The ladies just finished a meeting of the Distinguished Ladies of Purpose." The duchess stood taller. "It is a sewing group, which Priscilla leads."

He walked closer to his quarry. "It sounds fascinating. I did not realize you enjoyed sewing so much."

"Of course she does," The duchess responded for her daughter. "As a lady of the *ton*, it is one of her favorite pursuits."

Priscilla grimaced.

He couldn't stop himself. "Next to resting and shopping, I presume."

Priscilla turned a lovely shade of red. "Few would be interested in the Distinguished Ladies' Resting Guild," she said sweetly.

Her mother frowned, but he had to hold back a laugh. "Likely true. So tell me, what did you sew?"

"Sew?"

"At your guild," he prompted, "What is the subject of your current piece?"

For a second, a panicked look came in her eyes. Then they lit in mischief. "A vase."

"A vase?"

She smiled. An impish smile, undoubtedly meant to annoy.

It was adorable.

"A heavy vase. A big one."

Once more he had to hold back a laugh. What an unusual feeling. Likely she would love to bring the vase over his head. "A vase is such a nice subject. Many people also paint statues. Tell me, have you seen any unusual statues lately? Perhaps something that depicts a human subject?"

She turned pinker. And pinker. And pinker. "There were eight."

"Eight?"

"Eight vases."

The little minx. He laughed again.

The duchess couldn't seem to decide whether this was going well or not. "Tell us, Your Grace, what are your plans for this lovely afternoon?"

It was the perfect opening. "I thought I might go for a ride in the carriage. I was wondering if Lady Priscilla might want to accompany me."

Lady Priscilla's eyes widened, then narrowed. "I'm afraid I–"

"Would love to go!" The duchess shot in. "My daughter loves carriage rides, especially with a fine gentleman such as yourself. Isn't that right, my dear?"

"But it is–"

"Such a lovely day for riding," her mother finished.

Mother and daughter locked eyes. Finally, Priscilla looked away. "Yes, of course. I just need a few minutes to–"

"You're fine as you are. Isn't she, girls?"

Lady Emma and Lady Hannah nodded dutifully. "Of course, Your Grace."

The duchess smiled at the two ladies. And smiled. And smiled.

Emma turned pink. "I better go. I have to pick out a gift for my grandmother's birthday."

Hannah frowned. "Priscilla was going to help Emma choose a gift. The occasion is tomorrow."

"We can help Emma." Crawford stepped in. "I assume you have a chaperone?"

Hannah pursed her lips, but nodded.

"Then let's not prevent Lady Priscilla and the duke from their ride. If you would allow us, Peyton and I will accompany you."

"That. Would. Be. Lovely." Hannah spoke haltingly.

"Is that acceptable to you?" Peyton asked Emma.

Her cheeks an even brighter pink, Emma nodded.

The duchess clapped her hands. "Splendid. Have a wonderful time." In seconds, the efficient woman not-so-subtlety ushered the four to the front door.

A nice liquor would be required later to make it up to his friends.

The duchess was rubbing her hands as she returned. "Are you ready? I can act as your chap–"

"I will ask Aunt Lousia to accompany us," Lady Priscilla broke in.

Edmund relaxed. He would learn far more about Lady Priscilla without her mother's interference.

The duchess frowned, but did not contradict her daughter. "Very well. I shall tell her." And with that, the very eager duchess left her very innocent daughter very alone with a very eligible man.

Not very subtle.

Priscilla narrowed her eyes at the ill-hidden game. It was possible the duchess thought him too much of a gentleman to do anything that would force a betrothal.

More likely she was hoping he wasn't.

"I must apologize for my mother. I fear she has gotten the wrong impression of our relationship."

"Really?" He folded his arms across his chest. "And what impression is that?"

Two small spots of pink colored her cheeks. She lifted her chin. "I do not need to tell a man of your intelligence what is so painfully obvious."

He took a step towards her. "I appreciate your high estimation of my intellectual ability."

She shook her head, but a small smile played at her lips. "No one can ever accuse you of modesty, Bradenton."

He feigned an expression of indignity, hiding satisfaction she'd eschewed the proper "Your Grace." "Just the other day, I rescued a lady who was hopelessly lost. If I hadn't intervened she would still be searching for the entrance to the ladies' retiring room in the hedges. Yet I took no credit for such heroics."

"Perhaps the lady did not need rescuing. It is a little known fact that women can take care of themselves. She was perfectly safe where she was."

He gave her a wicked look. "She did enjoy

the statues."

She made a sound halfway between a cough and a laugh. "You sir, are completely inappropriate. What about all the stories of the powerful and dangerous duke?"

What, indeed? With Lady Priscilla, he was in rare form, less harsh, perhaps even lighthearted. It was a rare and tempting experience. "Not everyone is as they seem. Everyone has hidden facets."

She stared at him, sharp concern replacing the humor. It was curious, and also telling.

"Not everyone is so surreptitious." Her gaze didn't waver. "For some, what you see is what exists."

"True." He took another step. "Yet there is far more to *you* than the *ton* realizes."

She visibly swallowed. "Nonsense. I am exactly as I appear. Which is why you should take me at my word that we would not suit, Your Grace."

"Back to Your Grace, I see." Inexplicably drawn, he moved forward again. "You are fooling yourself. You were enjoying the conversation a minute ago, yet you keep reminding yourself we would not suit. Care to explain why?"

To her credit, she held her ground. "There is no grand reason. I simply believe it. You must discontinue this behavior now, before people get the wrong idea. Please do not consider me a challenge. I know how you are with those."

He stopped. "I did not realize you were so acquainted with my personal tendencies."

She hesitated for the briefest of instants. "You cannot be unaware of your reputation. Powerful. Tenacious. Unrelenting. Do not chase an unwanted prize simply because you wish to win."

He frowned. There was something familiar about the way she spoke. Answers lurked on the edge of his unconscious, puzzle pieces that didn't quite align.

He moved even nearer, placing just enough distance to avoid scandal should her mother return. "What makes you think I don't want the prize?"

"It does not matter. The prize does not wish to be caught."

"The prize does not always have a choice."

Her eyes widened.

He took advantage by moving even closer, in spite of the danger.

"We cannot be." Even as the words rang hollow, she pressed on, "What do I have to do to prove it?"

He raised an eyebrow.

Her lips set, and a determined look came into her eyes. "You do not affect me at all," she declared. "And I'll prove it."

Then *she* took his lips.

The kiss was not tentative. It was not passive,

friendly or in the least bit platonic. Borne of pure need, it was an onslaught of senses, a release of passion. Desire exploded as he pulled her close, demanding her surrender even as she pressed against him. He reveled as she moaned in sweet surrender.

Their lips tangled, hot and delicious, fiery frenzy. Heady need swirled around him as he sampled pure sweetness. She was all softness and generous curves, pure spirit and sizzling heat. He wrapped his arms around her, pulling her closer.

If she thought to prove herself unaffected, she was gravely mistaken, as he immediately took control. In that moment, he didn't want to let her go. Yet he hadn't a choice. Soon the duchess would return, and if she caught them like this, their future would be cast.

The thought was becoming more appealing by the moment.

He pulled back, yet didn't completely let go.

She gaped at him, heaving in great breaths, her expression raw and passionate. He, too, was not as in control as he pretended.

The sound of people in the hallway broke the sound of their breathing.

"It's my mother," she hissed. "Let me go!"

He looked down at her…

And tightened his hold.

CHAPTER FIVE

Dear Lord P,

I applaud your victory. Yet not all obstacles are easily beaten, and some may rise again, stronger, hardier and poised for victory. If you deign to describe your hindrances to me, I shall aid you in devising further strategies. In my career, I have fought and claimed victory against many foes, and look forward to more. Now I fight a battle with a greater opponent than ever before. Yet the prize is worth the battle.

I will be victorious.

Yours,
Edmund

P.S. We have conversed for over a year, and yet we have kept an unnecessary formality. Please address me as Edmund, as my good friends do.

"IS EVERYTHING ALL right?" her mother asked in a hopeful voice.

"Of course," Bradenton answered smoothly, with no sign he'd just been ravishing her daughter. "Lady Priscilla and I were debating a point, which she conceded to me."

She clenched her fists. "His Grace is unfortunately mistaken."

He raised an eyebrow.

She glared at him.

Her mother gave a nervous laugh. "I'm sure there's room for compromise. Do you want to share so we can give our opinion?"

Sure, Mother.

I claimed Bradenton didn't affect me.

To prove it, I kissed him.

The world exploded.

On second thought, I may have lost.

Kissing Bradenton seemed like a good idea at the time. Infuriatingly, it still felt like a good idea. But there would be no more of that. She moved towards her mother, away from Bradenton and his knowing expression. "It's nothing of any importance. The subject is closed. Permanently."

"Then you should go on your ride. I'm sure Aunt Louisa is excited."

Aunt Louisa wore the same scowl she always did and didn't respond. Her hearing had been failing for years, making her the perfect chaperone when one planned to loudly discourage a suitor.

Bradenton gestured her forward. Under her mother's watchful eye, she could do nothing but join him. He towered next to her, a paragon of power and strength. He leaned down and whispered so only she could hear, "Just so we're clear…"

"I won."

"LADY LOUISA, ARE you enjoying the ride?"

Aunt Louisa stared outside the carriage, scowling at people as they passed. She did not answer Bradenton's question.

It was a beautiful, sun-splashed day, and the eloquently dressed members of the *ton* were out enjoying rides in well-appointed carriages. Murmured conversations drifted through the air, set to the tinkling of polite laughter and children playing in the background. Freshly blooming flowers burst from gardens, their scents carried on a gentle breeze.

"She can't hear," Priscilla stated the obvious, even though Bradenton likely already guessed. "We have to write to communicate with her. So for instance, if I say a certain duke is overbearing and dictatorial, she would have no idea."

"I see." He expertly guided the horses. "And if I were to say a certain lady is beautiful and fascinating, she would not hear me."

Do not blush.

Do not blush.

Stop blushing!

She fought to remain emotionless. "I'm sure she's heard enough insincere sentiments to judge false flattery."

"It's the truth." His tone was genuine now, as he paused to look at her. "I'll admit many suitors wax poetic, but I am not one of them. I do not lie, and I do not exaggerate."

Priscilla swallowed. The close friend she knew from her letters did not tell untruths. He simply had no need.

People respected him no matter what he said.

Suddenly the atmosphere became far too dangerous. At least the kiss remained thankfully unmentioned. "Tell me about your work with social causes," she blurted. She grimaced. She had only meant to change the subject, not sound so eager.

"Are you truly interested?"

"All good members of society should be," she said carefully.

He studied her for a moment. "Much of it happens with the dukedom. It is vital to be present for my tenants, as well as everyone ruled by Parliament. I ensure the welfare of those under my care."

Priscilla nodded. A lady waved at Bradenton from a nearby carriage, then another and another. Not that it mattered. She barely remembered the twenty-two women who had waved so far.

Bradenton nodded back, but did not stop. "Beyond my personal responsibilities, I fight for those without a voice. Right now we are focusing on improving working conditions in the factories. We just had some success."

Despite her resistance, warmth spread through her. "That's wonderful. You must be very pleased."

His expression remained neutral, yet emotion lurked beneath it. "It's difficult to celebrate when so much remains to be done. I had hoped to achieve more by now. You should see the conditions, the children–" Just as his voice rose, he stopped. "Forgive me. This is not an appropriate subject for a gently bred lady."

"Of course it is." Guided solely by instinct, she placed a hand on his arm. She withdrew it quickly when he gave her a sharp look. "Cruelty flourishes with ignorance, and those who turn away do nothing to change it. Women and children are just as much victims of poor treatment as fully grown men. All people, no matter their station or gender, should be aware of society's ills."

He looked at her intently. She had surprised him, more than she intended, yet she couldn't stay silent on the cause that usurped her heart. She simply couldn't pretend it didn't matter. Not after all the hard work she – they – had done. Still, she must be cautious. If she kept slipping, he could connect her to his mysterious colleague.

Perhaps a new subject would be safer. "What do you do when not meeting your responsibilities or championing your causes?"

He relaxed ever-so-slightly. "I attempt to sleep occasionally."

She smiled. "You must have something you do for leisure."

When he didn't respond, her smile faded. Did the man truly do nothing but work for others? "What you do is important," she said softly. "But you should also make time for yourself."

Discomfort tinted his expression. "I attend balls, shows and other entertainment in the course of my duties. I am also a sportsman."

"That's obvious."

Well, just brilliant.

The scoundrel didn't even attempt to hide his bemusement.

Maybe she could make it better. "I mean I may have heard that you…"*Her ability to speak appeared to have disappeared.* "That you liked physical activity." *Wrong direction!* "Like sports, I mean, of course, obviously."

Mirth danced in his eyes. Thankfully, he did not comment on the fact that she had clearly lost her mind. "What about you? Do you have any hobbies beyond resting, sewing and getting helplessly lost under furniture?"

Rambling and making inappropriate comments. "I like to share my opinions."

"Excellent, because I have another question. Do you have a disdain for clever men?"

To the contrary, they were far too tempting. "I don't know what you mean, and if I did, I would say you are very impertinent."

"We've already established that." He made a graceful turn with the horses. "I am speaking of your suitors, the men you danced with at the Roxbury ball. They seemed unlikely choices for a lady of your position."

He had been watching her. Unease and frustration mixed with excitement and satisfaction, a tangle of conflicting emotions, amidst a major problem: how would she investigate if he was watching her?

"I am perplexed as to why you would watch me."

"Are you truly?" he said softly.

She felt herself color. Perhaps if she made it clear she would soon be engaged, he would retreat. "There is nothing unusual about the men I am considering. I imagine I will soon accept an offer."

Challenge lit his eyes. If she'd meant to scare him, her words seemed to have had the opposite effect.

"Tell me about your suitors."

"It would be inappropriate."

"Nonsense. I know most of the lords in the *ton*. Perhaps I can aid you in your endeavor."

She eyed him suspiciously. Far more lurked behind Bradenton's actions than he admitted. Still, if she did not answer his question, he might conduct his own investigation. "I have a list of suitable men."

He cocked his head to the side. "A list like one would make when heading to the fabric shop?"

She fought to keep a straight face. "Exactly."

"And who is on that list?"

"Many eligible men."

"Such as?"

She sighed. "The Earl of Castleberry, the Duke of Dewey and the Earl of Ridgeland."

"How fascinating. You are aware the Earl of Castleberry spends most of his time with rocks."

Exactly why she liked him. "I find his scientific interest interesting."

"He makes little beds for them."

"How kind."

"And gives them names."

"Sounds adorable."

"He talks to them."

And we have another entrant to the "I'm not that desperate" list.

"The Duke of Dewey has a similar fascination with plants."

"That's different," she protested. "Plants are alive. Many people enjoy botany."

Bradenton raised an eyebrow. "He also talks to them."

Priscilla shrugged. "I've heard it can promote growth."

"Did he tell you they talked back?"

Well, great. "Now I know you're telling tales."

"As we've established, I do not lie," he said solemnly. "Dewey told me himself. But don't worry. I'm sure the plants have said only nice things about you."

She looked down so he wouldn't see her smile. "What about Lord Ridgeland? Not a plant or rock in sight."

"Perhaps not," he conceded. "But he prefers his ladies with four legs."

She parted her lips.

"You must know the man spends all day with his horses. He gives them each a name, first, middle and last, and coddles them more than a mama with a newborn baby. If you were with him, you'd be lucky if he spent any time wi–"

He stopped.

Looked at her.

Narrowed his eyes.

"You'd be lucky if he spent any time with you," he murmured. "But that's what you want, isn't it? I thought you muttered 'busy' under your breath when I asked about your requirements for a suitor. It makes perfect sense. You want to find someone who is so busy, he won't notice you living life exactly as you please."

That's right. Precisely. Give the man a prize!

"That's preposterous. I have many requirements for a lord, most of which were stipulated by my parents. He must have a title, sufficient funds and–"

"A preoccupation," he finished.

She folded her arms across her chest.

"Do not worry," he rumbled. "I understand."

She looked at him sharply. Had he deciphered more than her motives? "Understand what, Your Grace?"

"I understand why a woman of your intellect wouldn't want a man interfering in her life. Why you would want someone so busy he would allow you to do as you please."

Anger flashed through her, not truly at Bradenton, but at the unfairness he highlighted. "You can't understand! Everyone listens when you talk. No one doubts your ability to care for yourself or thinks you can't grasp the simplest of tasks. No one chaperones you, telling you what you can and cannot do. When I marry, I will become someone else's property. It's all I can ever be, even if I wanted to change the world!"

His gaze didn't waver, even as her voice rose until others looked over. Yet his neutral mask was gone, replaced by understanding, compassion. "Do you wish to change the world, Lady Priscilla?" he asked softly.

She caught her breath. He couldn't know she already did. "I was using it as an example. No matter what a lady is capable of, she will always be considered property of a man."

"I cannot truly understand the obstacles of the fairer gender, but I can comprehend your desire for freedom." His voice was low, serious. "I wish females enjoyed more of it."

"Do you really?" She studied him. "What about your wards? As their guardian, do you allow them free rein?"

He shrugged. "My sisters and cousins enjoy a great deal of freedom. They choose their endeavors, activities and even suitors."

"Truly? So if your sister decided to travel the world, you would let her go? What if your cousin fell in love with a no-good scoundrel? Would you pay for a wedding breakfast and send her on her way?"

His jaw tightened. "I have a responsibility to them."

"Exactly." She gestured with her hands. "You would tell your sister she is staying in England, and order your cousin to find another suitor."

He didn't deny it. "It is my responsibility to keep them safe."

"But shouldn't that be for them to decide? Shouldn't they be able to live their lives as they choose?"

He leaned back and regarded her. At the very least, he was considering her argument. It was more than most lords would do.

"I must walk a difficult balance. I would give those under my care freedom, as I wish for everyone. Yet I am also aware of the dangers of the world, especially for ladies. I give them all the freedom I can, while still protecting them."

"'Protect' is just another word for control."

"For me, it is not." He looked at her earnestly. "I take my duties seriously, ensuring my wards are not only healthy but happy as well. Freedom is part of that."

"And what of the lady you choose as your bride?" She was treading into dangerous territory, yet she couldn't stop herself. "Will you restrict her activities?"

"Only when they threaten her well-being. If that makes me controlling, then so be it. It would be far worse if I failed to prevent something dangerous, and she came to harm. In most ways, my wife will be able to live life as she chooses. Marriage doesn't have to be a prison sentence." He paused. "I will admit to something. I will not allow my bride to pretend she is not in the marriage. I wish for an actual union."

Something moved inside her, a longing for what could never be hers. She pushed it aside. Despite Bradenton's "goodness" he'd confirmed his protective and possessive nature. With him, she would never be free.

"Such unions are good for men, perhaps, but not so much for ladies."

He shook his head. "I disagree. While you may have to compromise in a true marriage, consider life with your current suitors. What would it be like?"

There would be vases. Many, many vases.

The only question would be whether to pay for them in installments or one lump sum.

"It would be fine. The men were very... interesting."

"Interesting? Were you actually awake?"

She fought the smile. "Of course."

"I imagine you learned a great deal about horses, plants and rocks."

"Can one truly know too much about rocks?"

"I believe one can."

"I imagine you were hoping for something to make them stop."

"I was considering the location of the nearest vase."

She clamped her mouth shut. She had not meant to admit that.

Bemusement lit his eyes. "I suppose I should be grateful there are no vases in the vicinity."

She simply couldn't help it. She smiled.

"And now I understand why vases were the subject of your sewing. Tell me, do you actually like to sew?"

Her amusement fled at the stark reminder of her subterfuge. He must never learn her guild had nothing to do with sewing and everything to do with social reform. "I enjoy it as much as the average lady."

He inclined his head at the vague response. "You do not like to talk about yourself, Lady Priscilla. While others may not notice, I do."

Yes, he did. He noticed everything. Perhaps she could share something so he wouldn't search for everything. "I am a typical lady. I enjoy most subjects ladies do."

"You keep a busy social calendar."

"I am not one to sleep all day in preparation for the night's events. I attend gardens, festivals and so forth."

"Do you like museums? There's an interesting new exhibit on display at the British Museum."

She relaxed at the change of subject. "I saw it. It was quite fascinating."

He nodded to another waving passerby, then turned back to her. "I agree. What was your favorite part?"

"I enjoyed the statues and the paintings, but the miniatures were my favorite. I know you thought they were childish, but they had a unique quality to them."

He narrowed his eyes. Stared.

Her breath hitched. What had she said?

Something she shouldn't have known.

"How did you know I thought they were childish?"

She forced her voice to stay light. "You said so, didn't you? At the dance?"

"We haven't discussed the exhibit before now."

"I thought you mentioned it. Perhaps you simply look like the sort of man who would think miniatures silly."

He continued to stare.

This was why contact outside their letters was dangerous! She had to distract him, but how? In that moment, she thought of only a single subject powerful enough. "I'm sorry about the kiss!"

His eyes widened in surprise, a rarity for the stoic man. She blanched as he glanced around. Had she been too loud? If anyone heard…

Thankfully, no one was within range. "Lady Priscilla, you do realize the consequences of your actions?"

All too well. "I'm sorry." She lowered her voice. "I just wanted to apologize. The kiss was simply my clumsy way of making a point. I do not normally behave in such a manner." Heat crept up her neck.

His expression softened. "Do not worry, my dear. I hold you in the highest esteem. I am rapidly seeing the true Lady Priscilla."

That was exactly what she feared.

"What point were you trying to make?"

She straightened. "That we are not suited. That the connection you speak of is mere fiction."

"I would challenge you lost that battle." His voice deepened. "However, if you are unsure, we could test it again."

Yes!

Splendid idea!

Please, please, please!

"Your Grace, none of that!" Her disgruntlement was badly feigned and unlikely to fool him. "The subject is now closed. Permanently."

The spark in his eyes challenged every word.

Yet he was a gentleman and allowed her to change the subject. They conversed without further incident, touching upon a variety of matters, large and small. In his letters, Bradenton was an excellent conversationalist, spinning fascinating tales into enjoyable banter, and in real life he was even better. She simply couldn't resist his clever wit and enigmatic charm.

She was not the only one who noticed. Nearly every eligible lady and their mama greeted him with enthusiastic waves and bright smiles. It bothered her more than she would ever admit, yet even more concerning was how Bradenton acted with the lords who greeted her. His response was an authoritative stare, yet it conveyed the message of a thousand words. The lords quickly went past, yet even his silent sabotage couldn't upset her. She thought nothing could.

Until something did.

It happened so quickly. One moment they were in the middle of a lively discussion on foreign affairs, and in the next she saw a nightmare. The confrontation was extraordinary for the difference of the combatants. The aggressor: a large burly shopkeeper, tall, thick and angry. His target: a little boy, scrawny and dirty, no older than six.

Immediately, the situation became clear. The little boy clutched a piece of bread with one tiny bite taken out. The shopkeeper, his face bright red with fury, was yelling and shaking the child. The boy screamed in fear, yet people ignored him as they walked by, unconcerned, apathetic, as if they didn't even see the assault.

He could murder the child in broad daylight, and no one would even notice.

"Stop the carriage!" She tried to stand, but an iron hand stopped her.

Bradenton had yet to see the fight. "What are you doing, Priscilla?" He held her tightly. "You can't stand while the carriage is moving!"

"I have to get out!" The boy was struggling, but the shopkeeper held him in a firm grip, shaking him like a rag doll. "I have to stop it!"

"Stop what?" he demanded, even as he pulled back on the reins. "Calm down. What's wrong?"

"I need to save the boy! Let me out!"

"Wait just a minute. I'll bring the carriage around."

"There isn't time!" The shopkeeper was too large, too rough. If he kept shaking the boy, he would inadvertently – or purposely – do irreparable damage. She had to stop it now.

When another carriage moved close to them, Edmund released her to get a better grip on the reins. It was her chance. As the carriage slowed, she stood, opened the door…

And jumped.

CHAPTER SIX

Dear Edmund,

Remember not all battles can be won, nor should they be. Even the Duke of Bradenton could face an insurmountable foe. We do not always understand the forces against us, or the motives and reasoning of our opponents. I, too, face a significant obstacle. I am confident, yet still I wonder if I will win.

And sometimes I wonder if I want to.

Please forgive my ponderings. It has been a tumultuous few days. I appreciate the work you have done, and plan to continue my work soon. Soon, I will target Lord Cattlyn, who votes against us, even though he seems apathetic to both sides. Perhaps I will find something to sway him.

Yours,
Lord P

P.S. I appreciate your invitation to address you as Edmund. I do wonder, however, if there was an ulterior motive in asking for another name. You are welcome to address me as P.

PURE FEAR.

It was not an emotion to which he was accustomed, or could even remember, yet when Priscilla hiked up her skirt and jumped from the carriage, images of a horse trampling her forged pure terror. When she made it to the ground on both feet, relief as he'd never known it flooded him.

Relief that died when she ran through the street, narrowly missing that trampling horse before disappearing into the crowd.

He didn't wait an instant.

He took just enough time to secure the carriage, quickly promising a young man a handsome reward to make certain no one touched it. Lady Louisa looked shocked, but seemed to understand he was going after her niece.

Then he jumped down and ran.

A million emotions reignited fear. Fury and frustration, pure helplessness and sharp doubt. Why had she run? What had she seen? That it involved danger was obvious – by her panicked tone, the matter was life-threatening.

He threaded through the thick crowd. The streets were jammed with people enjoying the brilliant day, moving this way and that, roaming the walkways, haggling with vendors and bustling into shops. Fortunately his height gave him an advantage, and he spotted her over the crowd. His heart thundered as she confronted an ugly, burly giant of a man. The man was glaring at her with treacherous intent, leaning forward as if poised to strike.

If the brute touched Priscilla, Edmund may just forget he was a duke.

He barreled forward, focused and intent as the seconds ticked by in agonizing slowness. Finally he reached her. She was clutching a little blond-haired boy, and the big man was standing above them, fists clenched.

"I don't care what you say, lady. The boy tried to steal from me. It's not my problem he doesn't have parents!"

Priscilla pushed the sobbing boy behind her back. He clutched the piece of bread as if his life depended upon it. "He was desperate and hungry. I shall be happy to provide the cost of the loaf."

"I don't want your money, lady! I'm tired of these little thieves having fun at my expense." He cracked his knuckles. "I want retribution."

Fiery heat thundered through Edmund. Yet he showed none of it as he stepped forward and spoke in a low, cold voice. "If you touch what's mine, I will exact retribution."

The shopkeeper was large. He was burly. He was muscular.

Edmund was *more*.

The ruffian looked around, froze. Took in Edmund's large form, the fine clothing…

And paled. "My Lord, I–"

"Your Grace," Edmund corrected.

The man turned even paler.

"That woman is the daughter of a duke," Edmund bit out. "Do you have any idea of the power her father wields? The power I wield?"

The man looked like he was about to swoon. "That won't be necessary! I apologize, my lady. If I had known who you were, I would have acted differently."

"It shouldn't matter who I was!" Priscilla hissed. "You attacked a little boy because he was desperate enough to snatch a tiny piece of bread. You, sir, are a monster."

The man turned crimson, and Edmund's anger grew. Didn't Priscilla realize the danger she courted? Before the man could respond, he stepped in. "Apologize to the boy."

The man stiffened. "The boy is a common thief."

A muffled sob came from the child. He buried his head in Priscilla's dress.

"You are the criminal," Edmund growled.

"Do you think the authorities will care about bread when I report you for attempted murder?"

The man's face shriveled. "Please, Your Grace!"

Edmund took a deep breath, fought for control. Torn between civility and primitive instinct, it took every ounce of strength to stop himself from lunging.

He turned to Priscilla. "Are you well?"

She nodded.

"And the boy?"

"I think so."

The shopkeeper had no idea how lucky he was. "I will grant you the mercy you denied the boy. You will never touch another child again. You will not yell, strike or harm them in any way. Do you understand?"

Sweat pouring down his face, the man bobbed his head eagerly. "Of course, Your Grace."

Edmund leaned in. "I have friends all over London. If I ever hear of you abusing another soul again, I will have you arrested."

"I understand. Thank you, Your Grace."

Without another word, Edmund pivoted, grasping Priscilla in the same motion. He did not ask, because he simply couldn't contain the overwhelming urge to hold her.

Priscilla's eyes widened at his touch. She parted her lips, likely to protest, yet stopped at his expression. Something passed between them, something strong, powerful and completely inexplicable.

"We're leaving," he declared.

"I will not leave the boy."

Her voice was strong with only the slightest quiver, the pinkness in her cheeks the sole betrayal of an otherwise perfect facade. His admiration for her swelled. She had just confronted a violent monster, risked her life to save a boy she didn't know, yet instead of breaking into hysterics, she stood as tall as her petite form allowed, her head notched up and her hair windswept in the brisk breeze.

She was magnificent.

He looked at the tiny form attached to her dress, the little boy even now trying to burrow closer. He knelt down and said softly, "Does anyone care for you?"

His lips quivering, the child shook his head.

"Where do you live?"

The boy blinked, his eyes shining with tears. Slowly, he pointed to a filthy alley, where several adults slept on the ground, surrounded by what likely composed their earthly possessions.

Edmund breathed deeply, taking a moment to compose himself. He stood. "No child that tiny, young and vulnerable should be alone in the world. We won't leave him."

Priscilla looked at him suspiciously. "We

won't?"

"Of course not. Clearly he needs a caretaker. We will discuss details in the carriage."

With that, he leaned down to the boy. The boy flailed his arms in a mighty fight, but a few whispered words calmed him enough to allow Edmund to lift him. With one hand holding the boy, and the other securing the lady, he strode back to the carriage.

Anger borne of fear still simmered, so he didn't say a word, and neither did she. Of course, it didn't stop the people from staring at them as they drew past. No doubt this escapade would reach the entire *ton* by evening, exaggerated and embellished until it belonged in a fiction novel. By the end they would be claiming he bested a lion.

Yet while it would leave tongues wagging, it took place in the open, and wasn't the sort of scandal that would require anything but time. It certainly wasn't enough to require a betrothal, although his grasp on her arm would lead to speculation. But with no further signs of an impending match, the speculation would die down.

He reached the carriage and paid the boy double what he promised. He helped Priscilla up, then ascended himself, still holding the child. Lady Louisa wore an expression of pure relief, and even gave Priscilla an embrace as she entered the carriage. She looked at the boy curiously, but didn't say anything before looking once more out of the carriage. Settling the child securely in the middle seat, he urged the horses into motion.

He waited until they were away from the crowds and in the wide-open lane before turning to her. He had his speech all prepared. He would stay calm and in control, unemotionally explaining that what she did was dangerous and that she must never do it again.

Instead, he growled, "What were you thinking?"

She stiffened. "Pardon me?"

"I asked what you were thinking." He moved the horses forward, a little quicker for his agitation. "How could you jump out of a moving carriage? Do you have any idea what could have happened?"

"I know what would've happened if I hadn't gotten to the boy before–" She halted, glanced at the still quivering child. She lowered her voice. "I didn't have time for you to amble over there. Besides, I waited for the carriage to stop."

"You didn't even tell me you were going to jump. It's a miracle you didn't break a limb!"

"What would you have me do?" she demanded. "I didn't have a choice!"

Edmund drew a deep breath. The little boy was so tiny, so emaciated and helpless. Renewed fury flashed through him. Yes, something had to be done, and immediately, but it should have been *him*.

"I'm not saying we shouldn't have helped the boy. Of course we needed to intervene. If you had explained, I would have taken care of it."

She glared at him, her eyes flashing. "I was perfectly capable of rescuing the child. If I see someone in danger, I'm going to help, no matter the risk."

"You will not put yourself in danger again," he ordered, his voice rising with every word. "Next time, you will tell me, and I will handle it. I'll lock you in your room to keep you safe if I have to."

She gasped. "How dare you! You aren't my guardian! You have no right to tell me what I can and cannot do. Besides, you won't be there next time."

"We'll see about that," he thundered.

She sat back, folded her arms. "I imagine you'll never want to see me again after this."

Never see her again? The very thought sent fire through his blood.

He breathed deeply. How had he allowed himself to lose control? She was safe and healthy and whole. That, and the rescue of the boy, were all that mattered. He took a moment, and when he spoke his voice was quieter, controlled. "Of course we will meet again. I know I'm being harsh, but you have to understand. When you jumped into the street, I felt–" He stopped, shook his head. "Let's just say I am not a man accustomed to fear."

For a moment she stared at him, then she softened, her anger visibly fading into compassion. Her voice was barely above a whisper. "I'm sorry I worried you, Your Grace."

"In the future, you will allow me to face all danger."

She looked down. "I cannot promise that."

He touched her face, lifting her chin so she gazed at him. "And I cannot stand back while you place yourself in peril. I will do whatever is necessary to keep you safe."

It was a promise he intended to keep.

With the fury of earlier vanquished, they did not talk more. Priscilla turned her attention to the boy, who had finally calmed down and was staring at them with eyes far too large in his gaunt face. He probably hadn't had a decent meal in his entire life. That would change now.

Edmund expertly led the carriage through the busy streets, his thoughts swirling as the boy described how he stole scraps of food to survive. His story was heartbreaking, especially for how common it was. Society needed more safeguards to protect these poor children.

As he expected, Priscilla was soft, kind and gentle, soothing the child. Even Edmund grew calmer as they rode through the streets. Finally, they approached the Sherring townhouse.

He stopped the carriage and helped Priscilla and Louisa down, then descended with the little boy. He handed the child to her and the reins to the handler. "I will be a few minutes."

Priscilla hugged the boy tight. "That's not necessary, Your Grace. You are welcome to take your leave. I will arrange for the boy's care."

Surprise coursed through him, although it shouldn't have. Of course she would consider the child her personal charge. "You don't have to take responsibility. I'm happy to find an appropriate place for him."

She clutched the child tighter. "I will not have him in an orphanage or put to work. He needs someone to care for him."

"Of course. I have no intention of sending him to an orphanage." Abuse and neglect ran rampant in such places, which were not much better, and sometimes worse, than the streets.

She paused. "You don't?"

"Of course not. I was going to find a good family to adopt the boy. As a *son*, not a worker."

She held his gaze for a minute more, then relaxed. "I should know you well enou–" She stopped, sighed once more. "I'm sorry I misjudged you."

Normally, he cared little about what others thought of him, yet Lady Priscilla's opinion mattered. "He deserves a good home, a place where he can grow and flourish. It's what every child needs."

The boy watched them with wide eyes, even as he clutched Priscilla.

"Are you my new mama?"

Priscilla looked down in surprise.

The little boy colored. "It's just my mama had to go. She was sick, you see." His little lip quivered. "She told me to be brave. She said if I was very good, I may get a new mama."

Priscilla's eyes sheened with liquid emotion. "You are getting your new mama," she whispered. "I'm bringing you to her right now."

She smiled softly at him, then at Edmund. "There is no need for you to search for a family. My cook adopted a young boy I brought in from the streets a few years ago, and it was immediate love. She talked about wanting another little one, a brother for her boy. Of course this one is too young to work, but I can give Cook the resources she needs."

So she had done this before. He wasn't surprised. "That sounds perfect."

She turned to a footman. "Please fetch Mrs. Fitzgerald."

The footman nodded and promptly obeyed. A minute later, a plump middle-aged woman came dashing out of the house. Her blond hair was frizzy, her cheeks ruddy, but she had a natural prettiness highlighted by clear blue eyes and a kindly face. She stopped in front of Priscilla, but her gaze was riveted on the little boy. The little boy stared at the woman and blinked.

Priscilla smiled. "I know you mentioned you would like another one, Mrs. Fitzgerald. This tiny one is alone, and could use a family to call his own. If you'd like–"

"Yes!" With a beaming smile, the woman opened her arms wide. "Yes. Yes. Yes!" She stopped, blushed. "I mean, that would be most suitable, my lady. Hello, little one."

The little boy looked at Priscilla, who nodded. The child then turned to him, his large eyes seeking approval. Something shifted in his own heart as he nodded. The boy would now have a home and a future. And most importantly, *love*.

The boy ran to his new mama. Her eyes sheening, she gently lifted him into her arms.

"Oh, are you a wee thing." Mrs. Fitzgerald clucked. "We'll get right to work fattening you up. I hope you like to eat." With a polite nod, she turned back to the house. "Tell me everything you like to eat. Now Mr. Fitzgerald, that's your new papa, he's going to be mighty pleased to meet a little man such as yourself. We're going to have such good times…"

The voices faded as the woman disappeared into the house. Edmund shook his head, but an involuntary smile graced his lips. He was accustomed to helping people, yet seldom did he

get to see firsthand the fruits of his labor. It was…
extraordinary.

Priscilla gazed after the cook, her expression
one of pure happiness. Something stirred within
him.

"He'll be happy," she murmured. She turned
to him, her eyes shining brightly. "I know I didn't
say it before, but thank you. I appreciate what
you did for him, and for me."

"It was my pleasure."

For a moment, they stared at each other.

In the next, someone not-so-subtly cleared
her throat. "Isn't this a sight to see?"

Edmund fought not to cringe, even as Priscilla showed no such discretion. The Duchess of
Sherring looked as if she were about to break into
a song and dance of rapture. "Did you children
have an enjoyable afternoon?"

"Catherine, I think we know what type of
afternoon they had." In stark contrast to his wife,
Priscilla's father was serious and stern. "It's why
we rushed home."

Edmund grimaced. He'd expected word of
their misadventure to spread, but he never
anticipated it to arrive the moment they reached
home.

"Bradenton, I'd like a word."

It was an order, not a request. Of course, he
could refuse, but he had a feeling their goals
converged. "Of course."

Priscilla stepped forward. "I don't think His Grace has time for a meeting now. He was just telling me about a matter requiring his immediate attention."

The only urgent matter involved Priscilla. "Thank you for your concern, Lady Priscilla, but you misjudged my words. I'm happy to meet with your father."

She was clearly not happy, yet her choice had been usurped. She gave him one last long look as she followed her mother into the house.

Then he walked into the meeting that could change everything.

"WHAT ARE THEY discussing? What's taking them so long? I should go in there."

"Don't you dare!" The duchess stepped in front of Priscilla. "You will not bother the gentlemen when they have important matters to discuss."

Priscilla gazed down the hallway to her father's office. Short of hiking up her skirts and leaping over her mother, she would have no say in the discussions that could upend her life.

Not even if her father was soliciting an offer from Bradenton at this very moment.

Her mother confirmed they'd heard about their misadventures, told by friends who'd told friends who'd told friends. In their version, there had been five burly shopkeepers, two wild dogs and a runaway horse. Her parents were obviously displeased, holding her solely responsible, of course.

She forced herself to calm. They could hardly force Bradenton to extend an offer. His only crime was his high-handedness in grasping her, and it took place in public and with mitigating circumstances. Certainly nothing blatant enough to cause a scandal worthy of betrothal.

It didn't mean her father wouldn't ask for one.

It didn't mean Bradenton wouldn't comply.

"They're discussing me! I should be in there."

Her mother didn't deny it. "There's nothing to worry about, Priscilla. Your father and I like Bradenton very much. He's a fine gentleman."

They had no idea how good he truly was. It was all the more reason she couldn't marry him. After their incident, he'd shown his true protective nature, lecturing her and then forbidding her from any and all danger. If they married, he would have the legal right to lock her away just as he'd threatened! No doubt he would forbid her from investigating.

Of course, her secret identity as his informant also complicated matters. There was no way to know how he would react to the truth, but one thing was certain: He would be furious.

"I don't understand you, Priscilla. What's

your game?"

Priscilla looked at her mother. "What do you mean?" she asked carefully. "I have no game."

"Yes, you do." The duchess folded her arms across her chest. "You say you've accepted your father's decision regarding marriage."

"I have. My dance cards are full. I even created a list of eligible suitors."

"I noticed." Her mother grimaced. "Are you aware one of them talks to rocks?"

She definitely needed a new list. "I thought you supported interesting hobbies. In any case, your requirements were a title, wealth and upstanding reputation. Every single man on my list meets those requirements." *And, yes, one also talks to rocks.* "Why are you are pushing me towards Bradenton?"

"Because I want you to be happy."

Priscilla started. She had expected her mother to complain the men were not as high-ranked as Edmund, were not as wealthy, talked to inanimate objects. She never expected happiness to matter. "I chose men best suited to my needs."

"You're not going to convince me you'll be happy with a man who speaks to rocks. I know my daughter. You are searching for a man who will leave you alone."

Priscilla's breath hitched. Who was this insightful woman? Where was her mother, whose singular goal in life was to secure her daughter a favorable match? "It shouldn't matter who I marry, as long as they meet your requirements. You know *ton* marriages better than anyone."

"I love your father."

Priscilla stared. Her parents acted with affection, yet they didn't speak of love. She certainly never expected her mother to admit it. "You are fortunate. Love is not often seen in *aristocratic unions*."

"Exactly." Her mother moved forward, took her hand. "I was not given any choice in my marriage, yet I am grateful for it every day. My parents specifically choose someone well-matched beyond the title and wealth, someone who shared my likes and dislikes, my goals and aspirations. That is what I want for you, Priscilla, and you are not going to find it with a man who speaks to rocks."

Priscilla moved back, out of her mother's reach, yet she could not escape her shrewd gaze. "Perhaps not, but that doesn't mean I would be happy with Bradenton, or anyone else for that matter. With a man like him, I'd have to surrender everything!"

She snapped her mouth shut.

"You underestimate Bradenton," her mother said quietly. "Do not give up something precious because of fear."

Priscilla didn't trust herself to say more, so she just nodded. She should dismiss her mother's words, consider them a ploy to get her to agree to the favorable match. Yet her frankness shook her.

"Excuse me, Your Grace," a footman approached. "The Countess of Danvers is here to see you."

"Oh yes." The duchess smoothed her dress. "Send her to the blue room and tell her I'll be there in a moment."

The footman departed, and the duchess gave Priscilla a small smile. "Please consider what I said."

Priscilla nodded, wishing she truly could. Yet a life with Bradenton was far too dangerous. He would take control, shattering the path she'd chosen. For now, she would continue to fight, even as the truth remained:

She may not have a choice.

THE DUKE OF Sherring was a tall man, fit and hearty despite his age. His hair was mostly black with fringes of grey, his eyes a piercing green. He possessed the regal bearing of his position, the confidence and skills of a lifetime of leadership.

"Come in," He gestured Edmund forward into a well-appointed office. Unlike the gaudy excess of Roxbury's office, this one held subtle hints of luxury in quality furnishings and imported luxuries. "Can I offer you refreshment?"

Edmund shook his head, declining an undoubtedly superb vintage. He preferred his facilities at their sharpest for what could be a very substantial conversation.

"I am dismayed by this afternoon's events," The duke wasted no time with trivialities. "Is it true that Lady Priscilla jumped out of your carriage and into an altercation with a shopkeeper?"

Edmund hesitated, nodded. "A most unfortunate incident. I can assure you Lady Priscilla is unharmed. She saved a little boy."

Sherring sighed, yet pride shined in his eyes. "My daughter wants to save the world. From the time she could write, she sent letters to Parliament urging them to help the poor. She sent so many, they filled an entire barrel."

Something stirred within him. A memory, as if he'd heard the story before.

"She is a very special lady, a true rare breed. I would keep her forever if I could, but her well-being is too important for such selfishness. She needs someone young and strong to care for her, especially when she gets one of her ideas." Sherring swirled his drink. "You probably realize the decision to marry was not her own."

Edmund nodded once more.

"She thinks I betrayed her, but allowing her to run wild forever would be far more of a disservice. If you hadn't been there today..." His voice trailed off.

Memories of raw fear struck Edmund, powerful even now. "I will not allow Lady Priscilla to come to harm."

Sherring studied him, his shrewd eyes taking in everything. "No, I don't suppose you would, when she is with you, of course." He stood taller. "Now that the immediate danger is alleviated, I am concerned for her reputation. I want her to make a favorable match, although I do not understand some of her choices. Do you know one of her suitors talks to rocks?"

Edmund held back a chuckle. "All too aware."

"Priscilla needs a strong man, a man not afraid to do what needs to be done to ensure her well-being, protect her from herself if necessary."

He agreed.

The duke paused once more. "If these escapades continue, people will start to talk. It will start to affect Priscilla, and hence my family. So my question is, Your Grace, how serious are you?"

Edmund straightened.

Sherring was not attempting a trap. He was a man who loved his daughter deeply and wanted the best for his child.

Edmund did not need to consider his answer. "I am most serious."

Sherring smiled. He lifted his glass. "To the future."

They exchanged farewells, and now he did partake in that fine vintage. When he walked out of the office, Priscilla looked at them with eager eyes, yet he only smiled mildly. "A productive meeting."

As he departed, he could feel her wary eyes on him.

SHE WAS BEGINNING to understand what Lord Castleberry saw in rocks.

They were consistent. They didn't pretend to be one type of rock and then turn out to be something altogether different. They didn't talk back to you, weren't condescending.

They certainly didn't take liberties they had no right taking!

"My lord, this isn't why I wanted to chat with you!" She jumped to the side, barely missing the bony hand of the overreaching lord.

"What else could a woman possibly want to discuss with a man?" Lord Higgins replied, as if a female having anything serious in her mind was beyond comprehension. "Come here, pretty flower."

Priscilla squeaked as she darted around him. Fortunately, Lord Higgins was uncoordinated, slow and clumsy, especially since he was well into his cups. Goodness. Who went to the theater foxed?

Fear assaulted her. Not for herself physically, but at scandal. Rumors were the man was looking for his third wife.

It should have been an easy investigation. During a break in acts, she would catch the lord in the hallway for a quick chat about politics he was unlikely to remember. She had barely gotten a word out before he started chasing her like an overgrown schoolboy, managing to corner her into one of the prop rooms. Now she had to get out before someone noticed.

"Come here, my darling."

She firmed up her stance. He was standing in front of the door, but it didn't matter. One way or another, she was leaving. "Goodbye!" she said sternly, walking to him instead of away. Only he stood in front of the only escape.

"Please move!"

He grinned lecherously. "What will you do to convince me?" He closed his eyes, puckered his lips.

She punched him in the nose.

He squealed and cursed, but veered to the side. She dashed around him, and opened the door to a thankfully empty hallway. She turned quickly. "You should be ashamed of yourself. And if you dare insinuate anything, I'll tell my–" She stopped, smiled. "I'll tell Bradenton."

The lord's eyes widened, and he gasped. "Don't worry! There's no need to tell anyone about your misunderstanding."

Her misunderstanding? She humphed, but didn't respond as she fled. Yet another failed investigation. At least Bradenton hadn't been there to see it.

TIME TO INVESTIGATE.

It had been far too long since *he* had pursued a target.

Edmund prowled the corridors of the theater house, nodding to others as he passed, yet continuing a brisk stride that disavowed any who thought to stop him. He had no time for idle chatter in these few minutes in between acts. Not if he wanted to find Priscilla.

She was here with her family, at the play that was the talk of the town. He had watched her in her box, yet the moment the curtains fell, she fled. Disappearing seemed to be a hobby of hers, far more common than sewing or resting. It made him distinctly uncomfortable.

"I recognize that look."

"So do I."

Edmund neither slowed nor responded, even as Crawford and Peyton picked up their pace to keep up with him.

"My goodness, he's so focused, he doesn't even see us." Crawford grinned.

"What do you think he is looking for?" Peyton added.

"Don't you mean whom?" Crawford corrected.

"Most assuredly."

Edmund held in a sigh. "Have you seen her?"

With no need to voice the name, his two friends exchanged amused glances. "It's come to all that?" Crawford inquired. "Not a good look, old chap. I would set about securing her sooner rather than later."

The idea had definite appeal. "For now I would settle on knowing where she was. And most of all, making certain she isn't putting herself in danger." *Again.*

"I don't know where the fair Lady Priscilla is, but I do know the location of Lady Hannah and Lady Emma. Since the three are cohorts, perhaps we should ask them."

"Why do you know where Lady Hannah is?" Edmund asked as he followed Crawford down another corridor to one of the quieter theater sections, which mostly contained storage rooms and offices.

Crawford grinned. "The lady seems to have a penchant for trouble. Just doing my duty as a gentleman."

It was far more than that, but Edmund didn't inquire further as Crawford slowed before an ajar door. The lights were off, yet the sound of female voices belied its emptiness.

"Where is she?" Lady Hannah's timbre was clear. "She's supposed to be back by now, with valuable information."

"You don't think she's in trouble, do you?" Lady's Emma's softer voice crooned.

Suspicion gave way to concern, then concern to worry. It took all his control not to burst into the room, demand Lady Priscilla's location and scheme.

"She's fine," Hannah soothed. "Priscilla has done this many times."

"She's had trouble before. She just hasn't said anything."

They paused. As the seconds ticked by, his anxiety grew. He would not be able to wait much longer.

"Perhaps we should go look for her," Emma sighed.

"Let's give her just another minute."

It was a minute more than he was willing to spare. Just as Edmund moved forward, a hand on his arm stopped him.

With a finger over his lips, Crawford gestured to a figure in the distance.

Priscilla.

Pure relief flared as she hurried closer, showing no indication she had seen them. A group of matrons stepped in front of her, stopping her progress. Even from a distance, he could see her anxiety at being waylaid.

Yet for him it was an opportunity.

"I have an idea," he whispered to the two men. "But I need you to get Hannah and Emma away from here."

Peyton nodded, as Crawford rubbed his hands together. "No problem."

With quiet movements, the men entered the room. A commotion sounded a moment later, as Peyton and Crawford led two protesting ladies from the room. Edmund kept his back turned as they passed, then glanced back to Priscilla, who was still engaged in conversation, before ducking into the room.

The space was all darkness and shadows. Clearly the women had not wanted to alert others of their presence, and now it worked to his advantage. He moved as far into the shadows as he could, hiding behind a large prop. She would neither see nor easily reach him.

A minute later, the door opened.

"Hannah? Emma?" a low voice whispered. "Where are you? I can't see you."

He had to acknowledge her, yet how? Perhaps if he just made a noise, she would think it was one of her friends. He gave a low grunt.

There was a pause.

If it didn't work, he would just come out and–

"I'm sorry I'm late. The lord got some ideas..."

He couldn't stop a low growl.

"Don't worry, Hannah. I punched him in the nose."

Anger melted into satisfaction, then back to anger. When he found that lord…

She sighed. "I got nothing from him, absolutely nothing. It's all Bradenton's fault!"

What in the world had happened, and how was it his fault?

"Bradenton wasn't even there. He doesn't have to be." Footsteps thudded, the clear sound of her pacing. "His existence is enough! I'm always so worried he'll show up, I'm making mistakes. That's how I accidentally ruined what could have been a very productive afternoon." She sighed. "I know the question you are too polite to ask: why am I always thinking about Edmund?"

For a moment, Priscilla said nothing, yet he could imagine her with her hands on her hips, her cheeks flushed.

"I have no idea!" she exclaimed. "It was that kiss. Oh goodness, I didn't mean to admit we kissed."

She breathed out. "Emma, Hannah, I just don't know what to do. He affects me like no other, and not just because of what we are to each other."

What were they to each other?

"I pretend he infuriates me, but in truth, he's

amazing. He's so much more than a gorgeous, eligible lord. He's kind and giving, thoughtful and so very smart. And *delicious*. Oh goodness." She gave a nervous laugh. "Did I just call a duke delicious? Despite everything, I want Bradenton to grab me and give me another kiss that makes my insides sizzle." She sighed. "You've been so quiet. Tell me what you think."

It was time. He moved out of the shadows.

The scream rattled the entire room.

CHAPTER SEVEN

Dear P,

While victory is never assured, I have been successful in the vast majority of my quests. At the risk of sounding too self-assured…

I am confident in my triumph.

Be careful with your investigations into Cattlyn. While he is not as dangerous as some lords, he is extremely intelligent and crafty. I am dealing with such an opponent right now. Constructing a plan is difficult, especially when instincts demand you take control of the situation. How do you plan to conduct your investigation? If I can assist in any way, you need only ask.

Yours,
Edmund

P.S. Do any additional letters accompany the P? Idle curiosity, of course.

IT WAS A dream. Or a nightmare. Or both.

Bradenton was here. He heard her admit she punched a lord, complain about her failed missions and call him delicious.

Oh yes, and say his kisses made her inside sizzle.

Options:

Find a vase.

Turn invisible.

Pretend she was lost on the way to the ladies' retiring room.

A sliver of light from the door illuminated his features. His expression was neutral, betraying nothing. "Good evening, Lady Priscilla. I trust you are well."

"Have I turned invisible?"

His lips twitched. "I'm afraid not."

"Is there a vase in the room?"

"Heavens forbid."

"Would you believe the entrance to the ladies' retiring room is under that chest of drawers?"

He folded his arms across his chest.

Her body heated, uncaring of the inopportune moment. He was muscular, powerful, extraordinary. "I suppose you heard everything I just said."

"Every. Single. Word." He took a step closer. "And I have some questions."

She fought for strength. "Why are you here?

Where are Hannah and Emma?"

"Your friends are in Crawford and Peyton's most capable hands. As for why I am here, I was curious about where you keep disappearing to, and why." He stepped forward. "So tell me, Lady Priscilla, who were you meeting?"

His scent surrounded her, and the urge to surrender to his control hit. She stood taller. "It was not for any scandalous reason. I simply had a matter to discuss."

"What matter? With whom?"

"It is none of your concern."

"It is if you had to resort to punching him in the nose to get past him." His eyes flashed, as for just a moment, he showed his true power. "I would very much like to talk with him."

Her heart stumbled. Bradenton was not a man to be trifled with. "While I appreciate your chivalry, it is completely unnecessary. Clearly you misconstrued my words."

"Perhaps we should discuss the other things you said."

"You heard incorrectly!"

"I'm sorry?"

"You obviously misunderstood. I said you were… mischievous."

"Are you sure, because it didn't sound like that? In fact, it sounded like–"

"Audacious?"

"No, it started with a D."

"Ah, yes, disastrous."

His voice deepened, its husky cadence flowing through her like smooth honey. "And what about your comment about our kisses? You said my kisses made your insides–"

"Fizzle."

He let out a low chuckle. "Close, my dear, but not quite."

She held her nose up. "That was indeed what I said."

"Then I will have to issue a challenge."

"A challe–"

He pressed his lips to hers.

She couldn't fight. Not him, not her own misguided urges. Not when the handsome, kind and *delicious* man assaulted both her senses and her body. His intoxicating scent surrounded her, a taste of liquor and pure male. He wrapped his arms around her, pulled her closer.

"Curtain!" A voice outside yelled.

She pulled away, jerking so fast she nearly fell. "What are you doing? What am I doing? What are we doing?"

The passion in his eyes betrayed he was as affected as she. "Would you still like to deny what you said?"

She clenched her fists, but the words wouldn't come. Only one option remained:

Escape.

Without another word, she spun and threaded through the props, miraculously not tripping as she pushed open the door. Fortunately, no one paid her attention as she bustled back to her seat.

But her insides?

They sizzled.

"I ARRANGE THE rocks in order of importance, according to their rank."

How did she get stuck in another dance with the Earl of Castleberry?

"I explain my reasons so there are no hard feelings, of course."

It didn't seem right to clobber a man who was clearly not well.

"Of course all the female rocks are the lowest status."

On second thought, a vase might be appropriate.

A voice emerged from behind her, deep and powerful as it sent shivers down her neck. "I'm sorry to interrupt your dance, but a certain lovely lady is summoning you. She desperately needs your assistance."

Castleberry's eyes widened. He licked his lips as he took in the interloper's serious demeanor. "Really?"

"Oh yes. She said she was very interested in your… rocks."

Castleberry's eyes darted between Priscilla and the far end of the ballroom, where lords and ladies in shimmering finery and sparkling jewels danced under the candlelight. Cattlyn's ball was an unmitigated crush. "Lady Priscilla, would you be so kind as to excuse me? I hate to leave, but if someone requires my expertise about rocks, well, you understand."

Priscilla fought to keep a straight face. "Of course, my lord."

He gave a short bow and hurried away.

Bradenton stepped into his place. "May I?"

Even as she shook her head, she put her hands into position. "You know I can't refuse in front of everyone."

"I was counting on it."

They started to dance, immediately falling into perfect rhythm. "I suppose I owe you for relieving my suffering. I am curious, though. Did a lady truly ask for his expertise?"

"Of course." He swung her around. "And she was indeed a beautiful woman. She was also a great-grandmother."

Priscilla couldn't stop the smile. "If he wasn't about to share his views on the inferiority of female rocks, I might feel sorry for him."

"I have no remorse," he rumbled. "He made the decision to leave the most beautiful lady at the ball."

She swallowed, peering down at the pale blue satin slippers that matched her dress. "Do not start telling untruths, Your Grace."

"I never say anything I don't mean." He

pulled her closer. "You are extraordinary."

She blushed.

"It is fortunate there are no vases nearby," he whispered.

"Quite fortunate for conniving dukes." Yet truthfully, she had no desire to clobber him. Kiss him? *Yes, please.* "Tell me, Your Grace, how fares the hunt for a bride? And if you'd like a count, two hundred and fifty-two ladies are currently watching you."

"My endeavor is progressing well." His eyes were serious. "I have no doubt all will turn out as I hope."

Her heart skipped a beat. "Are you certain?"

His fingers tightened. "Absolutely."

They twirled again, and she looked out over the sea of people. She may have jested, but many of them watched, the men with smiles, the ladies glaring. Something sour swirled in her stomach. "Your number of admirers grows by the minute."

He smiled, as if he knew the path her thoughts had taken.

"Who are you considering for a bride?" She clamped her mouth shut. "I'm sorry, that was impertinent."

"It's quite all right. You shared your suitors with me. I am considering many, including Lady Betty Thompson, Lady Rachel Butler and the Carlyle sisters."

"They are completely unsuitable."

Surprise, then quickly amusement, lit his gaze. "You don't say? What in particular is objectionable about them?"

Really, nothing. They were all diamonds of the first water. Yet, somehow completely, utterly, most definitely wrong for Edmund. "They talk to rocks."

"Do they now?" He chuckled lightly. "I'll keep that under advisement."

The song ended, yet instead of exchanging farewells, he looked at her speculatively. "Do you have a partner for the next dance?"

She should lie, or at least make up an excuse. She shook her head instead.

"Excellent. Then I shall take another."

Of course he commanded instead of asked, yet she was powerless to resist. Every minute in his presence courted danger, yet something compelled her to remain.

The next dance was a waltz, and she moved even closer to him. A comfortable silence ensued, as she enjoyed simply being in his arms.

"Tell me about your family," he asked conversationally. "I haven't seen your brothers. Have they returned to London?"

"Not yet. One of our cousins is recovering from a serious illness, and they are helping with his estate." Although she normally enjoyed her brothers' presence, their absence now was a blessing. They liked and respected Bradenton. No doubt they'd be pressuring her to marry him immediately.

"Do you get along well?"

"I love them, and they love me. They have always been kind and affectionate."

He cocked his head to the side. "But something bothers you."

She hid her surprise. She was adept at hiding her dissatisfaction, yet somehow Bradenton saw through her facade. "They don't realize I'm a grown woman. They treat me like I'm still in the schoolroom."

"I'm sure they are just trying to protect you."

"I don't need protecting."

He smiled softly. "A big brother remembers his sister's first smile, her first steps, the first time she said 'I love you.' He remembers a tiny thing in braids following him around, giggling at every word. He wants to shield her from all the dangers of the world."

She softened. Undoubtedly he was thinking of his own younger sisters. "Are you close with your siblings?"

He nodded. "I would do anything for them. I'll admit to being overprotective, but it's just because I love them. They are beautiful, kind and smart, sometimes too much. In fact, they remind me of you."

Priscilla smiled. She had only met them a few times, because they had not launched yet, but she remembered sweet, precocious little girls.

"Even as children, they were sneaky little things. They even managed to trick me for an entire summer."

This she had to hear. "Do tell."

He sighed, but a smile played on his lips. "One day, they tiptoed past me, munching on apple tarts and carrying a bag almost as large as them. They looked so guilty, I demanded they show me the contents of the bag. Yet when I looked, it was only their art supplies. The next day, the same thing happened, two little tart-munching girls with a big bag. This time it held their dolls. When it happened again the third day, I let them pass, to fool them, but then I checked the next day. This time the bag was filled with their toys. Every day for the whole summer, they did the same thing. Sometimes I checked, sometimes I didn't, but the bag never held anything that wasn't theirs."

An image of a flummoxed Bradenton amidst two mischievous little girls flashed in her mind. It was endearing. "Did you ever figure out what they were up to?"

"Oh yes," Bradenton grinned. "Turns out they were indeed smugglers."

"But you said everything in the bag belonged to them."

"Indeed."

"Then what did they smuggle?"

"Apple tarts."

Priscilla chuckled. "They carried the bag to distract you."

"Exactly. Cook was beside herself over how she misplaced two tarts every single day."

She laughed again. "So what did you do? March them to the constable and demand he lock them up?"

"Not quite." His eyes shined. "I told them that next time, they should include me in their scheme. I loved Cook's apple tarts."

She blinked in surprise. "You didn't get them in trouble?"

"No. I probably should have, but Cook was such a mean curmudgeon. She hated children and never let them have any sweets. I considered it a little taste of justice." He chuckled lowly. "Plus, they were simply adorable when I caught them."

She shook her head. No one would believe the duke let his kid sisters get the better of him. Maybe he wasn't as harsh as she imagined.

"Soon I will have to choose their husbands."

Or perhaps she was right all along.

"Choose their husbands? Don't you mean *they* will choose?"

"Of course."

Yet something about his tone wasn't quite genuine. He would give them some freedom, yet when it came down to it, he would make the final decision. It was why she could never surrender herself.

But she did not want to break the contented mood, so she told him about her good-natured rivalry with her own brothers, including the time she hid under blankets and pretended to be a ghost. They were both smiling widely as the dance ended.

"You have a lovely laugh, Lady Priscilla."

"As do you, Your Grace. You should use it more often."

"Perhaps I should." He gazed steadily at her. "You must admit our discussions are more enjoyable than a conversation on rocks."

"Of course not," she teased. "I've been waiting for you to mention rocks this entire time. In fact, right now I'm going to go outside and talk to a rock."

"Truly?"

"Truly."

They both laughed again. And as they bowed, she didn't miss all the stares, from the ladies, from her parents, from the entire ton.

She was in trouble.

"YOU'RE SMILING." THE words were spoken with surprise, astonishment even. Especially since Edmund just put down a losing hand, surrendering a small fortune to Crawford.

The money was of little consequence. Yet he

was shocked at how easily he was showing his other hand, his satisfaction with Priscilla's courtship. "I'm sorry. My mind was elsewhere."

Crawford collected his earnings. "Usually you trounce me, but today I've won everything but your favorite horse."

"It's not as dire as all that." He never wagered what he couldn't afford to lose, and he could afford to lose much.

Peyton leaned in. "So what were you thinking about? And by that I mean who were you thinking about? And by that I mean how is Lady Priscilla?"

Edmund couldn't even find the motivation to growl. "She's fine. I appreciate you helping with Lady Emma and Lady Hannah the other day."

"It was no chore," Peyton said. "Lady Emma is a calm and timid lady."

"Not Lady Hannah." Crawford grinned.

Edmund gave his friend an inquisitive look, but Crawford didn't elaborate.

Peyton shuffled the playing cards and dealt another round. "How is your other hunt? Any luck finding your mysterious informant?"

Edmund palmed his cards. "That endeavor is as frustrating as ever. He is immune to all my efforts, and I'm no closer to discovering his identity than when I started. He could be any lord of the *ton*."

"No more clues in the letters?"

"Nothing blatant."

"It's too bad you can't watch him investigate."

"Exactly." Edmund looked at his cards, but the symbols blurred before his eyes. Slowly, he put them down. "Maybe I can."

Peyton looked up from his hand. "Maybe you can what?"

"Maybe I can catch him in the hunt."

"How? I assume he doesn't tell you the location of his investigations."

"Not where," Edmund grinned. "But whom."

Crawford shrugged. "Even if you know where, that doesn't tell when. You can't catch him a month after he searches."

"No, but I may be able to deduce it." Edmund's excitement grew. "Think about it. If you wanted to investigate a lord, would you break into his home?"

Crawford frowned. "Probably not. The risk of discovery would be too great."

"Exactly. But when could you search a lord's home with far less risk and a better chance of explaining yourself if caught?"

Crawford stared at him for a moment, then slowly grinned. "A party."

"Precisely!" Edmund sat back. "If my informant is already in the house for a party, he could easily slip away to conduct some sleuthing. If someone catches him, he can simply claim he got lost."

A foggy thought infiltrated the back of his mind, as if he were forgetting something important.

"Lord Cattlyn doesn't usually vote with us. Is he on your list?"

Edmund started. "Not only is he on the list, but he was the last target Lord P mentioned."

"Which means…"

"He could investigate tonight." Edmund ran a hand through his hair. Lord P could be out there, putting his life in danger this very moment.

"If your informant investigates during the party, when would he make his move?" Peyton asked. "He couldn't spend all night wandering the house."

"True." There had to be a way to narrow down the timeframe. "He wouldn't attempt it during dinner. Someone would miss him."

"And he wouldn't do it at the very beginning or end," Peyton offered. "The crowd is far thinner then."

"Which means he'd probably search at the height of the party…"

"Which is right around now."

"What are you waiting for?" Crawford gestured to the cards. "Fold and head out!"

Edmund picked up his cards. "I'll do this instead." He placed down a royal flush. As the others groaned, he collected all he'd lost and then some. "Hopefully I'll have as much luck finding my mysterious informant."

Crawford threw down his cards. "He doesn't stand a chance."

He was counting on it.

"YOU'RE GOING TO get caught."

It was a distinct possibility. The question was who would catch her. Lord Cattlyn?

Edmund?

"I have no choice," Priscilla whispered to Emma, who was trying to convince her to abandon the investigation, and Hannah, who wanted to join her. "I haven't gotten any good information in weeks. I have to find something."

"So talk to Cattlyn," Emma implored. "Maybe he'll slip."

"I already tried." Priscilla looked across the ballroom, to where the loud and garish lord was simpering at ladies half his age. "He's not as careless as he seems."

"So let's discover his secrets and blackmail him."

"Hannah!"

"We already agreed blackmail is not an option," Priscilla said firmly.

"I didn't agree," Hannah grumbled.

Priscilla ignored it. "But a quick look around the house is worthwhile. With this crowd, no one will notice if I slip away. But I need to hurry. My parents will realize if I miss dinner."

"What about Bradenton?"

Priscilla swallowed. How could the simple mention of his name produce such unease? "What about him?"

"You danced multiple sets with him, and your carriage ride was… unusual."

Priscilla held back a sigh. Everyone had heard of her "adventure," which now included Edmund besting a dozen men and carrying her away as she swooned. "He considers me a challenge, nothing more."

"Are you sure?" Hannah frowned. "Because the way he looks at you…"

"Is nothing special."

"What about the way you look at him?" Emma asked softly.

Priscilla swallowed the truth. "Edmun– Bradenton is unsuitable for me, and that will never change. I must go."

Hannah hesitated for just a moment. "Just in case, we'll keep watch while you're gone."

Priscilla nodded. She took a deep breath…

And walked into the unknown.

SOMEONE LURKED IN the shadows.

Edmund couldn't see his face, or even his outline, but the signs were there. Doors left ajar, imprints in otherwise perfect rugs, objects that looked as if they'd been recently disturbed. But the most telling sign of all: the soft cadence of footsteps ahead.

He'd searched for minutes before he heard them. He followed the sound, quickly encountering the open doors and other clues. The hallways he walked through were dark and quiet, making the lurker unlikely to be a servant or member of the family. The areas led to the private areas of the home.

Exactly where his informant would investigate.

Of course he could be wrong, and it could be someone with a perfectly legitimate reason to be skulking in the shadowed halls. Or it could also be someone with a darker ulterior motive. Yet there was a distinct chance it was his informant. He was so close.

And getting closer. The footsteps had grown louder, the rustling heavier, in the darkened hallway. He moved with stealthy speed, careful not to make any noise. So far, he'd been quiet enough to avoid detection. He pushed open a door.

It creaked.

Suddenly the noise ahead of him stopped. No more rapid tattoo of footsteps, no rustling and no shuffling. He could imagine his target frozen, as he discovered he had been followed.

The subterfuge had been compromised. The prey knew he was being chased, the predator revealed his presence. Whoever roamed the halls was not supposed to be there.

Edmund's heart thundered, flooding his muscles with strength. Time to discover the identity of the mysterious Lord P.

He sprinted down the hallway.

CHAPTER EIGHT

Dear Edmund,

Your past successes may give you confidence, yet not all battles are the same. Instead of fervently pursuing your quarry, consider whether it is a battle you should be fighting at all.

I struggle with the same indecision. It is difficult when you want something so badly, knowing it can never be yours. Sometimes you just have to accept, acknowledging that yours is a different path.

I have various methods of investigation. Of course I employ careful planning, yet instincts and fortune also play a role. I find persistence is paramount to any endeavor. It is an attribute you undoubtedly share. Yet consider that sometimes, it is better to fold.

Yours,
P

P.S. There are indeed letters after P. They are Iamnotsoeasilycaught.

SHE WAS CAUGHT!

The creaking was no natural sound, no idle settling of the house. Someone was following her! She'd suspected it for a while, yet had dismissed the soft sounds as her imagination. The door's groan made it clear:

She was being hunted.

Her heart thundered in the silence, and she had to force her breathing to remaining even. Who was it? A servant, Cattlyn, *Bradenton*? Whoever it was had clearly made efforts to conceal his pursuit. It was no longer necessary.

He had found her.

What was he going to do? The silence stretched into seconds that felt like hours. Yet no matter how much time passed, she was not safe. Undoubtedly he was waiting, biding his time before he pounced.

The entire project had been useless. She had passed what felt like a dozen rooms, yet they were all empty, with no help to provide. Now she'd be lucky to escape without discovery.

Where was her pursuer?

Who was he?

Heavy footsteps broke the silence.

She couldn't stop a muffled squeak as someone thundered towards her, not yet visible but growing louder with every moment. She twisted around. How could she escape in a wide-open hallway with no doors and no windows? There was no desk to climb under, no dressers to hide behind.

No escape.

She couldn't give up! She spun again, and saw it. A heavy tapestry hung from the ceiling, reaching to the floor. Unlike when she hid under Roxbury's desk, her outline would be visible, even in the blackness. Yet it was her only hope.

She darted to the tapestry. The wine-colored fabric tangled in her hands as footsteps slammed against the ground. She found an opening and lunged. Pressed against the wall, she froze, held her breath.

Someone entered the hallway.

She couldn't see her pursuer, but solid footsteps betrayed his presence. Then…

"You've been captured."

Her heart stumbled.

Bradenton.

It was the same phrase he uttered in the garden. How ironic. Did he know it was her? Had he followed her from the ballroom?

Did he know she was Lord P?

She heaved in musty air, coating her lungs with the tapestry's thick dust. There was nowhere to hide, no escape and no excuses. He would know she had a hidden scheme, and this time he would almost certainly connect her with Lord P. They had discussed Cattlyn in their last letter.

She stayed silent save for tripped-up breaths, waiting for the tapestry to be swept aside, praying that it wouldn't. His presence towered over her, crowding her back where there was nowhere to go. The fabric shifted as he grasped the edge. Ever-so slowly, it moved…

Suddenly, the movement stopped. She released a breath, even though the reprieve was undoubtedly temporary.

Then a voice, calm, controlled, filled with the power only Bradenton could yield. "Is it you, Lord P?"

She stifled a cry. He must not have seen her, but tracked the sounds and signs she left behind. He knew he was following Lord P, not Priscilla.

In a moment, he would learn he followed both.

Responding wasn't even possible. Her breath caught in her throat, all lies, facades and misdirection utterly hopeless. All she could do was wait while Bradenton seized victory.

"I hope you forgive me." Bradenton's words were low, controlled. "I know you wish to remain in the shadows, figuratively and literally. Yet although we have never met, I consider you more than a colleague. You are a friend, and I cannot allow you to take these risks on your own."

Once he found out who she was, he was more likely to lock her in her quarters than support her investigations. Of course, he didn't have any true power over her, but she knew how he worked.

He always took control.

"If you are concerned because we have some sort of connection in the real world, please do not be. I know the man you truly are. Maybe not your name or title, but the true person. Won't you come out?" he prodded softly. "Talk to me? I would like to know whom I call friend."

She didn't move, barely dared to breathe. Was there any chance he would leave, grant her secrecy? For a moment, he didn't speak, and the slightest spark of hope surfaced.

Then the tapestry shifted.

He was opening it, and this time he wouldn't stop. Her ruse was up, discovery a moment away. She squeezed her eyes shut, waiting for the shock, the anger. The total loss of control.

It moved slowly, slowly, slowly. Cool air flowed in as a sliver of light appeared. It grew bigger…

"Your Grace! Your Grace! Where are you?"

All movement ceased. Edmund still held the tapestry, yet froze at the sudden words, distant and yelled.

"Someone is coming." The fabric snapped

back, just as the call came again, from closer this time, heralded by heavy footsteps.

The discoverer had been discovered.

Would she be?

"Don't worry. I'll protect you."

Her breath hitched. This was his opportunity to unmask her, yet he was shielding her instead.

It was simply who Edmund was.

"I'll lead them back to the ballroom. Wait a few minutes before following."

She nodded even though he couldn't see, swallowing emotions she couldn't name. Her heart lurched as his presence withdrew, as he moved rapidly away.

Then there was someone else, no, judging by the footsteps, two others.

"Your Grace, there you are. We've been looking for you everywhere!"

"We're so glad we found you!"

Priscilla breathed out. Her saviors had arrived.

"Lady Emma and Lady Hannah, what are you doing here?" Edmund betrayed nothing of the discovery he'd almost made. "Is everything all right?"

"We were worried when you wandered into the closed wing. We thought you might have gotten lost." Although it had to be feigned, fright laced Emma's voice, rising in pitch with every word. Impressive. Timid Emma always fought against subterfuge, yet she was clearly a gifted actress.

"Is everything well, Your Grace?" Hannah asked. "What are you doing here?"

"I was simply searching for a moment of quiet." Bradenton's voice was neutral, measured. "I appreciate your concern, but you needn't have worried. I was just about to return the ball. Let me escort you."

They must have started moving because whatever was said next was too low for Priscilla to hear. Still, she waited a good few minutes before leaving her hiding spot, peeking out first before racing back to the ball. The sooner she returned, the less chance Edmund would notice her missing and realize she was his mysterious informant. Unfortunately she had to take a different path, longer and winding, in case he was watching for his informant's return.

She emerged back to a party in full momentum. The crush soothed her slightly, for even Edmund couldn't see everyone through the jostling throng. Now he was nowhere to be seen. If only she could escape, beg a headache and return home. Yet she couldn't leave until she discovered what he knew.

If he knew.

Just because he hadn't swept aside the tapestry didn't mean he hadn't deduced the truth. He may have noticed her missing in the minutes before his trek, or after, when she took so long to return. He may consider anew her escapade in Roxbury's garden, link her with his informant. He was extraordinarily clever, his eventual discovery of the truth nearly inevitable. But had he discovered it yet?

Just as she took a step to find him, Emma and Hannah burst from the crowd. With a grateful smile, she allowed them to lead her to a private corner.

"Are you well?" Emma whispered.

Hannah was more frank. "Did he discover the truth? What is he going to do? Do you need passage to America?"

"He doesn't know the truth, or at least I don't think he does." Priscilla breathed deeply. "He was about to learn it, though. I was hiding behind the tapestry."

Emma gasped. "You were there when we caught him? Did he see you?"

"No." She shivered at the memory of the shifting fabric, the cool air as he exposed her inch by inch. "He was about to pull it back when you arrived."

"My goodness." Hannah shook her head. "A few seconds later…"

"I would have been caught."

Emma put a hand on her shoulder.

Priscilla took another shuddering breath. She had to stay calm and collected to confront

Edmund. Speaking of acting…

"You surprised me." Priscilla turned to Emma. "You were quite the actress."

Emma blushed. "I'm just grateful we were there in time."

"As soon as we saw him leave, we followed," Hannah said. "Unfortunately some matrons waylaid us, which is why we weren't there sooner."

"You made it soon enough." Priscilla glanced back to the crowd, but Edmund was still not in sight. "Did he ask where I was?"

Hannah frowned. "It was the first thing he asked. But don't worry. We told him you were in the ladies' retiring room."

Bloody Hell.

Hannah watched her carefully. "You don't look relieved."

"I am. It's just…" She rubbed the back of her neck. "I think he's suspicious of my activities."

Emma paled. "But you said he didn't see you."

"That doesn't mean he won't figure out I'm investigating." She clutched her skirt, rubbing her hands against the soft fabric. "Bradenton is too clever by half. Last time we were at a ball, he caught me in Roxbury's garden. Now he almost caught me again. If he realizes I have an ulterior motive…"

"He may realize the woman he's hunting is

hunting others?"

Hunting. Priscilla's breath hitched at the word. Although she tried to deny it, Bradenton was hunting her, in more ways than one.

He was getting closer on both counts.

"He's smart enough to discover the truth," she said quietly. "The only question is whether he has."

"You should talk to him."

Hannah frowned at Emma's words, but slowly nodded. "I hate to say it, but I agree. You have to find out what he knows."

She took a deep breath. "I will find him."

"What are you going to say?"

"Hi Bradenton, guess what? I investigate lords and convince them to vote for my measures."

Emma's eyes widened before she smiled. "You're joking."

"Of course." Yet what would happen if she revealed the truth? No more apprehension, no need to watch her every word.

No escape.

No, exposure wasn't an option, at least not if she had a choice. Now she had to discover what he knew.

This time it was not difficult to find Edmund. She simply searched for the largest crowd, and there he was, surrounded by high-ranked society members. He glanced towards the door leading to the hallway. Even though she had taken a different path, she was far from safe. He had to know multiple exits existed.

Standing tall, she set off towards him.

He noticed her immediately. His eyes lingered, studying, searching, contemplating. She waited for an accusation, shock, anything to suggest he knew their true connection, yet he betrayed nothing.

"I'm afraid I must now excuse myself. It's time for my dance with Lady Priscilla."

They had no such dance, yet she kept her expression serene as the group turned to her with a dizzying mixture of interest, envy and spite. Edmund showed far more than casual interest, practically announcing his suit for the world to see.

She gave her best "daughter of a duke" nod and accepted Edmund's arm. She kept silent until they were in each other's arms, starting a perfectly timed waltz.

"I stole a dance, and you didn't say a word," he murmured. "Are you ill?"

She looked into eyes the color of the twilight sky. "Of course not, Your Grace. In fact, I was just about to complain about your insolence."

"Were you?" He spoke without humor. "Has something distracted you?"

She shook her head. "I have not forgotten your imperious behavior. What if I planned to dance with another lord?"

"I would have said you couldn't hide from me."

She stumbled, pitching forward into his arms. Bands of iron captured her, pressing her against his hardness amidst a million sensual sparks. In the next moment, he released her, so smoothly no one would suspect it was more than a slight misstep on her part and a helping gesture on his.

She knew better.

He narrowed his eyes. "Are you all right?"

"I'm fine."

"Are you certain?" He held her tighter than normal, effortlessly gliding her through the steps. "You seem flustered, and Hannah said you were in the ladies' retiring room." He paused, frowned.

Oh no! He mustn't connect the two excuses. "I was simply helping a friend. She was upset about one of her suitors, and I consoled her."

He gazed at her carefully.

She swallowed. Now she had to wander into more dangerous territory. "Hannah said you were roaming the halls. I don't blame you. This is quite the crush."

"Indeed."

She paused for a moment, but he didn't continue. "Did you enjoy your walk?" she prodded.

"It was not as beneficial as I hoped."

She breathed out.

"Don't worry, my dear. It was just a temporary setback. I will soon accomplish my goals."

She stumbled again.

This time she caught herself before she fell into his arms. "I'm sorry," she mumbled as she righted herself. "I'm not normally so clumsy. I must still be distracted with my friend's predicament."

He stared at her with indistinguishable emotion. "Do you wish to share her dilemma? Perhaps I can provide assistance."

As every thought in her mind seemingly vanished, it became clear this had been a mistake. She simply couldn't focus in his presence. Soon the dance would be over, and she could avoid him for the rest of the night. For now, she had to come up with a response that sounded coherent. "She was upset because of her…" What in blazes had she said?

"Suitor?"

"Exactly, a suitor!" She eyed the door to the ballroom. If she took a leaping start, she may be able to reach it before he started running.

Or he might capture her.

"She has a suitor who is completely unacceptable. No matter how she tries to dissuade him, he won't give up."

Challenge sparked in his eyes.

She swallowed, pressed on, "It really is quite silly of him, of course. If she won't take him, there's nothing he can do."

"Really?" He leaned in, his voice low, dark. "Are you certain?"

Not even a little.

"Of course. No matter what a lord demands, a lady still has to say her vows."

He dipped his head. "If the gentleman is in a position of power, her resistance may prove insufficient. I know you do not like it, Lady Priscilla, but that is the way of the world. Of course, her family must ensure the match is suitable." He frowned. "Is the suitor a bad man?"

She was taken aback. "Well, no…"

"Does he mistreat her?"

"Definitely not," she replied automatically.

"Is he very old? A spendthrift? Surrounded by scandal?"

She pursed her lips. "None of those things."

"Then if you don't mind my asking, what exactly are the lady's objections?"

"He's an overbearing, authoritative tyrant."

He grinned.

She growled.

He spun her in a dizzying circle, taking advantage to hold her closer. "Your friend may want to consider surrender. Sometimes, the future is inevitable."

"Or she could clobber him with a vase."

Edmund threw his head back and laughed.

She sniffed into the air. "I'm just saying that's

what I would do."

"My little spitfire." He held her closer. "I have a feeling her suitor will be able to control the situation."

"*She* will succeed."

He leaned nearer. "Victory is his."

The dance came to an abrupt end.

She let out a breath, watching the man watching her. In the end, they both knew they were discussing no friend, but at least the subject had turned away from Lord P. For now, she would take no more chances. "Thank you for the dance. I'm afraid I will be unavailable for the rest of the evening. I must seek out my mother to inquire about dinner arrangements."

An odd expression entered his eyes, part triumph, part slyness and all power. "Perhaps we will be together sooner than you think."

She narrowed his eyes. "Your Grace?"

"If I was your friend's suitor, I would ensure I had sufficient time to conduct my coup."

What had he done?

"Our host was kind enough to allow me to help with the seating arrangements."

Her breath hitched. "You didn't."

"I did." He leaned in. "You're not going anywhere. And while we are together, you will describe exactly what happened when you disappeared."

This. Was. Bad.

CHAPTER NINE

Dear P,

I always conduct my endeavors with careful thought and deliberate action. Whether for political causes or personal undertakings, I do not let anything stand in my way.

By the stalwart way you guard your secret, I suspect you are as determined. Do not add another number to your count of my inquiries, for I am not again asking you to reveal yourself. Instead I ask another question:

Why?

Why are you hiding from me? Why have you kept your identity a secret? Do we know each other? Do you fear me?

Whatever it is, I would like the opportunity to address your concerns and allay your fears. Perhaps I could even persuade you to change your mind…

Yours,
Edmund

HE WAS LUCKY there were no vases nearby.

Edmund had seen duelists with less outraged passion than Priscilla. Her cheeks were tinged pink, her eyes flashing a brilliant emerald. She did not realize her fiery challenge only made him want her more.

She was glorious.

Yet she was also distracted and out of sorts. She claimed it was her friend, yet the suitor she'd described had obviously been him. Of course her friend may have had a similar situation.

Or there was no friend.

"You arranged for us to sit together?" She glared at him. "Do you realize how high-handed that is?"

"Yes, I do."

"Domineering?"

"Quite."

"Tyrannical?"

"Indeed."

She put her hands on her hips, removed them when she noticed several people staring. She lowered her voice. "Do you have anything to say for this?"

Her challenge had the opposite effect intended, casting the urge to learn more about his beautiful partner. "I'm simply exploring something with the potential to be magnificent."

She colored slightly. "What if I don't want to be explored?"

He fought to keep his face passive. Did she have any idea of the images her words produced? In a moment, he could reach out and caress her soft skin, watch as it flushed pink under his administrations. Move into her territory, assert his dominance. It had been far too long since they kissed.

Soon, he would remedy that.

"You don't have a choice," he responded softly.

She couldn't hide her emotions. Not her desire when they touched, her enjoyment at their conversations or her laughter at his jokes. The more time he spent with her, the more it became clear she'd make the ideal duchess. Yet more than anger lurked in her expression. Apprehension and concern, emotions but not the cause.

"What is it, Lady Priscilla? You may be steadfast in your denials, yet you clearly enjoy my company. Now you are acting like a fox trapped by a hound. What changed?"

She looked away. "Nothing. As I said, I have had a difficult evening. If it wasn't for my family, I'd leave right now."

"Are you in some sort of trouble?"

The thought her secret could involve some sort of actual peril sent sharp discomfort through him, shocking in its breadth and depth. Could she be in danger? Was something, or someone, threatening her? The urge to discover her secrets took on newfound importance – and urgency.

She grimaced, as if his question held irony. She looked away again. "No. Everything is well."

By her haunted expression, that was clearly untrue. Yet her lips were as tight as a spy's, and further interrogation now would be useless. Yet he was a persistent man, and a patient one.

He would continue to search for her secrets.

"LADY PRISCILLA JUST told me how much she adores your rocks."

Bradenton was going to find himself at the wrong end of a vase.

"We had an entire conversation about her affinity for them."

Daughters of dukes do not get sent to Newgate.

"She said she looked forward to hearing all about them."

And if they did, it would be worthwhile.

It was a nightmare, no a nightmare within a nightmare. She already knew she'd be sitting next to Bradenton, pretending he didn't affect her with every smoldering look. Of course she'd be near her mother, who was already counting grand-babies on two hands. But now the sly duke managed to surround her with the suitors on her list, including her favorite rock-loving earl.

Why? No doubt to make their idiosyncrasies seem all the more frustrating. He was wagering she wouldn't want to spend every day talking about – or to – rocks.

He was right.

"That's wonderful." Castleberry gushed. "Tell me, what is your favorite rock?"

The type that can be used to clobber one very satisfied looking duke. "I like…" He had named the rocks a thousand times, yet now she couldn't remember a single one. "The really…" *Everyone was staring at her.* "Hard ones."

Bradenton choked back a laugh while the others looked at her indulgently.

Bradenton turned to Lord Ridgeland, whose fascination with horses went beyond even the most fervent fan. "Lady Priscilla is also quite interested in horses. Of course this is your area of expertise."

Oh no. Such a statement could only have one consequence.

A speech on every single horse Ridgeland owned.

A very, very, very, very, very long speech.

Priscilla tried to stay interested. She really, truly tried. After all, she hadn't yet crossed Ridgeland off her list. Yet by the end of the twenty-minute diatribe that ended with Ridgeland insisting his stallion could best a man at poker, he was most certainly off the list.

It was then the Duke of Dewey's turn to discuss his plants. By the time he was fifteen minutes in, she was considering clobbering *herself* with a vase. The only other person who managed to get a word in was Bradenton, to whom everyone listened, of course.

"What plants grow best in your garden?" Bradenton asked her.

"Let me answer that." Dewey chuckled at Priscilla. "It's quite all right, my dear. I wouldn't expect a lady to understand the complexities of nature."

She gritted her teeth. If only men understood what it was like to be judged solely on gender. Yet she nodded, because a duke's daughter did not argue with a lord in public.

Apparently, the same could not be said about a duke.

"Actually, Lady Priscilla understands far more than the average person." Edmund's voice was deceptively low. "To suggest otherwise is unacceptable."

Dewey paled. "I wasn't suggesting Lady Priscilla was in any way inadequate," he stammered.

Others looked on in silence, their expressions ranging from shock to pity to contemplation.

Emotions tumbling, Priscilla stared at Bradenton. His eyes blazed in challenge, devoid of any amusement or scheming. He was not trying to impress her, but simply defend her.

Because helping people was what he did.

She swallowed feelings she could not afford to feel, emotions far more dangerous than anger. "I'm sure he didn't mean anything."

"Of course not!" Dewey sputtered, his face as bright as his favorite rose variety. "I regard Lady Priscilla very highly. You must know that, my dear."

"Of course," she murmured to Dewey, even as she watched Bradenton.

He held her gaze. Gone was the challenge in his eyes, replaced instead by compassion, concern.

She swallowed, nodding slightly. They did not need words to communicate.

What else could he decipher?

"I believe ladies are as capable as men, and in some cases more so." Edmund now spoke to the group, as conversation instead of accusation. "I believe society would benefit if ladies partook in activities not currently available to them."

Priscilla parted her lips, fighting a surge of desire. Other woman coveted flowers and jewels, but she'd take valor over the most flawless diamond.

The others gazed at him in surprise, yet not a single spoke against him. The respect he commanded made him the most important fighter for their cause.

"What do you like, Lady Priscilla?" Dewey turned to her, clearly trying to regain his footing. "We've shared our interests. What are yours?"

"She likes vases."

Why that little–

Priscilla closed her eyes, opened them to universal befuddlement at Edmund's statement.

"Is that correct, Lady Priscilla?"

"Yes it is." She smiled at Bradenton. "I particularly like very large and heavy vases."

Bradenton grinned.

"Of course my daughter also enjoys more traditional things," her mother broke in, looking back and forth between her and Edmund. "She even leads a sewing group."

Priscilla held back a sigh.

"Your guild has been most beneficial for my family," Castleberry spoke up. "As you know, my sister Olivia is in it."

For the first time, Priscilla gave Castleberry a genuine smile. Olivia was compassionate, vibrant and hardworking, and a true asset to their cause. It was hard to believe the clever woman was related to Castleberry. "She is very gifted."

"We'd given up hope of her ever pursuing a more…" He hesitated, glanced towards Edmund, "Traditional role. She even tried to sneak into Parliament once. We were so happy, if a little bewildered, when she showed interest in your group. She always claimed to dislike sewing." He stopped, flushed as if realizing what he was saying. "I'm just glad she found a suitable diversion."

Edmund narrowed his eyes ever-so-slightly. "I gather her work has improved."

Uh-oh.

Castleberry smiled widely. "Oh yes, I imagine it has."

"You imagine?" Edmund frowned. "You don't know?"

"Olivia is extremely shy," Castleberry explained. "She won't let us see her work."

Lady Olivia was anything but shy. She was bold, assertive and fiercely intelligent. Yet she refused to sew in protest of her strict family, not even small pieces for the ruse.

"That's impressive." Edmund turned to her. "You even attract ladies who don't care for sewing. Tell me, what else do you do during your meetings?"

Learn how to pick locks, trick lords and select the most appropriate vase for clobbering. "We talk about the usual matters, Your Grace. It's all very innocent."

At the word "innocent," his gaze sharpened.

She clamped her mouth shut. This was why she couldn't be near him. Incriminating words simply slipped out. *She who protests too much…*

"My sister loves to sew." Edmund gazed at her. "Perhaps she could attend one of your meetings."

"No!" she cried.

Her suitors froze.

Her mother looked like she was about to faint.

And the suspicion in Edmund's eyes increased a thousand times.

"I'm sorry," she choked out. "I didn't mean she can't join… when she is older."

Edmund's raised an eyebrow. "She's too young to sew?"

"No, of course not." She clenched her fists until her fingernails pinched her palms. "We discuss matters for grown women. She would be bored silly."

"Perhaps." His gaze bore into her. "Yet with her launch next season, she already attends select social functions."

"Of course." Priscilla looked around for help, but the others simply stared, as if watching some sort of stage show. She pressed on, "Still, I believe it would be terribly boring for her."

He continued his scrutiny for a moment more. "I'll yield to your discretion," he finally murmured.

She let out a breath, but no relief came. She had given him yet another clue.

It was her mother who acted an unlikely savior, garnering everyone's attention with a wide smile. "Now that that is settled, I was wondering if everyone could help me with a conundrum."

Edmund answered for the group, "We are at your service, Your Grace."

She nodded. "At my country estate, there is a rare bird, a prized specimen known for its elegance and beauty. It is not caged, but lives among the gardens, coming and going as it pleases." She paused for a moment. "Not everyone agrees with my decision to leave it in the country. Many who visit encourage me to bring it to London, where it can be lauded and enjoyed by the *ton*. Of course, I would have to enclose it in a cage so it would not escape."

She looked to the men. "I would like your opinion. Should I bring the bird to London for the world to enjoy? Or should I leave her in the country, where she can remain free among the gardens?"

Priscilla frowned. The bird her mother referenced was indeed a prize, and all who came to the estate enjoyed its beauty. Visitors had mentioned the possibility of bringing it to London, but her mother always dispelled such suggestions immediately. She loved the bird far too much, she explained.

What was she up to now?

"Bring her here," Castleberry answered first, his voice booming with certainty. "I'd love to see such a rare specimen."

"She does sound splendid," Dewey agreed. "I'm sure she'd be fine in London. She'd get plenty of attention."

"It's just a bird," Ridgeland added. "I agree with the gentlemen. Share her with the world."

They all turned to Edmund.

He pursed his lips. "You say the bird always returns to the gardens? You do not worry of it escaping?"

The duchess smiled. "There is nothing from which to escape. The garden is its home."

"In that case, let it remain free. It has already given you the gift of its beauty. Enjoy it and let those who visit admire it. Do not cage the beauty you love, or you may lose it."

Her mother stared at Bradenton, and a slow smile came to her lips. "I believe I will." She turned to them all. "Thank you for your advice."

Priscilla swallowed. Her mother's inquiry held far more meaning than readily apparent.

She had no more time to consider it, however, as a cacophony sounded through the hall. An army of servants arrived, burdened with heavy platters of creamy cheeses, plump fruits and colorful salads. The conversation died down as the guests turned their attention to the veritable feast, and soon only soft crunching and murmurs of approval sounded.

Thankfully, the conversation turned to lighter fare once it resumed. Edmund's enigmatic charm ensnared the group, yet she could not relax, not even as he lightened the mood. He did not allow her to remain quiet, however, constantly asking questions and encouraging comments. He asked several more times about her sewing group, and she answered as casually as she could. It didn't matter. Once Edmund's suspicions were raised, nothing short of revealing the truth would satisfy them. It got so bad, she actually asked Castleberry about his latest rock.

Somehow, she managed no more major incidents as they continued into far more mundane conversation. Yet, she was far from safe.

No one escaped the Duke of Bradenton.

"I ASSUME YOU'RE looking for my daughter."

Bradenton hid his surprise as the Duchess of Sherring materialized behind him, approaching with a stealth he usually associated with her daughter. Her intuition was correct. He was indeed searching for his wayward prey.

Normally he stayed far away from match-making mamas, but right now he was more interested in the help she could provide. "I am indeed. Do you know where she is?"

"I do."

Edmund waited for elaboration, but none came. She was looking at him with the same shrewd wisdom as when she inquired about her bird. It had seemed more than a simple query for advice, more like some sort of test. By her smile, he had passed.

Was it a parallel to Priscilla? Of course he did not want to cage her.

It didn't mean he had any intention of letting her go.

"If you would be so kind as to direct me, I would be most grateful."

"Of course. She is in the gardens. Walk along the path until you see a tree with purple flowers in front of a row of hedges. Behind the hedges, you will find a lovely little moonlit garden. I believe you will find her there."

She did not offer to guide him, which was surprising. Was she essentially sending him to meet her daughter alone? Suspicion borne of countless attempts at entrapment rose.

It must have been obvious, because she smiled. "Do not worry. I have no plans to stumble upon you. I simply believe you have a few things to discuss."

His estimation of her rose. She may be a matchmaking mama, but she truly had her daughter's best interests at heart. He bowed. "Thank you, Your Grace."

"Of course. Do not forget my daughter is a very special woman."

He completely agreed.

Finding Lady Priscilla would have been impossible without her mother's assistance. It still took a few minutes to locate the entrance to the garden. Glancing around to make certain he was alone, he stepped behind the wall of green.

He stopped. Stared.

She literally took his breath away.

Bathed in moonlight, Priscilla was pure loveliness, an ethereal angel come to life. Golden curls framed a heart-shaped face, an artist's masterpiece of creamy skin, ruby red lips and sparkling eyes. Generous curves filled out the glittering gown, pure, feminine beauty. She was stunning, and yet what was on the inside was even more extraordinary:

The intelligence she hid so well.

The strength few could emulate.

The kindness so rare.

She was reclining on a bench, gazing up at the stars. Suddenly she looked up, her lips forming a perfect O. "What are you doing here? How did you find me?"

He frowned at the vulnerability in her voice. That he was the source of it was disconcerting but inescapable, at least for now. Soon she would understand she had nothing to fear from him.

"I had a little help finding you," he admitted. He walked closer, gesturing to the ornately carved bench. "May I?"

Her nostrils flared as she took in the small

space next to her. He thought she was going to deny him, but instead she sat up taller. "Of course."

He hid his satisfaction. She had a will of iron. Yet he tested it as he sat on the hard slab, closer than he should have, not as close as he wanted. It was not truly meant for two, especially one as large as him, and he brushed against her. Satisfaction surged at her quick intake of breath, the awareness she could not hide.

"I suppose my mother provided the assistance." Her eyes darted to the opening in alarm. "Should we leave?"

He shook his head. "She promised she wouldn't intrude, and I believe her. Since this garden is so well hidden, it's unlikely someone else will stumble upon us."

She pursed her lips, yet didn't argue.

"I actually came to apologize."

Her eyes lit in surprise, and suspicion. "Apologize? You?"

He lifted an eyebrow. "Shocking, isn't it?"

"Indeed." Bemusement entered her expression, and she relaxed slightly. "Which of your many transgressions would you like to apologize for?"

"My many transgressions?" He feigned indignation. "May I ask the crimes to which you refer?"

"Pursuing me when I have no wish to be

pursued."

Guilty. "A fabrication."

"Conspiring with my parents?"

Guilty. "Never happened."

"How about making all my other suitors seem inferior?"

She closed her eyes, opened them. "Pretend I didn't say that."

"Never." He grew serious. "But my apology does relate to dinner. It was never my intention to cast you as anything less than accomplished. I'll admit to exaggerating your interest in your suitors' activities, yet I did that to highlight how singularly focused they are. I did not foresee them using it to cast doubt on your abilities. You are a woman of rare talent, and I hold you in the highest esteem. For how they made you feel, I apologize."

Her gaze softened. "While I will accept your apologies on the other matters, I do not accept this one."

His jaw set.

She put a hand on his arm. "Because there is no need for you to apologize. You did not disparage me; they did. You defended me when others judged me solely on my gender."

He frowned. "But I put you in an impossible position. Few command their level of expertise, and I should have guessed they would attribute your lack of knowledge to your gender."

"That is their error, not yours. I appreciate what you said, and what you did. It truly matters." She sighed. "They listen to you. Everyone does."

He touched her cheek. "But not you."

She smiled lightly, licked her lips.

Clearly, she was trying to end him.

"There is another matter for which you should apologize."

He looked into fathomless eyes. "Oh?"

"Our kiss." Her voice had lowered to a whisper, and her eyes darted to his lips. "It has been far too long since our last."

It was a hint. A suggestion. A command. She couldn't ask the question, but he knew the answer.

"For that I am most definitely sorry." He leaned down. "I shall make it up to you immediately."

Spectacular. No other word could describe the kiss, or the woman. She tasted of chocolate and cream, and the urge to claim her surged through him. He wrapped his arms around her, pressing her supple form against his length. Her skin was as soft as petals, her gardenia scent a tantalizing aphrodisiac.

She was so delicious, so soft. So perfect.

They kissed and kissed and kissed. He drank in every moan, caressing, smoothing, *fondling* those delicious curves. He ran a hand through her hair, twirling the sultry locks. Desire swirled, accompanied by a thousand tangled emotions. She was where she belonged.

Yet the noises of the party reached them, and reality fought for acknowledgement. He was a gentleman, he reminded himself once and then a hundred times as he finally pulled back, barely regaining the control only she threatened. Then they just held each other, heaving in breaths, hanging on to what far transcended passion.

As he lifted her hand for a final kiss, he made a silent promise. One day soon…

She would be his.

RULES A LADY should ignore:
Never pretend to be a man.
Never dress like a man.
Never visit a gaming hell to spy on a man.

Priscilla had sneaked through lord's homes, spied on criminals and conducted covert investigations. Yet this was a first.

A gaming hell.

The *ton* would not approve. Her family would not approve. And Edmund?

He would lock her in a tower.

Yet as she sat in a corner booth in Diamond Dust, one of the rowdiest gaming halls in London, none of that mattered. Nor did it matter that the place reeked of cheap spirits or that it was filled with men who would be shocked if they knew the paragon of propriety walked the hall in breeches. If Lady Priscilla couldn't investigate, Lord P would have to take his place, dressed like the man she pretended to be.

The transformation had been more jarring than she'd imagined, but after two hours spent dressing, fussing, tucking and binding, she resembled a young lord. Hopefully Lord Roxbury would think so, too.

She picked up her cup and took a swig of liquid courage, barely managed not to spew it across the dimly lit room. Her eyes watered as fire singed her tongue and burned her throat. She stood. She could do this.

She strolled, no strode, to Roxbury's table.

Roxbury sat with several other lords at a Vingt-et-un table. She clutched her pin money tightly, plastering a smile on her face. "Mind if I join you?"

Roxbury snorted as the other men gave her looks.

Right.

Men do not ask, they simply do.

"You got money, lad?"

"Of course." She held up the money, with the largest on top to make it appear more substantial.

He grunted as she slid into the narrow seat. The pungent odor of spirits, sweat and urine assailed her.

"You even know how to play?"

She nodded, carefully counting out the money for the round. The others snickered at the amount, but it couldn't be helped. She needed it to last until she elicited some information from Roxbury. The play started.

"Wake up, boy, it's your turn."

"Sorry." Priscilla quickly made her move and winced as a senseless mistake handed her an immediate loss.

Roxbury grinned as he collected his earnings. "I like the way you play, boy." He looked closer, and his smile faded. "Hey, you look familiar. Have I seen you before?"

She swallowed. "I'm Peter. You went to school with my cousin, Frankfurt."

He continued to stare. Hopefully he was too inebriated to realize he didn't know anyone named Frankfurt.

Sweat broke out under the thick wool she used to bind her breasts. If he discovered who she was…

"I do remember him. Funny for such a big guy to have a puny cousin."

She forced a smile. "Yeah, well, he said they always looked up to you."

Roxbury puffed out his chest. "Course they did. Nothing's changed in that respect."

If she wasn't so nervous, she would have snorted. No one looked up to the vicious man. "I can see why. You're a real leader around here."

He grinned wider. "You may be small, but you've got some sense in your head." He clamped a meaty hand on her shoulder. "You and I are going to be good friends."

She let out a choked laugh.

What had she gotten herself into?

"DO YOU KNOW that boy? You've been staring at him all evening."

Edmund frowned, yet did not look at Crawford. Instead he kept his eyes on the… boy. The diminutive form perched on a chair next to Roxbury, holding a mug half as large as he was.

"There's something strange about him."

The boy had glanced at him, too, the first time with panic in his eyes, and several times after that, although he quickly looked away. Edmund tried to peer closer, but his features were undefined from across the dim hall. Now the boy slumped down with his hat low on his head.

Peyton took a swig of his own drink. "His outfit shows him as quality. You probably know his family."

"Perhaps."

"Why does it matter anyway?"

Edmund frowned. Why did it matter? Yet there was something familiar about the boy, and an insistent feeling he should recognize him, that it was *important.* "I just can't think of it, and it's puzzling me. I don't care for mysteries."

"We know that." Crawford sat back and relaxed. "How long must we remain here?"

"Not long," Edmund promised. "I like these establishments as little as you. Yet nothing has been effective in changing Roxbury's vote. I was hoping he'd be more amiable when into his cups."

Peyton looked over at the drunken man. "Hard to imagine he's ever amiable. Are you planning to let him win?"

Edmund grimaced. "I was going to try reasoning with him first. Or perhaps offer some sort of wager, where I might win favor for our measures."

Crawford leaned forward. "You want to bet for his vote? Is that allowed?"

"You think Roxbury cares what's allowed?" Edmund took a final gulp, then put down the glass. He stood and started towards the Vingt-et-un table.

As if he sensed his approach, the boy glanced his way. For a moment, he looked about to flee, but then he hunched lower, shifting towards the wall. By the time Edmund arrived, he was turned fully sideways, with only the top of his cap and the back of his jacket visible.

Stranger and stranger.

Roxbury was not happy to see him. "What

are you doing here, Bradenton? I thought this place was above the lofty lord."

Edmund gave him a mild look. "There are far better entertainments available, yet sometimes I like to sample the less tasteful offerings."

Roxbury's gaze darkened. Although he was a lord, his abrasive tendencies excluded him from many social events. He more than deserved it, yet Edmund was here to build connections, not break them.

He inclined his head toward the piles of money in front of Roxbury. "I see fortune has smiled upon you."

Roxbury brightened. "Jealous, are you? Even the famous Bradenton fortune can't match me tonight."

Roxbury's holdings were a fraction of Edmund's, and if he continued gambling, it wouldn't last to his heir. Yet he didn't mention it as his attention once again strayed to the figure next to Roxbury. "Is he the source of your luck?"

Roxbury guffawed, slapping the boy's back. The youth jerked forward, only just managing not to fall off the stool. "I'm just showing him how to play. He looks up to me."

By the way the boy stiffened, Edmund very much doubted that. He tried to see his face, but he'd pulled his jacket up so high, it covered his cheeks, almost meeting the bottom of the low-slung hat. "What's your name, son?"

The boy mumbled something unintelligible.

The sense of familiarity hit again, now a thousand times stronger. He touched the boy's shoulder. "Why don't you turn around, lad?"

Under him, slender muscles tightened, and the boy lunged out of his grasp. "Had too much to drink!" he gasped out. "I'm going to cast up my accounts!"

Edmund moved back, but frowned. The boy had nursed the same drink the entire evening. Even a lightweight like him shouldn't be drunk. "You need some water?"

He shook his head.

Roxbury took another swig of his cloudy brown drink. Unlike the boy, he was well on his way to getting foxed. "Leave the scamp alone, Bradenton. Not everyone prefers you." He gave a lecherous grin. "What's wrong with you anyway? Having trouble with the Livingston chit?"

Edmund gritted his teeth, fighting the urge to break something, mainly a smug, vicious lord who took advantage of every woman he could find. The man wasn't fit to utter Priscilla's name. "There's no problem with that."

"Oh yeah?" Clearly unaware of the danger he was courting, Roxbury leaned in. "Has she given you any favors? I must say, she is lovely. Sometimes the prim and proper ladies are the most wild underneath, if you know what I mean."

If he was careful not to kill him, perhaps no one would notice if he broke a leg or two.

"I'm not here to discuss Lady Priscilla."

"Really? If you're not set on her, mind if I take a go?" Roxbury grinned widely. "Just a little taste?"

Forget the vote. He was just going to destroy the monster.

He glared. "You will not touch Lady Priscilla. She belongs to me."

The boy gasped.

Edmund froze.

There was something about that gasp.

He turned back to the boy. Leaned closer. Took a deep breath… of gardenia-scented air?

That was when he knew.

CHAPTER TEN

Dear Edmund,

I cannot explain why I must hide my identity except to say exposure threatens all. It is a risk I cannot afford.

I know you will not like this answer, but please accept it. Stop trying to uncover my identity and instead focus on the social causes that need us. I have enclosed information regarding Lord Cattlyn, which will aid in your endeavors. I will continue to search for information so long as you cease your inquiries into me. Already it has affected our work...

Yours,
P

IT HAD BEEN going so well. With every drink, Roxbury had grown more and more talkative; with every question, he offered increasingly useful information. She'd learned about several mistresses as well as other promising details.

Then Bradenton arrived.

He hadn't followed her. She'd arrived far before him, and had been careful to study her surroundings every step of the way. Likely he was here for the same reason as she, to investigate on the day neither had a major ball to attend.

He didn't know who she was when he came to the table.

He knew now.

It was apparent the second he did. The quick intake of breath, the tensed muscles, the shocked reflection glinting off the glass mug.

Their eyes locked. Then suddenly…

She was lifted out of the chair.

She gasped as she was slung over a hard and large shoulder, as she landed against a solid body she knew so well. Muscular arms snaked around her, powerful bands holding her as securely as iron shackles. She kicked and struggled, yet it was useless.

She was captured.

Roxbury shot up. "What in blazes are you doing?"

"This belongs to me."

Roxbury swore, stammered, sputtered. He took a drunken step, then looked at his piles of money. With an unfocused shrug, he slumped back down. And her?

She was still being kidnapped.

"Put me down!"

Edmund paid her no heed as he stamped through the gaming hell like a gladiator holding a trophy of victory. Hard muscles flexed under his shirt as people darted out of his way, staring and pointing and yet not intervening. They delved closer and closer to the exit as he carried her to a destination unknown.

"He's the little brother of one of my friends." He patted her rear. "It's time for him to go to bed."

"Why you!" she squealed. She opened her mouth to demand he release her when he pushed her into his thick coat. His heady scent filled her nostrils.

"Do you want someone to recognize you? Keep your head down!" He stopped briefly to talk to someone. Oh no – Crawford and Peyton were here! Now she voluntarily stilled, until he moved once more, exiting the hell with her in his firm possession. As they entered the crisp night, she resumed her struggles. "Let me go!"

"No."

She yelped as they ascended into a closed carriage, as he murmured something to the coachman she couldn't make out, as the door slammed shut. He deposited her in the seat next to him. A moment later, the carriage jerked into motion.

She lunged to the door, but he was too quick. He grasped her arms and brought her into his lap.

Heat flooded her.

"How dare you! Let me go this instant. You have no right to kidnap me!"

He looked at her incredulously. "You were the one traipsing through a gaming hell. Do you have any idea what would have happened if they discovered you were a woman?"

"No one was going to discover the truth. I look just like my brother."

"You look nothing like a man," he growled. "The only reason I didn't realize sooner was because you were turned away. The moment I caught your scent, it was obvious. Not too many men smell like gardenias."

She cringed. One forgotten detail.

"Do you know what could have happened?" he thundered again.

"Nothing! Perhaps a minor scandal, but they were gentlemen. I would have left immediately."

"You think they would have just let you leave? Half those men were foxed! What if Roxbury learned the truth?"

She suppressed a shudder at the thought of the beefy, corrupt man. "He would never guess. I'm dressed like a boy."

"You may be dressed like a boy, but any red-blooded male would see you're all woman." His voice came out low, husky. "Nothing can hide your beauty."

From anyone else it would have been meaningless flattery, yet from him it held untold meaning. The fire burning in Edmund's eyes belied deception, pooling heat in sensitive spots.

"Those breeches hide few secrets, Priscilla."

Her heart slammed against her ribs. Anger fled, replaced by desire. She couldn't stop herself from reaching out, touching his heated chest. A thousand whispers warned of danger, yet she ignored every single one.

He looked down at her hand, back at her lips. "I suppose I will have to prove it to you."

He did not wait an instant.

The kiss was intoxicating, tasting of brandy and heady male. He pressed his lips to hers as he grazed her curves, smoothing sensitive skin underneath the thin fabric. Pulled against his solid body, she could not shield her femininity.

He ran his hands along every inch, cupping her back to press her tightly into him. She moaned as she pressed closer… and closer…

The carriage hit a bump.

Priscilla yelped as they bounced up and down. It was enough to break the spell. She pulled back, rubbing her swollen lips with the back of her hand.

He gazed at her with the intensity of a hungry lion.

She put a hand in front of her, as if it could

stop the powerful man. "This was a–"

"If you say it was a mistake, I'm going to do it again."

She looked at him. Clenched her jaw. And just barely managed not to claim it was a mistake.

"Do you understand you are no less desirable in boy's clothing?" he ground out.

She could scarce deny it. Which meant, if someone else had realized…

Stop it. She knew the danger going into the investigation. "It was worth the risk."

"Worth the risk?" he ground out. "Why were you really there?"

"I was there to–"

She froze. *Blazes!* The kiss had her so befuddled she almost blurted out the truth. "I– I was there to see what it was like, of course. It's ridiculous men experience all these wondrous things while women are expected to sit home and sew."

His eyes narrowed. "I thought you liked sewing. You started an organization dedicated to it."

Woops.

"And you call a gaming hell wondrous?" He folded his arms across his chest. "You can't be serious."

"Perhaps wondrous was the wrong word. Let's call it an adventure. And although I like sewing, it is not an adventure."

"Acting as Roxbury's good luck charm was an adventure? You're going to have to do better than that." He flexed his muscles, and her breath caught. Battling equal wits, she sometimes forgot how physically powerful he was.

"I didn't mean to get trapped next to him. I simply wanted to experience a gaming hall."

"But you approached him."

Heat crept up Priscilla's neck. He *had* been watching her. Did he know she targeted Roxbury directly?

Did he know why?

She had to redirect the conversation before he figured out the truth.

She notched up her chin. "Vingt-et-un is one of the few games I know. I didn't realize he was there until I went up to him," she lied.

"Roxbury is gregarious, oafish and loud. How could you possibly miss him?"

She shrugged.

"Why do I keep catching you in all sorts of strange places? First Roxbury's garden, then next to him in a gaming hall." He stopped. "Gracious, Priscilla, please tell me you and Lord Roxbury aren't–"

"No!" she screeched.

"Then why were you truly there?"

"I told you. I want to experience all life has to offer, even and especially activities not deemed ladylike. I was having a lovely time before you kidnapped me. You had no right to carry me out like you owned me." Feminine power infused her. She held out a finger. "I demand you stop this carriage right now."

He leaned back. "No."

"Yes!"

"No."

"Yes!"

"No."

She clenched her fists. "I live life as I choose. If I want to gamble in a gaming hell, I will."

"And if I want to kidnap you, I will." He flexed his muscles. "I will not allow you to put yourself in danger."

"You will not allow it?" she sputtered. "You have no say!"

"What do you think your parents would do if they learned of this?"

She gasped. "You wouldn't."

His bold gaze belied her denial. "You'd have a hard time denying it."

She wouldn't have a chance. If her father knew she snuck into a gaming hell, every choice she had – or thought she had – would disappear in an instant. He'd marry her to the first suitable lord he could find.

Bradenton.

"If you do that, I'll never speak to you again," she hissed.

For a moment, he said nothing. As the carriage hit another bump, she looked out the window. They were nearing her home.

"You will never go to a gaming hell again."

"You have no right to make demands."

"I have every right."

"Based on what?"

"I don't think you're ready to hear that."

Her heart lurched. She couldn't, wouldn't, go there. "Would you agree to the same?"

"Priscilla…"

The voice held a warning. She had no intention of obeying him, yet she refrained from saying so. Hopefully he would take it as an affirmative.

He sighed. "No one hurt you, right? Did or said anything that troubled you?"

Unwittingly, she softened. "Except for Roxbury's odor I was perfectly safe."

"I only want to protect you."

She swallowed as warmth infused her, even as she fought it. She could resist an overbearing brute and high-handed tyrant. A chivalrous crusader? Not so much. "I must live my life, Bradenton. If you tell my parents, life as I know it will be over." She swallowed. "As a gentleman, will you keep your silence?"

He gazed a moment more, slowly shook his head.

Her heart stumbled.

"All right."

She let out a breath.

"For now."

The breath caught in her throat.

"I promise to not say anything tonight, yet I reserve the right to speak if something changes. I will see you safe, whether you like it or not."

She opened her mouth to protest, yet he stopped her with a raised finger. "Do not test me, Priscilla. Keeping silent goes against everything in me."

It was less than she hoped, yet more than she feared. She had no choice to take it. "Thank you, Your Grace."

The carriage came to a sudden halt, not in front of the townhouse, but in back. Edmund pointed. "I assume you weren't planning on entering through the front door. I will watch to ensure your safety."

"That's not–"

His harsh look stopped her.

She took a shuddering breath. "Fine. But remember, you are not responsible for me." She rose as eloquently as her tight breeches allowed, brushing by his taut muscles as she threaded to the door. With a curt nod good-bye, she descended the carriage and walked into the darkness.

As the cool night air tickled her sensitized skin, the breeze carried his final words. "Not yet, Priscilla. Not yet."

"How can I investigate while someone is investigating me?" Priscilla slammed her hands on the table, remembered that ladies were not supposed to slam hands on tables, and slammed them harder. She paced back and forth, too agitated to stay still.

"He shows up to every single event I attend. He demands a dance, or two or even three!"

He also managed to steal a kiss. Or two. Or even three.

"How he does it is a mystery. With so many competing events, someone must be sharing where I will be. Once I changed plans at the last minute, and he still came to the ball. Before me! Of course, getting access to anything and everything is easy for him. Hostesses compete for the opportunity to entertain the most lauded duke of the *ton*."

She stopped pacing. "I don't know what to do. I won't chance investigating while he is there, and he is *always* there. I haven't gotten anything useful in a month."

Emma gave a hesitant smile. "You found information about Lord Cattlyn."

Priscilla shook her head. "That was sheer luck. Once I discovered how much he admired Lady Letitia, I was able to recruit her to change his mind. She did a splendid job."

"If I recall, she returns his affection," Hannah remarked.

Priscilla nodded. "There's to be an announcement soon. With her influence, hopefully we won't have to worry about his vote again. Yet there are so many others whose votes are vulnerable. I can't do anything while Bradenton watches my every move. He acts like we're betrothed." She suppressed a shiver. The words were spoken in indignation, yet other emotions surfaced. Craving. Desire. Longing.

"Are you certain you don't want the match?" Emma asked softly.

"Of course not." Priscilla stomped her foot. "Bradenton is one of the most powerful men in the *ton*. If he discovers my identity, he'll take control of everything."

"But how do you feel about him?"

She suppressed a shiver. "I feel hunted."

"Yes, but what else?" Emma pressed. "You've gone against many lords, but you've never been so passionate."

"I'm not passionate about him." *Well, except for the kiss. And the other kiss. And the kiss she was currently imagining.* "I am not passionate about him," she repeated louder and stronger. "I am frustrated by his pursuit. I'm scared he's going to succeed. And I'm not entirely certain I don't want him to."

She swallowed emotions she hadn't meant to reveal. In truth, Edmund inspired many feelings, and not all of them were bad. He was indeed like chocolate. The more she tasted, the more she craved.

"Oh darling," Emma's expression softened. "Have you considered telling him the truth?"

"Don't you dare!" Hannah admonished. "If she reveals her identity, we're all finished. We'll be sentenced to a lifetime of embroidery, tea rooms and the pianoforte. Just give it time. Bradenton is actively searching for a wife. When he finds a suitable bride who is *not* Priscilla, he will cease his investigations, and everything will be like before."

"Exactly," Priscilla agreed. And if the thought of Edmund with another woman made her think of vases, she would just ignore it.

"Girls, are you ready?" The duchess breezed into the room, garbed in a fashionable blue dress, matching shoes and a decorative hat. She was holding a small silk bag.

The ladies straightened as Priscilla frowned. "Is it already time to go to the modiste? I thought our appointment wasn't until this afternoon."

"We need to leave now." Her mother beckoned them forward with ruthless efficiency. "You'll need more than a few hours to order new gowns and all the accompaniments. Hannah and Emma, your parents entrusted me to help you."

Priscilla grimaced. She'd much rather be plotting her next move than being pinched, poked and prodded. Yet there was no stopping a duchess intent on the modiste.

Her mother held up the bag. "You received a gift."

Priscilla accepted the parcel as she walked to the door, with the ladies trailing behind. It was soft, silky, and surprisingly heavy for its size. "Who is it from?"

Her mother shrugged. "There was no card, and the footman who brought it left immediately."

Priscilla frowned. She received many gifts, yet typically the suitor claimed credit with verses of poetic prose. "Perhaps there's a card on the inside."

There was a card, but no name. She unfolded the crisp square paper and read, "For the safety of all."

She opened the bag to reveal....

The smallest vase she had ever seen.

It was tiny and delicate, only a few inches in height and intricately carved from a piece of mahogany. Covered in detailed miniature paintings and encrusted with sparkling gemstones, it truly was a work of art. Rubies, sapphires and diamonds glistened as she turned it under the light.

"Extraordinary." Her mother leaned in. "Who do you suppose it is from?"

"I can't ima–"

She stopped. Remembered the message.

For the safety of all.

She tried to hold back the laughter. Really, really tried.

Failed spectacularly.

The other ladies looked at her in bemusement as she laughed in a most unladylike manner, giggling until her eyes moistened. How Edmund found such a small vase, she would never know. She turned the vase over, and something shiny fell out.

She sobered immediately.

Emma gasped, and even Hannah's eyes opened wide. Priscilla bent down and slowly lifted the heavy golden chain from the floor. A huge diamond solitaire dangled at its end, sparkling in the light, casting a rainbow of colors from its fathomless depths.

"Goodness," Emma whispered. "Is it real?"

The duchess took the necklace. "I've seen this piece before. It's from a very exclusive jeweler whose wares are only available to a select clientele." She pointed to a small symbol on the chain. "This is his mark. The price is as massive as the diamond." Her mother gave her a long look. "Your secret admirer is quite extraordinary. Do you have any idea who he is, Priscilla?"

She didn't have an idea. *She knew.*

Her heart thumped in her chest. The vase had been a clever and amusing gift, but there was nothing humorous about the diamond. It held meaning, importance, a *message*.

Suitors did not send priceless diamond jewelry. They sent flowers, chocolate, cards of poetry. Edmund was conveying something far more important with the necklace.

"Put it on."

She looked up. "Mother, no–"

"Yes." Her mother's voice brooked no argument. "We are searching for gowns. I daresay you will wear the necklace when you wear them. You can see what best complements it."

"But we don't even know who sent it."

"We don't?"

Her mother stared at her. She could continue to feign innocence, but the truth could not be denied. It was Edmund.

"Something like this should not be taken lightly," Priscilla said quietly. "If the gentleman sees me wearing it, he may make assumptions–"

"You will wear the necklace, Priscilla."

Priscilla regarded her mother for a moment more. Finally she breathed out. "As you wish."

Her mother smiled, patted her arm. "It's all right, my darling. All will be well. But we must hurry. We do not want to keep Bradenton waiting."

Priscilla's breath hitched. "Bradenton?"

"Did I forget to tell you?" Her mother smiled. "The duke asked for assistance in purchasing gowns for his sister. We're to meet him in half an hour."

The vase was definitely way too small.

"TELL ME AGAIN why we're here."

"Because my duchess-to-be will soon arrive, and I need her where she can't escape." Edmund rubbed his hands together. "Hopefully, my sister can convince her I'm not nearly as controlling as she believes."

"You *are* that controlling." Crawford examined a piece of lace like it was some foreign creature. "And does she know she's your duchess-to-be?"

"I'm not going to answer that."

Edmund pushed aside a curtain of jewel-colored silks to view Sophia. Normally his mother would accompany his sister to the modiste, but he needed an excuse to enlist the duchess' help. His sister was looking far too mature with her golden curls and bright blue eyes, and a dress that made her look older than her years. He was not the only one who noticed, but his piercing glares ensured she was left alone. He always made sure to keep his sister, and any men who would deem approach her, in view.

He turned back to Crawford, "I'd like her to see marriage will not be as dreadful as she assumes."

Peyton inclined his head. "Fine. That explains

why you are here. But why are Crawford and I here?"

"Because you are kind enough to distract Lady Emma and Lady Hannah."

"Ahhh." Crawford smiled. "I do not mind distracting Lady Hannah. The lady is refreshing."

Edmund looked at him frankly. "She dislikes you intensely."

Crawford smiled wider. "She does indeed."

"I do not mind entertaining Lady Emma." Peyton straightened his sleeves. "She is pleasant enough, even if she doesn't utter a word. And what about you, Bradenton? How goes your suit?"

Edmund grimaced. With her spirit, kindness and intelligence, Priscilla would make the ideal duchess, yet she remained resistant, defiant. "As frustrating as my search for my informant."

"You have no new leads?"

Edmund shook his head. "If only I had pulled the curtain back sooner. I've done a little investigating during several parties, but the only lurkers I found were..." He cleared his throat. "Indisposed."

"That must have been awkward."

"Indeed."

"Did Lord P mention the episode in a letter?"

"No, so I cannot even be certain it was him," Edmund replied. "One thing did change, however. Whereas in the past, we discussed specific lords to target, now he will neither suggest nor confirm any names."

"He doesn't want you to find him."

"Likely. But I have a plan." Edmund stood up taller. "He won't be able to hide the truth for much longer."

A gasp pierced the air.

All eyes turned to the door as the Duchess of Sherring, Lady Priscilla, Lady Hannah and Lady Emma entered, accompanied by an army of maids and footmen. Most smiled warm greetings.

Priscilla stared at him.

No matter how many times he saw her, her beauty stunned him. Today she wore a pale blush dress accentuated with tiny flowers and ethereal puff sleeves. It fit tightly around her ample bosom and skimmed gracefully over her hips. Ladies' fashion was not normally something he admired, or even noticed, but he couldn't help but appreciate how the silky fabric hugged her curves. Her creamy cheeks were flushed pink and her eyes shone brightly.

She was wearing his necklace.

The shimmering jewel lay nestled against her creamy décolleté, perfection among perfection, its beauty a glittering complement to the flawless woman. A surge of satisfaction emboldened him. He wanted to spoil her with all the riches in the world, give her everything she ever desired.

She caught his gaze lingering on the jewel

and visibly tensed. No doubt she knew its origin.

She was the one who had gasped. But why? She must have overheard his statement and assumed it pertained to her.

"Are you all right?"

Emotions flitted across her face, fleeting panic melting into concern and then neutrality. She straightened. "Of course. I was simply startled."

She gave no other explanation, and he didn't ask for one. Blatant questions wouldn't unlock the mystery that was Priscilla Livingston. He would have to be clever, and subtle, to uncover the truth.

He greeted the other members of their party. Upon seeing his friends, Emma smiled shyly and Hannah looked as if she'd eaten spoiled fish. The duchess took charge, immediately suggesting Emma and Hannah pair with Peyton and Crawford. All the ladies started to protest, but Crawford and Peyton led their respective charges away before they could formulate an argument strong enough to counter the duchess' clout. A true master of the *ton*, the duchess then declared herself in charge of Sophia, and stomped off towards the unsuspecting chit, beckoning the bevy of servants like a general heading to war.

And just like that, he was alone with Priscilla.

"I'm so glad you could meet us here. As you see, my sister is busy at work." He gestured to

Sophia, who juggled three bolts of fabric and four spools of lace. He laughed softly.

He turned to find Priscilla staring at him. He frowned. "Are you certain you're all right?"

"Perfectly fine," she said in a clipped tone. She studied the fabrics as they started to walk, but soon her eyes darted back to his. "What were you speaking of earlier?" Though said casually, an undercurrent of tension laced every syllable.

"Don't worry, my dear. I wasn't discussing you."

She looked even more worried.

He gently touched her arm, careful to angle her out of eyesight of others. "Truly. I was speaking of someone else."

She gave a strained smile. "So I'm not the only one you're investigating?"

Bemusement surfaced at her frank response. "No, but don't worry. The other is more business than personal. I wish to help a friend of mine, but he is being obstinate."

She turned back to the material and started sorting with ruthless efficiency. "What did your friend do to deserve your scrutiny?"

He frowned. Except for Crawford and Peyton, he hadn't told anyone about his informant, and he would not go into details now. Yet the urge to share with her was strong. "It wasn't something he did. I would like to help him."

Now she flipped through fabric at a dizzying

speed. His sister could spend half an hour on a single bolt before declaring it the ugliest thing in existence, but Priscilla barely gave them a second's attention. "If he does not wish for your assistance, why force it? Shouldn't he be allowed to solve his problems on his own?"

He shrugged. "Many in need of aid do not ask. I merely desire a more productive relationship."

She stopped, turned her bright emerald gaze on him. Clearly she didn't quite believe what wasn't quite true. "If he doesn't wish for your interference, perhaps you should allow him his privacy."

He stared. Something about the way she said that…

"We should help your sister!" Suddenly, she was leading *him* along, all but dragging him towards Sophia.

He shook his head. What had gotten into her?

"Lady Sophia, how lovely to see you again!"

Sophia looked startled, but quickly recovered. She gave a genuine smile. "It is an honor, Lady Priscilla. Your mother has been so kind to assist me, and I look forward to your insight as well."

Edmund's gaze turned mischievous. "Priscilla will be quite helpful. She loves spending time at the modiste."

Priscilla relaxed into a smile. "Ah, yes, my favorite pastime."

"Outside of collecting vases."

"Speaking of vases." The duchess put her hand on Priscilla's shoulder. "My daughter received the most unusual miniature vase this morning. It came with this diamond necklace. Isn't it stunning?"

"It is indeed." he murmured to the duchess, even as his eyes never left Priscilla. "Yet it pales next to its wearer."

Priscilla's cheeks tinged pink. Despite her attempts, she was not immune to his flattery.

"Did the gift please you?" he murmured.

"The vase was far too small to be practical."

He chuckled.

Sophia was looking back and forth between the two of them, her lips curving into a slow smile. "Lady Priscilla, will you be so kind as to give your opinion on these patterns?"

Priscilla nodded. Soon the ladies were in an animated discussion about fabrics, chatting and laughing like old friends within minutes. Priscilla was patient and kind with his sister, listening intently and offering sage advice. They shared similar personalities, marked by intelligence, consideration and clever wit.

They spent a few minutes consulting, then separated once more, the duchess tailing Sophia as she left to be measured, and Edmund following

Priscilla back to the fabrics.

Yet before they could start looking, a harried assistant came rushing from the back, clutching a small piece of paper. "Madame Fleur wanted me to give you the latest on your accounts." She reached out with the paper, but stumbled at the last minute. As she righted herself, the paper fluttered down.

Priscilla caught it.

The horrified woman backed up. "I'm so sorry, Your Grace! We had a huge rush order and I'm three gowns behind and–"

"No harm done." He held out a placating hand. "I certainly won't mention it."

The woman relaxed. "Thank you, Your Grace. Thank you so much." She scurried away.

Edmund waved after her, then turned to Priscilla. He stiffened.

She was reading the paper.

"Priscilla–"

"I can't believe it." Fury blazed in her eyes. "It says you fund accounts for over two dozen ladies."

He reached for the paper. "It's not what you think."

"Then what is it?"

He hesitated.

She snatched it back. "Tell me what it is." With every word, her voice grew in volume. Others looked their way, but she paid them no heed.

He should just tell her the truth, explain it was not as she assumed, yet something stopped him. This was personal.

"Wait a minute." Her stance softened, anger changing to confusion in an instant. "This account is for a sixty-year-old widow, this one is for a disabled grandmother and this one is for a woman who almost lost her home before a mysterious benefactor helped her..." Her voice trailed off. She pinned him with a look far stronger than anger. "These are charity accounts?"

"Yes, well..."

She softened further, held out the sheet. "I'm sorry."

He stood taller and took the paper. He folded it and placed it in his pocket. "No need to apologize."

"Of course there is," she said quietly. "I assumed something very bad, only now I understand. You're helping disadvantaged ladies with nowhere to turn. Do they even know you're their benefactor?"

He hesitated, shook his head.

She gave him a small smile. "How do you find out about them?"

He looked away. "Some I know personally, others I heard from gossip or general knowledge. Madame Fleur will sometimes suggest a lady in need."

"Does she contact them?"

He nodded. "She tells them an anonymous benefactor paid for their clothing. We provide everything they need to rebuild their lives."

"Everything?" Her eyes widened. "This isn't just about clothing. Did you save that lady's home?"

He'd done that and far more. It was a true injustice when people were left unable to fend for themselves, especially the most vulnerable. Fortunately, the Bradenton coffers were vast, and he had a talent for making money. "It's nothing."

She shook her head, gazing at him in an entirely disconcerting way. "Oh no, Bradenton. This is beyond special. It is extraordinary."

He grunted and moved back to the racks. He felt her smile as she followed behind him.

Now Priscilla searched through the fabrics slower and more focused, actually giving her attention to the task. He split his time between watching her and keeping an eye on his sister, who was smiling gaily, even with the serious duchess.

Priscilla noticed his perusal. "Your sister is delightful."

"Thank you. I can't believe her come out is next year."

She smiled. "You sound worried."

"A trove of rakes pursuing my beautiful baby

sister? What's there to worry about?"

Priscilla chuckled lowly. "Come now. It isn't as bad as all that."

"Sophia deserves someone who will make her happy. I'm also hoping she'll stay nearby." His sister moving far away to only correspond by letters every half year was simply unacceptable. He would encourage suitable *close* gentlemen.

"I bet you have a hundred requirements," Priscilla teased.

"Actually, five hundred and thirty-eight."

She chuckled, yet they both knew it was not a complete exaggeration. He would ensure his sister had a happy life, even if it meant being a little, or perhaps a lot, overbearing. Yet he didn't want Priscilla even warier of him. "As I said before, I will allow her to choose her own match."

Priscilla sent him a skeptical glance. "Truly?"

"Truly."

"But you must approve."

"I am certain we will find a choice that satisfies us both."

"I hope you allow her the freedom you claim. Your sister is very kind. We get along well."

"I am pleased to hear that." And pleased she mentioned it. It provided the perfect opportunity for further investigation. "Since you get along so well, perhaps you'll reconsider her attendance at your sewing guild."

She hesitated. When she spoke, the words were low, careful. "I still don't think it's wise. The conversation may not be appropriate."

He cocked his head to the side. "You speak of inappropriate matters at a sewing guild?"

"No, of course not." Pinkened cheeks belied the denial. "I meant we speak of things above her age. You do not want Lady Sophia growing up too fast."

If he had his choice, she'd remain in the schoolroom forever. But she was nearing womanhood, whether he was ready or not.

And he'd wager Priscilla's true objections had nothing to do with age.

"Castleberry's sister is in it. She's only a year older than Sophia."

"What a difference a year can make." Priscilla rubbed her hands together. "Let's discuss this next year then."

Likely she had no intention of ever discussing it. "Perhaps I should join you for a meeting."

She gasped. "You can't come! You are... a man!"

From anyone else, the explanation would have made sense, yet something else lurked behind her horror. Was there more to her sewing circle than obvious? "I was jesting, of course."

"Of course." She gave a lighthearted laugh, yet it rang hollow. She quickly turned back to the fabrics.

He would let it go for now, but he wouldn't forget. He added it to the list of clues surrounding the mysterious Priscilla Livingston.

For now, they both gave their attention to the task at hand. The tension between them softened as they returned to comfortable conversation, light jokes and amicable laughter. She knew what fabrics she liked, but was open to views beyond her own. He never imagined he would enjoy shopping for ladies' fashions, yet with Priscilla he did exactly that.

The fabrics came in every color of the rainbow, with countless thicknesses, textures and embellishments. She picked several in a variety of colors suitable to her age and position. Finally, they reached the greens. He grimaced.

"Let's skip these. I know you dislike them."

He halted.

She continued walking, then turned back. "What is it–" Her eyes widened, nostrils flaring.

They stared at each other.

A moment passed, and then another, as his mind reeled. "How did you know I dislike green?" he finally managed. His hatred of the color, and the reasons why, were only known by a select few, close friends and family who would never tell. How in blazes had she discovered it?

"I, um…" She stumbled on the words. "I don't know." She smoothed her dress. "No one told me. I just assumed because you never wear green."

"There's a difference between not wearing a color and disliking it. Do not evade me, Priscilla. How did you know?" He gave her a long hard stare. "The truth this time."

She sucked in a breath, hesitated. And finally, notched up her chin.

"You told me."

CHAPTER ELEVEN

Dear Edmund,

I am sorry for the quick letter, before I have even received yours, yet I must implore you again. I wish I could explain the dangers of revealing my identity, yet it would give away far too much. It is too late to change the path I have chosen. I can only say you would undoubtedly make the same decision in my position.

I beseech you to stop your investigation into me. It is limiting my ability to conduct my work. Remember why we fight. Changing society is all that matters.

Sometimes it is necessary to give up the things we want for the greater good.

Yours,
P

IT WAS THE truth.

He told her.

In a letter.

Edmund didn't merely dislike the color green, he despised it. It was the color of the awful outfit his mother made him wear on his thirteenth birthday. It was hot. It was itchy.

It was what he was wearing the day his father died.

And from that moment forward, he would never wear green again. Few people knew because he did not like to show weakness. He never explained why he told her.

Yet now, the truth ensnared her.

"I told you?" He spoke slowly. "Me?"

"Yes, of course, you." She moved forward, hiding the uncertainty churning in her stomach. "Don't you remember?"

He stared at her. "I have no recollection of doing anything of the sort."

"You did." She said it firmly, willing him to believe it. "You mentioned it offhand while we were dancing. I said something about liking the color of a lady's dress, and asked what you thought of the color green. You shook your head, like you really disliked it."

His eyes narrowed ever-so-slightly. "I don't recall that."

Of course he didn't. It never happened. "Perhaps you didn't hear me, and I thought you responded. You didn't explain why, so I just assumed you didn't like the color."

"And you would avoid it simply because I disliked it?" Incredulity laced his voice. "Not consider the shade at all?"

It made no sense, but she couldn't explain. "I didn't mean I would never wear green again. It isn't my favorite color, either, and there are so many choices."

"That's not what you said." His voice was low, controlled. "You said we should skip it because I disliked the color."

Yes, she had.

He folded his arms across his chest. "This isn't the first time you've inexplicably known something about me. The other day you mentioned my affinity for the newest play."

"Everyone likes the new play."

"You didn't ask if I liked it. You simply stated I had."

She took a measured breath. With every slip, he grew closer and closer to the truth.

"How did you know about the play?" He pinned her with his gaze. "The color? The museum exhibit?"

She heaved in a breath. He was one idle guess away from realizing his two quarries were one and the same. Only his utter certainty Lord P was male stopped him from making the connection.

"I admit it!" she shot out. "The reason I knew those things is I… I… I have been investigating you!"

"What?"

What?

Items she wished she currently possessed:

1. A vase.

2. A vase.

3. A vase.

"I've been investigating you," she said it slowly, more like a question than an answer. She forged on, "I've been asking for information about you."

Suspicion burned in his eyes. "Why?"

"I was curious. You know a lot about me, so I thought it prudent to learn about you. It was nothing too invasive, just a few questions here and there."

It was the best excuse she could formulate, and better than she'd hoped. It didn't truly explain her knowing about the color, since no one who knew would tell, but hopefully he would focus on her knowledge as a whole. If he didn't…

"Just ask."

She shot her head up. "What?"

"If you have questions, just ask. I'd be happy to answer."

She took a deep breath. "Of course."

He nodded, but took another long look.

She swallowed. By no means was this an exoneration. It was simply a reprieve.

"Lady Priscilla, forgive me for taking so long!" Like a savvier from above, Madame Fleur arrived in a flurry of silk, satin and blond curls. With green eyes and a tall, waiflike appearance, the sought-after modiste was as striking as her fashions. "Your Grace, I was just helping your sister choose gowns. She is going to be magnificent."

Edmund frowned, and Priscilla felt a stab of pity. No doubt he would find his sister's come out a challenge.

"I do not care how much I spend, but remember her age," he rumbled.

Madame Fleur held a hand to her chest. "Of course, Your Grace. She will be beautiful, but entirely appropriate."

His frown lightened only slightly.

The modiste turned to Priscilla. "But you, my dear, will have much more freedom."

The frown deepened once more.

Priscilla smiled. "I've been thinking about going a little more daring."

He scowled.

"Perhaps a lot more daring."

Bradenton looked like *he* needed a vase. "Lady Priscilla is jesting of course."

The modiste immediately nodded. "Of course, Your Grace."

Priscilla clenched her fists, yet didn't argue. Madame Fleur loved to gossip, and any histrionics would be shared in exaggerated detail with the entirety of the *ton*.

"Have you selected fabrics yet?"

Priscilla nodded. "I need several gowns for upcoming events. You may use the same pattern as last time."

"Actually, I have a new design." The modiste's eyes darted towards Bradenton. "I assure you, Your Grace, it is entirely proper."

Priscilla narrowed her eyes. "There has been a misunderstanding. The duke is only here to keep me company. The decision on what to purchase is mine."

The modiste looked towards Bradenton. Again.

Who didn't say a word.

Which in itself said a thousand.

Now Priscilla scowled. Even in a space typically reserved for women, he exerted his power.

"I have a dress already made in the new pattern. The particular gown is reserved, but if you like it, I can create one in the fabric of your choice."

"That would be acceptable."

Bradenton gestured to where his sister had reemerged. "I will consult with Sophia while Lady Priscilla is dressing. Madame Fleur, if you would be so kind as to let me know when she is appropriate, I will come."

"That's not neces–"

"Of course, Your Grace."

Priscilla growled lowly. She snatched up her skirt and turned on her heel.

Pure male satisfaction glinted in his eyes.

Priscilla followed Madame Fleur to the back of the large building. If the showroom had been cluttered, the workroom was overrun, with dozens of seamstresses dashing about, carrying pins and measuring implements amidst hundreds of trims, laces and embellishments. The sound of snipping scissors and quiet chatter filled the air, as they came to another door. Madame Fleur opened it to reveal…

The most beautiful dress Priscilla had ever seen.

It was a gown fit for a princess, or a queen. Crafted in shimmering ivory satin with an over-dress of gauze, the gown possessed intricate embroidery, satin pearls and delicate lace. Faceted diamonds lined the bodice, set in swirling designs, while tiny puff sleeves and a low neckline glistened with jewels, their depths alight in a rainbow of colors.

"Goodness," Priscilla breathed. "It truly is a work of art."

Madame Fleur flushed with pleasure. "Thank you. I do believe it's the most beautiful piece I ever created."

"I quite agree." Priscilla moved forward, reverently touching the bodice of the dress. "I can try it on?"

"Of course, my dear."

Madame Fleur and several assistants set to work. The dress felt nearly weightless as it floated around her, shimmering as she moved. They worked quickly and efficiently, soon tying the final ribbons. Priscilla felt a strange tick of nervousness as the others gazed at her.

Madame Fleur clapped her hands together. "Magnifique!"

The women broke into wide smiles, gifting praise. Their excitement was palpable, their compliments authentic, as they chatted, pointed and beamed.

Priscilla breathed deeply, turned to the mirror. Stopped. And stared.

She possessed many beautiful gowns, many expensive, extravagant and fantastic creations, yet none matched the masterpiece adorning her now. Ethereal fabric molded to her curves, whimsical, light and heavenly. Diamond embellishments glittered in the light, set among intricate beading and delicate lace. The gown matched the diamond necklace to perfection, as if fated to be together.

"My goodness," she breathed. "It is..."

"Exquisite."

Priscilla turned at the deep voice. Bradenton stared, his emotions hidden behind an expression of steel. Everyone and everything in the room disappeared as he captured her in his fiery gaze. "The loveliest vision I have ever seen."

Her breath hitched. It was the sort of statement she heard from a hundred suitors, yet it meant a hundred times more. She heated under his smoldering regard, frozen as he stepped towards her. He studied her every inch, casting a rare lightheadedness set to the tempo of her thundering heart.

"She is a work of art, is she not?" Madame Fleur murmured, moving back.

Priscilla closed her eyes, willing herself to break the moment. Lady Fleur would undoubtedly spill tales of this encounter the moment they departed, yet she could not feign nonchalance. Not with Edmund.

"She is beyond art." He shook his head as if to clear it, turned to the modiste. "The dress is sold, you say?"

Madame Fleur hesitated, nodded. "I'm afraid so. It is for Lady Drummond."

Priscilla started. Lady Drummond was a dragon in the *ton,* brusque, curt and feared. She was also a grandmother of twelve. "I've never seen her wear anything like this."

"Of course, not, my dear." Madame Fleur tittered. "I meant Miss Drummond commissioned it for her granddaughter." The modiste sobered. "A shame for the dress to go to the child."

Priscilla opened her mouth to protest, but Madame Fleur held up her hand. "I did not mean she does not deserve it. Every lady should look beautiful for their come out. It is simply not the right dress for Lady Clara. She is extremely pale, and this color will cast her as sickly. Someone with your coloring brings out its true beauty." The modiste sighed. "A light blue or blush would be acceptable and highlight Clara's loveliness. It was what she preferred and I encouraged, but her grandmother was insistent on ivory or white. I'm afraid neither the dress nor the lady will do each other justice. I wish Lady Drummond would allow me to create the dress in a different color."

Priscilla frowned. Lady Drummond was set in her ways, and few argued with her. Yet Priscilla sometimes wondered if she was as bad as society believed, for she donated generously to charitable causes.

"Can you recreate the dress?" Edmund asked.

The modiste shook her head. "I'm afraid not. The embroidery is one of a kind, secured from an exclusive artist in France. The lace is equally difficult to find, and I used my best diamonds on it. Of course, I can make something in the same pattern, but it will not be the same."

Rare disappointment surfaced. Priscilla spent little time on fashion, but she had never loved a gown like this. "Please create something in a similar pattern. Do you need measurements?"

"I have everything I need from your last fitting."

"Oh my dear!" Her mother beamed as she entered the room. "You look absolutely gorgeous."

"Thank you, Mother." Priscilla smoothed down the dress. "Unfortunately it is sold."

"Oh no!" her mother cried. "What a pity. Tell me you can create something similar, Madame Fleur."

"I will do my best." The modiste gave a strained smile. "It will be beautiful, of course."

Priscilla stepped down from the pedestal and turned to Edmund. "I need a few minutes to change. If your sister is ready to leave, please don't wait on me."

"Of course I will wait on you." Something flashed in his eyes. "After all, we still have much planned."

"I'm sorry?"

He didn't answer, instead glanced around the room.

"What are you looking for?"

"Just making sure there are no vases."

Her breath hitched. "What have you done?"

He gave a brilliant smile. "Since we are all together, I suggested to your mother we go on a picnic."

"And I thought it would be a wonderful idea." Her mother smiled in delight. "Don't you agree?"

Yes.

Then, the voice in her head disagreed, *No.*

Yes.

No.

Edmund leaned in so only she could hear. "Did you think you would escape so easily?"

No.

"THIS WAS SUCH a splendid idea, Edmund. I'm quite amazed you thought of it."

Edmund leaned over and ruffled Sophia's hair. "I do have them once in a while, poppet."

She giggled, and he softened. No matter how old she was, she still reminded him of that cheeky little girl who stole Cook's tarts.

He relaxed back into the soft green grass. They sat in a shaded clearing in Hyde Park, close enough to see the open carriages pass but far enough to have some semblance of privacy. It was a glorious day, the trees brilliant emerald against the baby blue sky, a gentle breeze bringing a tempering coolness. Birds soared above them, watching over the peaceful surroundings.

He smiled as he regarded his sister. "This isn't the only good idea I've had."

"It isn't?" Sophia's lips curled mischievously. "I hadn't noticed."

He grinned wider. "Oh you hadn't? You

seemed pleased when I allowed you to purchase three hundred and fifty-two dresses."

Sophia chuckled again. "I did not purchase three hundred and fifty-two dresses. Of course if you don't think I bought enough, we could go back and–"

"That's not necessary," Edmund quickly interrupted. Yet in truth the errand had not been as laborious as a typical trip to the modiste.

Not with Priscilla there.

He had been thunderstruck when he saw her in that gown. Floored, flabbergasted, over-whelmed and more. It was stunning, yet the lady was the most enchanting of all. She was a true diamond of the first water.

The dress had been made for her. Not literal-ly perhaps, but it was perfection. He knew Lady Drummond and what she truly sought. As soon as possible, he would pay her a visit and negotiate a deal that would be to the satisfaction of all. Whatever it took, he would secure the dress for Priscilla.

Then he would secure Priscilla for himself.

His sister made a face, and he brought his attention back to her. Of course, he did not mean to act the miser. "Purchase as many dresses as necessary. Whatever you need, financially or otherwise, you may always come to me."

Sophia's gaze softened, and his heart squeezed. His sister was turning into a beautiful woman. "I know that, Edmund. I was just teasing you."

"Just so." He deepened his voice, stiffened as he thought of launching his beautiful, vulnerable sister into society.

Considered how much a tower cost.

Priscilla smiled at his sister. As he'd hoped, the two ladies had taken to each other like old friends, perhaps too well, judging by Sophia's eager sharing of her childhood antics. Yet she spoke in good humor, with nothing severe enough to make Priscilla wary.

Priscilla bit into a juicy apple, and he forced himself to look away. He wanted to give her time to accept the inevitable before solidifying the match. Yet it grew more and more difficult to not claim her with each day.

Especially since he knew the ultimate outcome.

"How about we play a game?" His sister smiled widely.

Emma and the duchess immediately bobbed their heads. The others groaned, but agreed with good-humored smiles.

"Do you have a particular game in mind?"

"I do." Sophia's eyes sparkled. "Let's create a story. Each of us tells a small part, adding a twist or something unexpected. I'll go first." She rubbed her hands together. "Once there was a very handsome prince. He was brave and strong and loved by everyone in the kingdom. The day had finally come to find his princess." She stopped, her smile wide and dreamy.

"I'll go next," Crawford looked directly at Hannah. "There was also a princess in this tale. She was sweet and soft-spoken and always listened to her male relatives."

Edmund choked back a laugh. Crawford was grinning widely at Hannah.

And she looked like she was about to clobber him.

"I'll go next." Hannah smiled sweetly. "Unfortunately, the prince developed a terrible disease and all his teeth fell out. The princess decided she would rather create her own destiny, so she set out to conquer the world."

Everyone laughed, Crawford the hardest of all. He winked at Hannah.

She scowled.

"Fortunately, matters were not as dire as they appeared," Duchess Sherring jumped in. "The prince met a mysterious lady, only she was not as she seemed. She was actually a kind sorceress, and she restored his perfect teeth. He returned to his quest to find his princess."

"Who was having a fantastic time all on her own," Emma continued the tale. "She learned new skills, performed good deeds and helped many people. Everyone loved her."

"Especially the prince, because she was simply perfect for him." Peyton smiled at Emma, bringing a blush to her cheeks. "He set out to prove they were meant to be together. When a fierce dragon threatened her, he rushed to her defense."

"Yet his assistance was unnecessary," Priscilla said quietly. "She did not need anyone to rescue her. She saved the entire town and became a true heroine."

His turn.

"When the hero finally found the princess, he didn't try to change her. Nor did he stop her from conquering the world."

He watched her carefully, searching for any sign of emotion. With the last word barely out of his mouth, she broke in, "That's not true. He wants to turn her into the weak princess she once was."

"She was never weak." He gazed at her, willing her to see the truth behind his words. "She was always brave and strong. Yet together, they could conquer any enemy, bring peace and prosperity to the world."

"How can she believe that? In a world where she is less, how can she believe he'll allow her to be more?"

"Because he lo–"

He froze, yet his gaze remained riveted on the woman before him, as the world melted away. Priscilla's expression reflected shock, confusion and something far stronger: *hope*. He closed his mouth in measured movements, lifted his chin.

She met his stare with an unreadable one of her own. The others watched in stunned silence, their eyes parrying between the two of them, waiting to digest the next act of what was no longer a game.

Why had he said that? What did it mean? Not the literal words, but the instinctive impulse behind them, and the reaction she could not hide. He could not understand his own motives, much less the feelings she kept locked behind a chiseled wall of silence.

For now he could do nothing except remain silent.

It was not time for the story to end.

Chapter Twelve

Dear P,

Fear.

You may not recognize it. You may not understand it. You may not even realize it.

Yet this is what drives you.

Fear.

Through these letters, I have learned much about you, more than I know of some of my closest allies. Without the hindrances, judgments and misconceptions of physical personas, we "read" each other's true personalities. It is so clear.

What drives you is fear.

Do not let it triumph. Strength is not the absence of fear but the willingness to overcome it. You have talked about giving up what you truly want.

Just imagine if you didn't have to.

Yours,

Edmund

"So what do you think of Edmund?"

An image of Edmund flashed in Priscilla's mind, the challenge, desire, *emotion* as he bent down to brush his lips against hers. With a shallow inhale, she shook her head. "I do not think of him."

Only that wasn't true. She thought of him when she was awake. And sleeping. And breathing.

"Truly?" Emma asked with a grin. "Because that's not how you were acting."

Priscilla looked past Emma and Hannah to the rest of the picnickers. They had gone for a small stroll, but kept their voices low for the short distance. "I was just trying to be cordial. What about you two? You act… differently around Crawford and Peyton."

Hannah's expression turned guarded, and Emma blushed.

Interesting. "Is there something I should know?"

"I'm afraid not." Emma sighed, the tinge of regret tinting her eyes.

Priscilla put a hand on Emma's shoulder. "Are you interested in Peyton?"

"Half the ladies in the *ton* are interested in Peyton."

True. Both men were as eligible as Edmund.

"You are extremely eligible yourself, Emma. If you are interested in a match, you should pursue it."

Emma's cheeks darkened. "You're forgetting one problem."

"What's that?"

"I can't manage a coherent word in front of him."

Priscilla chuckled. "Emma, you are smart, sweet and altogether wonderful. Never forget that."

Emma turned pink and looked down. "It's too bad," she said softly. "He really is an interesting man." She turned to Hannah. "What about you? Crawford doesn't make you speechless."

Hannah snorted. "Hardly. I can think of many, many words to say to him."

"Are they words a lady should know?"

Hannah grinned. "Not even close."

They all laughed. "Why?" Priscilla asked. "He seems nice enough."

"He's an overbearing tyrant."

It was what Priscilla called Edmund, only the moniker wasn't truly accurate, neither for Edmund nor Crawford. They were both strong, powerful lords accustomed to leading, yet they also had a reputation for being upstanding gentlemen. "He certainly has a favorable view of you. Are you sure there isn't something there?"

"Only a sour stomach." Hannah folded her arms across her chest, even as her expression turned mischievous. "Can I borrow one of your vases?"

"Absolutely not!" Priscilla fought to keep her voice stern. "There will be no clobbering. Well, unless I'm the one doing it."

"So, back to you, Priscilla." Emma grinned. "Tell us again why you and Bradenton wouldn't suit."

"I'm looking for a man who talks to rocks."

"Oh come on." Emma laughed. "I know you don't want someone who talks to rocks, or plants or… what does the other one talk to?"

"Horses."

"Ah, yes."

"I don't think she should pursue him." Hannah's expression turned serious. "He threatens everything."

"We don't know that." Emma pressed closer. "Who knows? He may even help us."

Emma and Hannah exchanged a look. For not the first time, Priscilla wondered if they knew he was her mysterious colleague. She should just tell them, yet for some reason, she couldn't bring herself to voice the words. He was her secret.

"It's not just that." She stood taller. "There are other reasons why I can't be with Edmund."

Emma gave her a look. "Such as?"

"He takes control of every situation, charms

everyone and is too lickable."

Oh. My Goodness. Did she actually call him lickable?

Emma gasped. "What did you say?"

"Can we just forget I said that?"

"Never."

Emma looked at her earnestly. "If you can't be honest with us, at least be honest with yourself. We can tell you like him."

"No, you can't."

They gave her identical pointed looks.

"I'll admit I like him. But like a friend. Or a pet bunny."

"A pet bunny?" Now even Hannah laughed. "What does that mean?"

"Fine, like a pet lion."

"Now he's a lion?" Emma shook her head. "You really are confused."

"Well, how can I not be? The man is as gorgeous as a Greek god and as lickable as chocolate ice cream." Priscilla put her head in her hands. "There, I admit it. Are you happy?"

Could things get worse?

"What is lickable?" A deep voice she knew so well boomed through the air.

Ye, they could get worse.

Much, much, worse.

She peeked up and squinted at Edmund, leading his friends from behind a too close bush. His expression was neutral, yet his eyes lit with challenge… and satisfaction.

Betraying nothing, Peyton offered his arm to Emma. "It's almost time to leave. May I escort you?"

Emma blushed as she accepted his arm.

"And I will take you." With the definitive statement, Crawford took Hannah's arm and placed it on his sleeve.

Hannah scowled, but allowed him to lead her away.

Which left Priscilla and Edmund alone.

Plastering a smile on her face, Priscilla took a springy step back towards the others. "Shall we return?"

"Wait."

She froze, swallowed. "Yes?"

"I have some questions."

She looked at him carefully. "Yes?"

"You said you wanted to lick something."

Oh. My. Blazes.

He had heard. There was simply, positively no other explanation.

"You misheard me. I said I wanted to kick something."

The sides of his lips curled up. "You want to kick something?"

"Very much."

"I also heard you discussing mythology, particularly, Greek gods."

"I don't really care for Greek gods." She

edged back. "Really, I find they are all average. Below average even."

His lips twitched. "Greek gods are below average?"

"Absolutely, Now if you'll excuse me."

"What about bunny rabbits?"

"What about them?"

"Do you like them?"

"They are a little too soft, I think. But at least they are easy to lead. You simply pick them up and direct them."

He stepped closer. "Can you now?"

She nodded. Stepped back again.

"What about lions? They are far more power-ful."

"Yet equally as malleable. Just give them fresh meat, and they'll eat out of your hands like little kitties."

Bradenton smiled like the predator with which she had compared him. "Or he could decide you are the fresh meat he desires."

Her heart stumbled. She forced herself to stand tall. "Is there anything else?"

"One last thing. How do you like ice cream?"

She didn't respond. Didn't even try. Instead she spun on the ball of her foot and stomped back to the others, even as his gaze burned into her back. *Perfect.* Now he knew how she regarded him, specifically that he looked like a Greek god and was as lickable as ice cream.

No doubt he would never forget.

"HE IS THE greatest man I have ever met."

If only she didn't agree.

"He works tirelessly to help those in need."

With her hidden at his side.

"He may not show it, but he cares greatly for people."

That makes him the most dangerous of all.

"Of course don't tell him I said all that. It'll make his head as large as a hot air balloon." Sophia laughed gaily, seemingly oblivious to the turmoil churning inside Priscilla.

She looked across to the other carriage, where Edmund sat with the men. As if he could sense her perusal, he turned to her, and their gazes held in unspoken communication. She sucked in a breath of suddenly heavy air. What would it be like to have such a powerful man actually care for her? To be his? Just about every eligible lady in the *ton* wished it.

She was the only one who couldn't have him.

She had to remind herself why not: he would watch her every move, stop her investigations, control *everything*. "Isn't it a challenge?"

Sophia cocked her head to the side. "A challenge?"

"Having Edmund for a brother." She held up her hand when the girl opened her mouth in clear protest. "I didn't mean it in a bad way. It's just he…" She lowered her voice. "He takes control."

Sophia visibly relaxed. By the way she had come to his defense, she truly loved her brother. "Edmund is one of the most influential lords in the ton. He commands a great deal of power, and he expects others to follow. I won't deny the obvious."

Priscilla bit her lip.

"However–" Sophia held up a finger. "He is also smart, reasonable and above all, kind. He is not so rigid to demand our compliance without care to our happiness. He is willing to compromise. For instance, he is allowing me to choose my own match. The same cannot be said of many families of the *ton*."

It was true. Parents and suitors often came together to make the choice, leaving the bride without a voice.

"He also allowed you an extra year before coming out," Priscilla noted.

"Actually–" Sophia smiled. "That was his idea."

Priscilla looked at her in surprise. Many fathers and guardians wanted their charges to be settled as soon as possible. "Really?"

Sophia nodded. "Said he wouldn't mind having me around another year. He spoke casually, but I could sense emotions he wouldn't show. He has always made me feel loved."

The wall guarding Priscilla's heart cracked

just a little.

"Does he watch out for me?" Sophia asked rhetorically. "Undoubtedly. I do not have free rein, and he does not allow me to partake in dangerous activities. No matter how fun they may be."

Priscilla smiled at the girl's rueful expression.

"But is it worthwhile? Oh yes. He has never wavered in his devotion. And I love him." Sophia gazed at her brother, her gaze filled with adoration. "He's the best brother ever."

The wall all but crumbled. Edmund may be one of the most powerful men in the *ton*, yet he gave his sister unconditional love.

"He is pursuing you."

Priscilla straightened. By now everyone knew of his pursuit, since they danced twice – or more – at every event. Wagers had progressed from when they would get married to what they would name their first child. "He is considering many for his duchess," she said carefully.

Sophia shook her head. "Perhaps once, but not anymore. Although that doesn't stop them from trying. Just last night, three ladies tried to convince him to take private walks so they would be 'discovered' by their families."

An unexpected surge of anger hit. If one of them had been successful...

"Don't worry." Sophia put a hand on her arm. "Edmund is far too wise to succumb to such plots. He would never let himself be trapped into marriage."

Sophia nodded, even as her mind reeled. He had put himself in that position, multiple times. *With her.*

Sophia gazed at her with the same sharp intelligence as her brother. "Perhaps I should say he would never be forced into that position."

"Of course not," Priscilla replied quickly.

"I have a question for you."

She forced a breezy smile. "Yes?"

"How do you feel about my brother?"

Nameless emotions tumbled within her, powerful, conflicting, overwhelming. She fought against them, focusing on her life's purpose. Yet Edmund's life purpose mirrored her own: fighting for those without a voice, improving deplorable working conditions, championing the poor. His work gave power to her voice, communicated through ink and paper. He was so kind, so giving, matching her in so many ways. If only…

"I see," Sophia said. She hadn't answered the younger girl, yet her eyes shone with satisfaction.

"Oh no!" Priscilla shook her head rapidly. "It's not what you think. I think of Edmu– Bradenton solely as a friend. As I've explained, we wouldn't suit."

"You do not truly believe that, do you?" The satisfaction in Sophia's gaze turned to compassion. "Edmund will be a brilliant husband."

No doubt. "I do not wish to surrender my freedom."

"None of us do," Sophia commiserated, her tone far wiser than her years. "Yet it will happen with any man you marry. Unless your family will allow you to not make a match?"

Lips pursed, Priscilla shook her head. She glanced again at Edmund.

"He never loses."

"What?"

"Edmund. When he goes after something…" Sophia's voice trailed off, the rest unspoken. Yet the ending was as clear as the world surrounding them. What he chased, he got.

Now he was chasing her.

"No one attains everything they want."

"Edmund does."

Priscilla sucked in a breath. His sister was not exaggerating. In all the instances she could recall, he had always emerged victorious.

Would he emerge victorious now?

And…

Did she want him to?

"You're being summoned."

Priscilla started as a young girl with long, flowing hair waved at them from the window of a nearby building. The carriages slowed to a stop in front of a neat two-story bookshop with white and green trim.

"My lady, my lady!" The girl smiled widely, revealing two missing front teeth. "Miss Henrietta was just saying your book came in and–"

"Susie, hush!" A middle-aged, harried-looking woman burst out of the building. "My apologies, my lady. We didn't mean to interrupt your ride. Your book arrived, but you can get it any time."

"I do not mind stopping." Edmund called from his carriage, his voice easily booming across the distance. "We could spend a few minutes perusing the books."

"That would be fine–" Priscilla stopped. It would be fine, except for the book she ordered:

The Vital Campaign for Social Causes.

"Actually, I can come back later. I'm sure everyone wants to get home and–"

"Nonsense," her mother broke in, lifting herself off the seat. "I wouldn't mind browsing the bookshop for a while. An excellent idea, Bradenton. Is everyone agreeable?" Without waiting for an answer, she continued, "Perfect, let's go."

And just like that, the decision was made. Priscilla parted her lips as everyone started exiting the vehicles. After disembarking from his own carriage, Bradenton came to hers and extended his arm. She gritted her teeth, but took it, then let go as soon as she hit the street. She raced forward. She had to attain – and hide – the book before he saw it.

She hurried into the spacious shop. The airy space smelled of paper and fresh ink, emanating from thousands of tomes filling bookcases two stories tall. Normally she spent hours in the shop, perusing volumes on any and every subject, yet now she swiftly threaded her way to the back. And Bradenton?

He was right behind her.

How was she going to lose him? She looked around, noticed a certain lord disappear behind a bookshelf.

It would be wrong.

So very, very wrong.

Yet she was desperate. She spun around. "Your Grace, I just saw a friend of yours. He needs assistance."

"Who?"

"The name escapes me, but he is a good friend."

He cocked his head to the side. "How did you know he needed help?"

"It was obvious. You should hurry." She put a hand on his back, leading him away. "I think he's unwell. You should make sure he is all right."

The look in his eyes said he didn't believe her, but he continued. "I shall return in a minute."

Unlikely. By the time he extricated himself from the lord, hopefully she would have retrieved and hidden the book. Because when he discovered who that "friend" was, things would get *rocky*.

WHAT WAS SHE up to?

It had to be important, and likely related to her secret. Why else would she send him to Lord Castleberry?

The rock-loving earl.

After enduring an eternity-long diatribe on rock formations, he finally managed to get away by explaining he had to research towers. Now he strode to Priscilla. She was standing at the desk, bobbing up and down, shifting her weight from foot to foot. Why was she so nervous?

"I'm sorry, my lady. I know I put it right here." The shopkeeper frowned severely, as she sifted through overfilling piles of books. "I just don't kno– Oh, here it is!" With a triumphant smile, the clerk held up a large volume.

Edmund squinted, but was too far to read the title on the big black book. He strode quicker.

"Thank you!" Priscilla grabbed the book at the same time she saw him, and a look of utter panic entered her eyes. She dashed to the nearest bookcase and started peeling books off the shelf.

What in blazes?

He finally made it to her as she juggled the books in her arms. "Priscilla?"

She looked up as if shocked to see him. "Oh,

hello! I was just picking out some books. But I really don't need so many." She started putting the books back, one by one, without even looking at the titles. Finally, only one remained in her hands.

He folded his arms across his chest. "Care to explain?"

"I got the book I ordered."

He looked down and froze.

She looked down and gasped.

They read it together, *"A Complete, Comprehensive and Detailed Examination of Men's Underclothes (with Illustrations)"*

She looked back up.

Looked back down.

Parted her lips.

"Well, I, um, yes…"

"Can you explain?"

"Not really."

"Is there a reason you ordered a book on men's…" He cleared his throat. "Clothing."

"Well, yes, of course there is." She stretched her face into a smile as fake as a paste diamond. "Obviously."

"Are you trying to think of one right now?"

"Quite."

Amusement, confusion and suspicion tangled. Unless – He looked towards the volumes on the shelf. Could she have possibly switched books?

"It's for you!"

He turned back to her. "I'm sorry?"

She blushed. "The book, it's for you. I bought it for you, as a gift."

He just stared.

"Well, I could get you something else instead, since you clearly don't appreciate it." She returned the book to the shelf. "Let's see what would be good for you."

Then, she put her hand on *his* back and led him away.

He let her have her way, mainly because the small palm heating his back simply felt too good. Yet it was obvious she was trying to distract him. He would discover the truth.

She perused the titles, stopped, and smiled. "Now here is a good book for you." She handed him the thin volume.

Vases Through the Years.

"I think not."

She picked up another. "How about this one?"

A Complete History of Rocks.

"Not if it was the only remaining written work in existence." He firmly replaced the book on the shelf. "However, that does remind me. That good friend you sent me to–"

"Here's another!" She grabbed a thick brown book and thrust it at him.

He immediately returned *Horses are People,*

Too back to the shelf.

"Perhaps I can find one." He perused the topics. "Ah, yes, how about this?"

The Winning Strategies of the Lion. She stiffened. "There are tricks to best such a predator."

"You are mistaken." He curved his lips into a smile. "Perhaps I should look for a book on why Priscilla Livingston should stop keeping secrets from the Duke of Bradenton."

She sniffed. "No such book exists."

"Perhaps not. Why don't we go back to the books by the desk? I thought I saw something interesting–"

As he took a step, she looked positively panicked. She glanced around, fluttering her eyelids up and down. "Your Grace, I… I–"

"I say, Priscilla, do you have something in your eye?"

She put her hands on her hips, hissed, "I was about to swoon!"

He held in the laugh. What could be so pressing she was actually pretending to faint? "We should definitely head to the carriage, then. The quickest way is right past the desk."

"I'm sure it's not!"

Before he could move, the proprietress came from behind a bookcase. "Priscilla, I'm so glad you're still here! I found your book on the shelf. You must have accidentally returned it with the others. Here you go." She handed the book over.

Priscilla tried to cover the title, but she wasn't quick enough. It had nothing to do with any sort of men's underclothes.

It was a book on social action.

Her expression remained hooded, shuttered. "I will give it to my father instead."

He simply nodded, not revealing he had seen it. That she would order a book on social action was unusual, yet not completely unexpected. The steps she'd taken to hide it were far more telling.

What on earth was Priscilla Livingston hiding?

He had to do something to make her less wary of him, to trust him even. He thought back to the modiste. Hopefully securing the dress she so clearly loved would aid in his endeavor. One way or another, he would find his way into Priscilla's confidence.

THE REPORTS HAD not been exaggerated.

Lady Drummond truly was a dragon.

As Edmund walked into a formal drawing room decorated in shades of deep chocolate and black, the older lady made no attempt to approach, greet or even acknowledge him. Instead she stood in the middle of the room, her grey hair pulled ruthlessly back, her voluminous black frock covering her from neck to floor. She wore a scowl as severe as the dress, and a shrewd look that skewered.

The servant bowed and left.

"It's a pleasure to see you again," Bradenton walked to the lady, halting at a respectable distance. "You look well, as always."

"You know flattery doesn't work with me, Bradenton," Lady Drummond snapped. "What do you want?"

Edmund hid a smile, not unpleased. It was preferable to deal in a forthright manner instead of negotiating by the typical rules of society. "We recently visited Madame Fleur. She showed us the dress you purchased for your granddaughter, a unique ivory creation."

Lady Drummond's eyes narrowed, yet she didn't respond.

Edmund continued, "I am very much interested in purchasing the gown for a friend, only it cannot be recreated. Madame Fleur mentioned a different color would suit your granddaughter better. I was wondering if you would consider allowing us to buy the dress. Of course, I would personally commission a new dress that is just as brilliant for your granddaughter."

The eyes narrowed more, displeasure sparking off of them. "Madame Fleur should learn to keep her mouth shut. I will not waste your time, Bradenton. The answer is no."

He had expected no different. He also knew she expected him to argue. "Tell me, Lady

Drummond, what do you truly want?"

She pursed her lips into a tight slash. "I want the dress I ordered."

"Yes, but what do you hope to accomplish with it?" He held his hands out. "It is for Lady Clara's debut next week, correct?"

She gave a curt nod.

"So I assume you truly wish for a successful launch, correct?"

"Get to the point, young man."

He had not been called young man since his own grandmother had done so a decade ago, but he continued, "This dress will not aid Clara in a successful coming out. If anything, it will provide an obstacle. Madame Fleur said a gown could be made in a very pale color, which would complement your granddaughter's beauty."

Lady Drummond's gaze softened ever-so-softly.

"What you really want is for your granddaughter to be a success. If you allow me to help, I could do far more than an unflattering dress could."

Her gaze sharpened. "Don't talk in circles, Bradenton. What exactly are you offering?"

"How fares the guest list for the ball?"

"Sufficient." Yet Lady's Drummond's frown told a different tale. With so many competing events this time of season, it was difficult to attract a crowd, or at least the right kind of crowd. Many people feared Lady Drummond and stayed away.

"I saw you were kind enough to invite me. I have not yet responded." Of course he'd planned to reply with a negative. In his position, every night brought vast choices, and lately he chose based solely on Priscilla.

Lady Drummond cocked her head to the side, her expression thoughtful. "You would attend the ball?"

Clearly, she knew the benefit his presence would bring. He rarely attended smaller balls, and the *ton* would most definitely notice.

"Your granddaughter deserves the best start possible, don't you think?"

For just a moment, something akin to a smile passed by the older woman's lips, but it was gone in an instant. "You know, young man, you remind me of my–"

"Grandmother!"

They both turned as something large, bulky and furious thundered into the room. Bradenton straightened as a tall and muscular man planted himself next to the older woman. He wore a gentleman's suit, his black hair cut in a gentleman's style, but there was something wild about him. He turned his dark gaze on Edmund.

"Why are you bothering my grandmother?" he demanded, a slight Scottish burr tinting his voice.

Bradenton had met most of Drummond's grandchildren, but he had never met this man, if that was who he is. "I'm not bothering anyone," he replied calmly. "I simply came to discuss a business interaction."

The man folded his arms across his chest. "She is not interested in any business with you, Bradenton."

Edmund narrowed his eyes. "I'm afraid I do not recall us meeting."

"I'm Ken–" The man stopped, shook his head. "I'm Foxworth."

"My grandson recently inherited a dukedom." Lady Drummond turned to him. "I appreciate your help, but it's not necessary. I was just about to come to an agreement with Bradenton."

Foxworth's gaze softened on his grandmother, but it hardened when he turned back to Bradenton. "You will not make an agreement with this man." He stepped forward.

A lesser man might have stepped back, but Edmund stayed where he was. Foxworth might be large and muscled, but so was he, and well-skilled in the fighting arts. He never imagined needing them in Lady Drummond's drawing room, but he would defend himself if necessary.

Yet more than anything he was confused. The man obviously had some sort of hidden argument with him.

"You need to leave now," Foxworth growled.

"Get away from my brother!"

They all turned.

Lady Drummond lifted her hands. "Bloody Hell."

Edmund gaped as Sophia raced into the room and planted herself between him and Foxworth. She stood more than a foot shorter than both of them, but she pointed a finger at Foxworth and poked him in the chest.

Literally poked him in the chest.

"I will not allow you to hurt my brother!"

"What is the meaning of this?" Foxworth roared. He reached for Sophia.

Edmund saw red.

As Foxworth took a firm grip of Sophia's arm, Edmund prepared to lunge. His muscles were flexed and ready, yet he couldn't attack with Sophia in the way. Only the new duke simply moved her out from between the two of them and glared down at her.

"What do you think you're doing?" Foxworth growled. "Do you have any idea of the danger you put yourself in? You can't put yourself between two men!"

The sharpest edge of Edmund's anger fled. Foxworth hadn't been trying to hurt Sophia. He'd been trying to rescue her.

It would save him a pummeling.

Sophia glared at Foxworth. "I had to protect

my brother."

Foxworth looked at her incredulously. "Lass, your brother doesn't need you to save him. You will never do something like that again!"

Sophia put her finger out, stepped forward.

Edmund strode in front of her. "Foxworth is right. What were you thinking, stepping between us? You could have gotten hurt."

"Exactly." Foxworth opened and closed his fists. "You need to watch your sister better, Bradenton. She's going to get hurt fighting your battles."

"She does not fight my battles," Edmund growled. He looked down at his sister. "Never again, Sophia."

She was squirming and pink and extremely mad. "I can't believe I followed you here to help. And just as I was telling Priscilla you were not a controlling brute!"

"Listen to your brother, lass." Foxworth seemed calmer, even as he gazed at Sophia sternly. "I would never allow my sister to imperil herself."

"Kenneth!"

Lady Drummond put a hand on her forehead. "Of all the–"

They all turned as a young waiflike woman ran into the room. She launched herself at Foxworth. "You've arrived. I've been waiting all week! Well, all month, really, since I left, and I…

I am just glad you are here."

Edmund watched in amazement as the man transformed, every feature softening as he gazed at the blond-haired, blue-eyed beauty. He held her gently in his arms. "It is wonderful to see you again, lass."

Sophia softened as well. He looked down to see her staring, not at the newcomer, but at Foxworth, her lips parted and her gaze slightly unfocused.

He stiffened. "Sophia, if I move aside, will you promise not to attack the man who is three times your size?"

She nodded distractedly.

Edmund grimaced. If he could help it, this was the last time Sophia would be in close quarters with the untamed duke.

"If I had known there would be a party, I would have served tea and crumpets," Lady Drummond quipped, expertly regaining control of the meeting. "But as I am fearful of another dozen guests should I hesitate, I will take care of this matter now." She turned to her granddaughter. "Clara, am I correct you did not like the dress I commissioned from Madame Fleur?"

"It was a beautiful dress..." The girl hesitated.

"But you did not care for it."

Clara grimaced. "Not for me. It was gorgeous on the form, but ivory doesn't suit me. I have always preferred colors." She held out her hand. "I have seen many other debutantes in colors."

"That's true," Sophia said. "I'm planning to wear a color for my coming out next year."

Foxworth's gaze sharpened.

Edmund glared and pulled Sophia a little closer.

"And I assume you have someone whom the dress flatters more." Bemusement flashed in the older lady's eyes. "Lady Priscilla, I assume?"

Edmund inclined his head. "Her complexion is more suitable for the gown."

Lady Drummond pursed her lips, turned back to her granddaughter. "You would prefer I commission a dress in a different color?"

"Oh yes!" Sophia brightened. She clapped her hands together. "That would be wonderful!"

Lady Drummond sighed. "Then I will accept your offer, Bradenton." She held up her hand when Foxworth started to protest, giving him a stern look. He grimaced but said nothing.

Lady Drummond turned back to Edmund. "You will deal with Madame Fleur, and ask that she make the most flattering – and suitable – gown for my granddaughter in time for her ball. And I do believe your response to the event was an affirmative?"

Bradenton hid his smile. The older woman was as crafty as the most seasoned military leader. "Of course."

Satisfaction reached the older woman's eyes. "Perfect. Then I'm afraid I must adjourn this impromptu party. I would like to spend some time with my grandson, who has only just arrived from Scotland."

Bradenton inclined his head, and took a firm grip of Sophia's hand. "Of course, my lady. And thank you. I will instruct Madame Fleur to refund your accounts."

Lady Drummond waved a black gloved hand. "Too much accounting. Just put the money towards one of your causes."

Edmund stopped. Perhaps Lady Drummond was not what society believed. "Of course, my lady." He bowed.

He led his sister out into the brightly shining sun, the perfect complement to his day's success. Despite the complications with his sister, his spirits were buoyed. He had secured the dress for Priscilla and only had to attend Clara's launch in return. In truth, he didn't mind helping the young debutante, especially in light of her grandmother's kindness. The situation with Foxworth perplexed him, especially since he could not remember meeting the man, and he would have to be careful. He would definitely keep his sister away from the unpredictable Scotsman.

For now, he would retrieve the dress and bring it to Priscilla. Or perhaps…

This could be an opportunity.

There was something strange about Priscilla's sewing guild. If her excuse for not having his sister join was genuine, she would have changed her mind once she saw how mature Sophia was – her decision to come between him and wild men notwithstanding. With her refusal, his suspicions had grown regarding the group and its true purpose.

The dress provided the perfect excuse to arrive unannounced. He could arrive just as the guild ended, talk to some of the ladies, ask some questions.

And just perhaps solve the mystery that was Priscilla Livingston.

"OUR EFFORTS FOR the Berkshire Orphanage have been a complete success. Thanks to you, the children will have ample food for the next month."

Priscilla smiled at the extended clapping from the crowd, the largest she had ever hosted. She had carefully selected and invited several new members, and they were as enthusiastic about the cause as the seasoned participants. She had also extended their mission to include more than indirect actions. In addition to influencing votes, they now volunteered, donated and made changes in smaller measures.

"For several reasons–" *Or one infuriating man.*

"I have been unable to conduct my own investigations. Fortunately, I received another anonymous letter from my *Greatest Admirer*. It held a great deal of useful information, which I have passed along to my colleague."

The clapping sounded again.

"It's almost time to conclude today's meeting. Does anyone have any questions?"

Several hands shot up. Priscilla pointed to a lady in the back. "Yes?"

"Are you betrothed to Bradenton yet?"

Priscilla shook her head. Most in the *ton* thought it only a matter of time before an announcement was made. Including, most disconcertingly, Edmund.

"We've already discussed this. I am not getting engaged to Bradenton." She pointed to another lady. "Yes?"

"What does it feel like to be courted by Bradenton?"

Wonderful. Delightful. Enchanting.

"Quite boring, I assure you. Does anyone have a question that does not involve Bradenton?" She pointed at another hand. "Yes?"

"What are Bradenton's favorite things?"

A headache threatened. She didn't blame the ladies for being curious about the duke. He was a hero to them, a handsome, powerful man who championed the causes they cherished. In a world of elites, he was royalty.

"He likes rocks and vases. Now if there are no other questions–"

The door to the room opened. Everyone grabbed their sewing.

The duchess glanced around the room, her lips curving into a smile. "Priscilla, may I talk to you for a moment?"

"Of course." She nodded at the ladies. "That's all for today. Everyone remember to focus on your–" She cast a sideways glance at her mother. "Embroidery."

The ladies filed out, Emma and Hannah taking one last look before they left. Priscilla smoothed down her dress. "How can I help you, Mother?"

"I shall like to discuss Bradenton."

Priscilla forced her lips into a smile. "Yes?"

"Have you accepted his suit?"

Her breath hitched. "Has he–"

"No."

Priscilla breathed out. If – when – Bradenton asked, she may not have the power to stop what he started. "There is no reason to believe he will do so."

Her mother looked at her incredulously. "There is every reason to believe he will offer. His interest is obvious. He is only giving you time."

Was it true? Did Edmund consider their match inevitable, only granting her time to become accustomed to her surrender?

"What if I do not wish to marry him?"

It was not the question she intended to ask, yet it was the answer she needed. Likely her mother would simply say it was not her decision.

Yet instead the duchess sighed softly. "Do you truly wish not to marry him?"

Priscilla opened her mouth, yet the words caught in her throat. She parted her lips.

What was wrong with her? She didn't want to marry Edmund.

Did she?

It didn't matter. She *couldn't* marry him, not if she wanted to continue her all important work. "I can't."

"I see." The duchess studied her. "Your well-being matters a great deal to me. I would not push for the match, duke or not, if I did not believe he would bring you happiness." She sighed. "You suit incredibly well. Why do you resist what is clearly so right?"

Priscilla swallowed. "I have my reasons…"

"You are scared."

"Of course not!"

"I understand." Her mother gave a small smile. "Believe it or not, I was once in your position."

Impossible. Her mother loved being a duchess.

"I can see you don't believe me, but it's true. Do not misunderstand, I am happy in my role, and, as I shared earlier, I love your father."

Since the elucidation, Priscilla had noticed the love her mother claimed. It was obvious by the way her parents smiled at each other, the little touches when they thought no one was watching.

If she married one of the suitors on her list, she would never have that.

But she would be able to continue her mission. It was a sacrifice she had to make.

"Fear is a powerful emotion, Priscilla. I believe yours is unfounded, but you will never know if you surrender to it. You do not lose yourself when you marry a good man. And Bradenton is a very, very good man. I continued my own endeavors after marriage."

"It's not the same." Her mother dreamed of balls and luncheons and fancy rides through Hyde Park. She did not have a grand mission marriage would eliminate.

"Your father is determined for this match."

Priscilla darted her eyes up. While her father remained relatively permissible among parents of the *ton,* he was still a powerful duke. "How determined?"

Her mother put a hand on her shoulder. "You should prepare yourself."

Priscilla took a step back, shook her head. "No. He said he'd let me choose."

"He said if you didn't choose quickly enough,

he would make the choice for you."

"The season is only midway through. There are several lords who are quite interesting."

"You do realize one talks to rocks?"

Priscilla heated. "There are plenty of men who don't talk to rocks." *They talk to horses and plants instead.* "I've already gotten offers."

It was true. She'd received offers from multiple men: titled, wealthy lords who met her parents' requirements. Only she found a reason to reject each one. Some were far controlling. Others were biased against women. Still others talked to rocks.

Yet the biggest problem: They were not Bradenton.

Bradenton was sabotaging her. No man could compare to the intelligent, handsome and powerful duke. Several suitors had also abandoned their bids because of Edmund's pursuit. No one wanted to go against the powerful duke.

Her mother folded her arms across her chest. "You may have offers, but you have no betrothal. You turned them all down."

"I will accept one eventually."

"It might not matter if you do." The duchess set her features. "As I said, your father is determined for *this* match."

"He cannot force me to marry!"

"You and I both know he can and will," her mother returned. "They had a long discussion when he arrived."

Priscilla froze.

"What do you mean, when *he* arrived?"

"Bradenton is here."

This was bad. Very bad. Right now the ladies from the meeting would be streaming past the drawing room where Bradenton was most likely stationed. He already suspected the sewing guild was not as it seemed. Had he planned to question the unsuspecting members of the guild? Was it a coincidence or a plot? And the most important question:

Was it already too late?

"I ADORED YOUR vote on the factories last month!"

"I loved the orphans' initiative!"

"The best was when you stood up to that hideous Lord Roxbury in Parliament!"

Edmund took in the sea of women with great bemusement and a dash of confusion. Dozens of animated ladies crowded around him, far more than seemed typical for a sewing guild, and definitely more excited. Most were well-bred, yet some were clearly of the lower classes. This neither surprised nor bothered him, since he did not harbor the same biases as many of his fellow lords. What did surprise him was Priscilla's assertion Sophia would not fit in with the group.

He recognized several ladies of exactly the same age.

They all knew him.

He was accustomed to compliments, yet usually people applauded his title or his wealth, sometimes his physical prowess or sportsmanship. A group of ladies concerned with his voting record?

Most unusual.

"I appreciate your support." He turned to look at each one. "Ladies do not often take notice of society's ills."

"Oh, we care very much. In fact we love to discuss–"

"Shh!"

Several ladies hushed at once, sharing an almost comical expression of horror.

What in the world?

"Love to discuss…" he prompted.

The woman laughed nervously. "Love to discuss…" She looked around, as if searching for the answer. "Embroidery!" She held up her sewing triumphantly as the ladies around her giggled.

"Of course," he inclined his head. "Tell me, what do you like most about sewing?"

For a moment the ladies stared at him. Then everyone spoke at once, giving inane answers such as "needle" and "thread."

His suspicion deepened. "I would love to see

your work."

"Our work?" several echoed.

"Anyone's work." He gestured to the group. "Whoever would like to share. I've never seen the efforts of an entire sewing guild."

"Of course." One lady pulled a small piece of fabric, turned it to him to reveal…

A cock?

"Do you like it?" The woman asked eagerly. "I tried to be as realistic as possible. Have you ever felt one of these?"

For once, he was speechless.

"Bethany, you make a lovely *aubergine*." Hannah's lips twitched.

He nodded at her with a silent thank you. "It is a lovely aubergine."

The woman flushed pink.

Another lady held up her work. "Do you like it?"

What the mishmash of threads was supposed to represent was anyone's guess, although at least it did not resemble anything scandalous. The closest he could guess was a cow. A dead one.

He put on his best ducal voice. "It's lovely. I've never seen such a lovely… cow?"

The lady frowned, turned the work to face her. "It's a bed of flowers."

"And a splendid one at that." He leaned in. "I was just joking, my lady."

The woman brightened.

Several other ladies displayed their work. A few had obvious talent, yet the vast majority of pieces were poorly done or just plain confusing. By the time they had finished, his suspicions were no longer smoldering.

They had ignited.

He was not particularly knowledgeable about embroidery, but he had seen his sisters' efforts, and the work in other ladies' homes. He would have expected a guild dedicated to the sewing arts to be extraordinary. Yet most of these were poor, lackluster even. Priscilla's guild was not as it seemed.

If they didn't focus on sewing, what did they focus on?

With Lady Priscilla not yet arrived, this was his chance to find out. "Ladies, I'd love to hear what you discuss in your sewing guild."

"Sewing, of course," Hannah broke in, loudly drowning out the other replies.

"Of course." Edmund stepped closer to the lady he had made blush earlier. "Is there perhaps something else you like to talk about? I have the feeling this sewing guild is more than it appears. Am I right?"

The woman looked at him with wide eyes. Then ever-so-slowly nodded.

The taste of triumph rose within him. "My lady, do not keep me in suspense. Tell me, what do you really discuss at your sewing guild?"

The woman looked around nervously, bit her lip.

He lowered his voice. "Come on, you can tell me. I am on your side."

The woman blushed. Then in a very soft voice, said, "Social justice."

CHAPTER THIRTEEN

Dear Edmund,

Why does everyone mistake logic for fear? Although I cannot explain, the truth threatens everything. This is the reason I must stay in the shadows.

Not fear.

Definitely not fear.

I have heard you are searching for a bride. How goes the endeavor? As I am sure you are aware, many ladies of the ton are eagerly vying for the position. I assume you will find a nice, biddable lady who will follow your every whim.

I am also searching for a match. The matter has gained utmost importance in recent days.

Yours,

P

P.S. Not fear.

"SOCIAL JUSTICE."

Two small words.

Infinite consequences.

"Your Grace, what a surprise." Priscilla strode into the room, speaking before she even reached the duke. "I see you have met my sewing guild. Are they sharing details about our meetings? We talk about so many things. Sewing, of course, the latest fashions–"

"Social justice."

She swallowed. "We discuss society, like in every *ton* drawing room."

His eyes narrowed.

Sweat broke out under her stays as the ladies squirmed uncomfortably behind him. She had to regain control, and quickly. The first step was getting him away before someone said something else that was compromising. "Ladies, if anyone is interested, cook made her famous peach cobbler."

Clearly grateful for the excuse, and such a delicious one, the ladies quickly excused themselves. Emma and Hannah lingered, but Priscilla gave them a small nod. With twin frowns, they followed the rest of the ladies.

"A most unusual sewing guild."

Priscilla forced a smile. "There's nothing unusual about my guild. We cater to smart, strong women who like to sew."

He folded his arms across his chest.

She puffed out hers. "You doubt their intelligence."

He shook his head. "Not at all. They seem smart and thoughtful. I was curious about their devotion to sewing, however. I asked them to show me their work, and the results were a bit surprising."

No doubt.

"One of them showed me a flower bed that resembled a dead cow. Another showed me an aubergine that resembled…" He grimaced. "Something else."

A blush stole up her cheek. She had thought the first a dead horse. And the aubergine?

A cock.

"We do not require extraordinary ability to join the guild. It is simply a group where ladies can relax and discuss current events."

"Like social justice."

"We discuss anything and everything."

"Really?" he stepped forward. "Are you sure you don't have a particular focus?"

Her heart skipped a beat. "It's just a sewing guild."

"You're hiding something."

"Untrue." She was hiding many, many things. "I assure you, Your Grace, I am as I seem. Yet you have not explained the reason for your visit. I assume you did not come to see my sewing guild."

He did not respond.

She sucked in a breath. Had he come to investigate? How close to her secret was he?

"I need you to be honest with me."

She laughed nervously. "I have been honest with you. I told you we wouldn't suit–"

"That's part of your dishonesty." He moved closer. "I know you feel what's between us. Something is holding you back, and I want to know what it is. I will support you."

She opened her mouth to dismiss him, yet stopped. For just a moment, she considered *what if*.

What if she told him the truth?

What if she shared who they were to each other?

What if she revealed how she felt?

Exposure was looking more and more inevitable. If she revealed herself, at least she would have some control over the situation. Hopefully, he would understand why they could not be together and would continue to work with her.

"I'm trying to give you time."

She narrowed her eyes. Like her mother, he was acting as if the outcome was inescapable. Thoughts of honesty dissipated as he once more seized control.

"I do not need time." She angled her head to

view him. "I already made my decision."

"You accepted a suitor?" he asked sharply.

"No!"

At his triumphant look, she hastened to add, "But I've narrowed my search. Soon I will announce a betrothal."

"I see." His eyes flashed in challenge. "Then I suppose I will have to move quicker."

Her stomach clenched "Your Grace, why are you here?"

He held her gaze, edged forward. He sighed softly. "My intention was not to upset you, Priscilla."

She swallowed. As difficult as it was to fight his aggressive nature, she could scarcely endure his earnest one.

"I will tell you, but first, I've been dying to do this."

"Do wh–"

He kissed her.

Pure danger. In the drawing room where anyone could enter, she was powerless to stop the forbidden. He tasted of sweet perfection, wine and pure male. He was equal parts strong and tender, powerful and kind. She pushed closer, breathing in his scent. No matter how many times they kissed, he enraptured her.

She gave a soft moan when he pulled back, heaving in air, wading through a sea of emotions: satisfaction, desire, pure need. How would she ever convince him to halt his pursuit when she couldn't stop kissing him?

"I'm sorry."

The deep voice seeped into her mind, stealing her attention. She fought to appear unaffected. "You should be. You should not be kissing a lady in her home."

"I'm not sorry about the kiss." The wolfish smile returned. "I'm sorry about stopping."

So was she.

"But as much as I don't fear being forced to marry you, I'm trying to avoid you feeling so. My apology is for that risk."

"If you don't want me to feel forced, then end this courtship."

"I can't do that."

She tensed.

His face betrayed no emotion. "You wanted to know why I came."

Not trusting herself to speak, she nodded.

He walked to the table, where a large white box tied with a vibrant blue ribbon sat. She had been so preoccupied, she hadn't noticed it before. Yet it was extremely large, and expensive looking. "Gifts are not necessary." She took a deep breath. "Unless it's a vase. Tell me it's a vase."

He chuckled, and even she smiled.

"I'm afraid my sense of self-preservation is too large for that." He stepped back. "I hope you like it."

She walked over to the box and untied the ribbon. She started to lift the top. "Whatever it is, I cannot acc–"

She stopped. Swallowed.

It was the dress of her dreams.

"Oh my." Carefully and slowly, she lifted the gown. The fabric shimmered like liquid pearls, soft and elegant and nearly weightless in her hands. Faceted diamonds glittered in the light, casting fiery rainbows upon the intricate embroidery. Delicate lace trimmed the edges, intricate patterns with a quiet grace. "It's even more beautiful than I remembered," she whispered.

He smiled. "Do you like it?"

She didn't like it, she loved it. A shot of delight surged through her. "It's amazing." She held it close. "But how?"

"I spoke with Lady Drummond."

Unease flared. Before she could say anything, he held out his hand. "Don't worry, I didn't use any unscrupulous measures. I simply convinced her another dress would better suit Lady Clara, just as Madame Fleur said."

Priscilla gazed at him. There had to be more.

"I also agreed to attend Lady Clara's coming out ball."

That made sense. Lady Drummond was a shrewd woman. She knew Edmund's presence would be far more valuable to her granddaughter than any dress.

In the end, most everyone got something. She got the gown of her dreams; Clara got a dress better suited to her, and Lady Drummond got a fantastic launch for her granddaughter.

Edmund received nothing.

She sighed. "You have to stop doing this."

"Stop cajoling dragons into trading dresses? I'm pretty sure this is the first, and last, time."

She tapped his arm. "You know what I mean. Being nice."

"How else will I protect myself from your vases?"

She laughed lowly. "I insist on paying you back."

"There's no need. Lady Drummond refused a refund. She asked me to redirect her funds to charity instead."

Priscilla paused, smiled. "Perhaps the dragon has more smoke than fire. Not everyone is as they seem."

"Exactly."

She swallowed. This was not a conversation she wanted. "Still, you must let me pay you back."

"I absolutely refuse to take any funds from you." A light came into his eyes. "But there is one thing you can do."

No.

"Yes?"

"More than anything, Lady Drummond wants her granddaughter's come out to be a success. Unfortunately, Lady Clara has been the target of some vicious rumors, endangering both her reputation and the ball. They say she has gotten closer than appropriate to a gentleman. There is no proof, thus it has not caused irreversible scandal, yet it has dampened her upcoming debut."

Priscilla frowned. Society could be so cruel. "I can counter the gossip," she offered. "Say they were false, and that she is a diamond of the first water. With my position, it could make a difference."

But it was not all she could do. Like Edmund, her attendance would both elevate the ball and attract others. It would be a risk to be close to Edmund at so intimate an affair, yet how could she send her regrets when Lady Drummond gifted her the dress? "I will also attend."

Satisfaction lit Edmund's expression, and a complete absence of surprise. She clenched her muscles as once again the duke got his way. Perhaps the trade did get him something.

Her.

"Handwriting."

"Excuse me?"

"Handwriting." Edmund rubbed his hands together. "That's how I am going to do it."

Crawford looked at Peyton, who shrugged. "Do what?"

"That's how I'm going to discover the identity of my informant." Edmund looked out at the crowd overfilling Lady Drummond's ballroom. The ball was an unmitigated crush, far exceeding even the most optimistic predictions. Scores of lords and ladies walked the luxurious space, enjoying delicate appetizers and superb liquors.

He swirled the amber liquid in his glass, watching as guests danced, talked and laughed. Any one of them could be his informant. "I can't believe I didn't think of it earlier. Just because I didn't recognize the handwriting doesn't mean I can't find it."

"You just need to get a handwriting sample from every lord in the *ton*. Simple." Crawford raised his glass.

"It won't be as complicated as all that." Edmund pointed to a satin-covered book on the front table. "I can examine guest books, wagering sheets and even the daily correspondence. I may already have a matching sample."

"What if your informant is purposely changing his handwriting?" Peyton asked.

"Then I will have lost nothing." Edmund shrugged. "I may never find him, but it's still worth a try."

Their hostess walked up. As always, Lady Drummond wore uninterrupted black, yet the dress was softer than her usual ensemble, with less fabric and a more modern cut. While she did not smile, there was a gentleness that hadn't been present earlier. "Bradenton, a word?"

Peyton and Crawford bowed graciously. "We will see you later."

Bradenton turned to his hostess. "Good evening, Lady Drummond. How are you?"

"I am delighted."

He held in a smile. The slightest softening of her lips was the only visible difference between Lady Drummond's fury and delight. "That is wonderful."

"It is because of you. No, don't deny it." She held up a hand when Edmund started to protest. "You and I both know it's true. The ball is a far greater success than I could have ever hoped. You promised to attend, yet you did far more than that. How many people did you convince to come?"

A lot. He'd called in favors, told countless friends and solicited his family. The only thing he hadn't done was put a notice in the papers. "Lady Clara reminds me of my own sister. She deserves a successful launch."

"Thank you." The older lady studied him. "Not only is the ball a success, but the rumors plaguing my granddaughter have vanished. She is the happiest I have ever seen her."

He gave a genuine smile. "I am most

pleased."

"As am I. As you have gone beyond our agreement, I feel the need to respond in kind. Of course there is little I can offer a duke such as yourself, but I did hear Lady Priscilla has recently arrived." She paused, lowered her voice. "Would you care for some time alone with her?"

He allowed his lips to curve into a slow smile.

She interpreted his expression correctly. "If you go to the gardens and follow the path, you will come to a wall of red bricks with a single yellow brick. Push that brick, and a door will open into a beautiful, enchanted garden. If you decide to share it with Lady Priscilla, no one should bother you. That is, unless you wish to be bothered."

H stared at her in shock.

"Don't be surprised, young man. I see the way you look at her, and the way she looks at you. In my day, you'd be married with twins by now."

He choked back a laugh.

She remained sober. "Time is your enemy, Bradenton. You are both highly sought after. If she, or you, inadvertently found yourself in a compromising position, it would be disaster. I can ensure success."

He opened his mouth to turn down her offer. Stopped. Considered.

It was outrageous, contemplating what he

fought for so many years. Yet Lady Drummond was not incorrect in her assessment, however frank it was. If one of them became compromised with someone else…

No. He could not start their union like this. Priscilla would be furious with him for forcing her, and she may still try to escape. As long as the chance existed for her to accept his suit without subterfuge, he had to try.

If that didn't work…

"I appreciate the offer, but for now I will continue my courtship. I would love to view the garden, however."

Lady Drummond sighed. "Just don't tarry, young man. Is there anything else I can do for you?"

Once more he hid his smile. Others judged Lady Drummond severely, yet under the stern exterior she was charitable, kind and just. A shame she couldn't help him attain Priscilla.

He stopped.

That didn't mean she couldn't help him find his informant.

He had only just devised his plan to search for his informant's handwriting, yet perhaps someone was already familiar with it.

Like a matriarch who had known most lords since short pants.

It was not without risk. He couldn't explain why he needed the information or what he intended to do with it. Still, Lady Drummond was not one to gossip. He had brought a writing sample from one of the letters, a paragraph with no mention of their subterfuge. He disliked sharing it, as he had declined to do with Crawford and Peyton, yet it would be worthwhile if it led to his informant.

"I could use your assistance with a different matter. I wish to know the author of a letter." He held out the small paper. "If you could identify the handwriting, I would be most grateful."

Lady Drummond took the offering without comment, her lips turned down as she studied it. Her eyes darted left and right, her frown deepening.

She hesitated. And then…

"I recognize it."

He let out a slow breath.

"But I cannot recall whose it is."

Disappointment pierced him, all the sharper for its proximity to success. He reached for the paper, but she clutched it tightly in her bony hand, studying it once more.

"It's on the fringes of my mind." She sighed. "It's likely to come to me. Can I keep this?"

He nodded, anticipation muted but present. She may not have the answer right now, but her response was encouraging. As she said, she would likely remember.

Then he would have all the answers he needed.

"I DO NOT know how to thank you."

Priscilla smiled at the debutante of honor. As Madame Fleur predicted, Clara was resplendent in a pale blue gown embellished with sapphires and embroidered lavender flowers. It floated around her, flattering her pale complexion and casting her as a true diamond of the first water.

Priscilla smoothed down her own dress, a silky aqua creation with tiny beaded roses. It had not felt appropriate to wear the gown commissioned for Clara to her launch. "There is no need to thank me for your success. You are radiant."

Pink tinged Clara's cheeks. "I appreciate your kindness, but I am well aware of what you and Bradenton did for me. I never dreamed so many people would come to my ball. I've been here for a month, and I don't really have any friends–" Her eyes turned misty, and she swiped at them. "I'm sorry, I don't mean to be a watering pot." She took a deep breath. "What I'm trying to say is, thank you."

"I do not accept."

Clara's eyes widened.

"I'm referring to your claim you have no friends." Priscilla smiled. "You absolutely have a friend. Me."

"Oh." Clara's eyes sheened brighter.

"Now, none of that." Priscilla softly chided. "We don't want your eyes getting all red. Soon we'll arrange a visit, and I'll introduce you to some very nice ladies. Not that it will be necessary after this." She gestured to the large crowd. "I have a feeling you're going to be quite popular."

Clara's smile brightened the entire room.

A small commotion sounded from the side of the ballroom. Priscilla sighed. She recognized what, or rather who, was behind the fuss.

She gave herself a moment to study him. Edmund was magnificent in a pitch-black suit with an intricate cravat and crisp lines. He stood tall, his muscular build imposing, his hair shiny and smooth, his features chiseled. He was even more celebrated at the intimate party, immediately attracting a small crowd. Yet he seemed distracted, a slight frown as he scanned the ballroom.

When he found her, the world disappeared.

For just a moment they stared at each other, as she resisted the connection that grew ever-stronger. It urged her to go to him, to ignore the danger to claim what she so desired. What would happen when the inevitable end came, when she found a match, or he did?

Her heart lurched.

She shivered it away, stood taller.

He left his audience and threaded through

the crowd. He bowed. "Lady Priscilla, a pleasure as always."

He leaned in, far enough to be respectable, but close enough only she could hear. "I am surprised you did not dash behind a potted plant when you saw me."

She sniffed. "There was not a sufficiently large one."

The amusement in his eyes deepened. "Or perhaps you knew I would find you wherever you hid."

Her breath hitched. He was not merely referring to the ballroom.

"Would you care for a walk? Apparently Lady Drummond has an enchanted garden."

She looked at him in surprise. "Enchanted? Lady Drummond actually said that?"

"You know I do not lie."

Not like her. She swallowed back the words. "I can't believe you charmed Lady Drummond. Is anyone not enamored of you?"

"I have not yet captivated that potted plant."

"Actually, the plant was just remarking how dashing you were."

"Really?" He raised an eyebrow. "Then yes, I have charmed everyone. Come with me to the garden."

It was more command than request, yet Priscilla simply couldn't resist.

He touched the small of her back, leading her

forward. Tingles raced through her, bringing memories of touches and kisses, desire for more. She looked around, trying to divert her attention before she accosted him and made another memory in the middle of the crowd.

Laughter sounded from the refreshment table, where Clara chatted gaily with several girls. "I know how you charmed Lady Drummond."

"Do you?" He continued forward, even as he nodded to countless people. He exchanged greetings, but did not stop as they exited the ballroom into the crisp evening.

Like Lady Drummond, the garden was severe and muted, with perfectly pruned hedges, manicured trees and not a single flower in the sea of green. A few other people were enjoying the fresh air.

"How have I charmed the dragon?"

"You made her granddaughter's party a success. Instead of simply attending, you arranged for half of London to come."

What he did was stunning.

Just like him.

He inclined his head. "You did no less. In addition to dispelling the rumors plaguing Miss Clara, you encouraged others to accept as well."

"I may have mentioned it to my sewing guild."

His gaze sharpened.

Why had she mentioned the guild again?

"This was mostly you," she blurted out. "Why do you do it?"

The fire in his eyes lightened. "Why do I do what?"

The query was meant to distract him, yet she found herself truly curious. "Why do you work so hard to help others? What is your true purpose?"

He hesitated for a moment. "Do you know the feeling you get when you help someone?"

She gave a soft smile. It was the same feeling she got every time a vote went her way, or when conditions improved at one of the charity organizations she supported. "There's nothing like it."

"Exactly!" His mask dissipated, and for once he wasn't the commanding duke. Instead he was simply a man making a difference in the world.

"A dukedom is more than power and wealth. It's about responsibility and changing the world for the better. It's about helping people, no matter their social class. To bring joy to people, to make a difference in their lives. I would argue it's the true meaning of life."

She couldn't agree more.

He didn't aim for power or accolades. He did not care about being popular. He did it because he truly wanted to help people.

If he had been difficult to resist before, now…

She leaned in.

"Lady Priscilla," he said softly.

She straightened, heaving in a breath of flagrant air. What was she doing? Had he so intoxicated her she would kiss him right here, in the open?

His expression was unfathomable, yet for just a moment, something stronger passed through his eyes. He lowered his voice. "I will leave now. Wait a few minutes, then follow the path until you reach a red wall with a single yellow brick. I will meet you there."

A thrill raced through her. She should not agree, should not consent to once more being alone in his presence. Undoubtedly they would kiss again. Maybe twice. Maybe a dozen times.

After sacrificing so much for her cause, she deserved a little excitement before a lifetime of duty.

"I trust you can find your way?"

"Yes."

With one final look, he turned and casually strolled away. She waited. And waited. And waited some more, through a short while that felt like forever. Even when he wasn't with her, Edmund occupied her thoughts, her emotions. Every revelation made him more irresistible. It was almost like she was in–

No.

She pushed the thought down, away, because it never could be. Marriage would shackle her in virtual chains, stealing every freedom. No matter what he claimed, he would protect his wife.

She had to find a way to escape. Pain sliced through her, but it was the only way. Time was running out. What could she possibly do to change his mind?

She could tell him the truth.

What was once unthinkable may be her only hope. It was a risk, yet doing nothing held more danger, as he delved closer and closer to the truth. If discovery was inevitable, best it come from her. She could control the narrative, argue to continue their vital work. She would pursue her calling, and he would find a more biddable bride.

And her heart would break.

The door behind her closed as the last of the guests returned to the party. She stood straight and made a decision. She would do it. She would tell him the truth.

She forced herself to move, following the path to the unknown. In a few moments she came upon the red brick wall.

Where Edmund waited.

He seemed different. Or maybe she was different.

He held out his hand. "Ready?"

Not even a little. Yet she nodded as he opened a hidden door. With a deep breath, she followed him into the hidden depths.

Enchanted had been an understatement.

Magical. Captivating. Magnificent. No words could truly describe the veritable wonderland. Lady Drummond had worn nothing but black for decades, yet somehow created a garden brilliant with color, a rainbow of roses, hyacinths and tulips tangled in a dazzling display of natural beauty.

"It's amazing." She twirled around. "Absolutely breathtaking."

And fitting for what she needed to do.

She stopped and faced him. He closed the door to the garden, leaving them completely alone.

If she wanted to tell him, now was the perfect time.

How should she do it? Should she just blurt it out? *The roses look lovely and by the way, I'm your informant?* Should she start at the beginning? *When I was a child, my grandmother saved a baby and my life changed?* Should she use humor? *You're going to wish you had a vase when I tell you this.* There were a million ways to tell him and not a single one that felt right.

"Are you well?"

He stared as if he could see every thought in her mind.

She breathed deeply.

"You know you can trust me, right?" Edmund came closer. "No matter what it is, I'll understand."

She took another deep breath. Steeled her-self.

"It's time I told you the truth."

CHAPTER FOURTEEN

Dear P,

You possess far too many assumptions. You never know exactly how one will react in a given situation. Sometimes they will do exactly as you predicted. Sometimes they will behave as you least expect.

My hunt for a bride is nearly complete.
I am certain of my victory.

Yours,
Edmund

THE TRUTH.

He had waited so long.

Since the moment he discovered Priscilla hiding from unseen dangers, protective and possessive instincts urged him to discover what they were. To vanquish whatever demons chased her. To protect the woman he wanted for his own.

He touched her shoulder. "You can tell me anything. I will always support you."

She tensed, her eyes flashing with unease. The urge to sweep away the fear fired, to bear whatever burden she possessed. With the truth, he could do exactly that.

Yet indecision wavered in her expression, and she stayed silent, biting that luscious bottom lip.

"Whatever it is, I understand." He lowered his voice. "Nothing will change how I feel about you."

She breathed deeply. "What I tell you will come as a shock. You may indeed feel very differently about me."

His frown deepened. "No matter what you're hiding, or what happened in your past, I know who you truly are. You help people when no one is watching, change lives for the better." He caressed her arm. "This secret is tormenting you. Please let me help. I am a powerful friend."

She kept her gaze steady. "And an even more powerful adversary."

It was true, as others had learned, yet how could she ever think they would be adversaries? "Consider me a friend, a partner even." *Her soon-to-be-husband.* He didn't voice the last title, yet he had no intention of being anything less. "I wish you no harm."

"I know. It's just when you learn the truth, you may be…" She bit her lip. "Upset."

He expected no less. Priscilla was an intelligent woman. If she thought he would be displeased, she was undoubtedly right. Yet he had not lied when he said it would not change how he felt. Even if she gambled away her inheritance or had some deep, dark habit, he would still want her. She had become more than a desire, more than the fulfillment of a duty.

He could not imagine any outcome other than her becoming his.

"I have overcome challenges in the past. Whatever it is, we will face it together."

She looked down. "I'm telling you so you understand why we cannot be together."

He narrowed his eyes. What could be so substantial, she truly believed he would not wish to be with her?

"I've done things." She took a deep breath. "Things ladies are not supposed to do. I'm not as innocent as you believe."

Suddenly every answer became clear. How could he have missed it? Her explanation was literal.

She wasn't an innocent.

Jealousy surged though him, raw, blatant and unmistakable. Who had she been with, and why? Did she have feelings for them? Had she been forced?

A thousand and one questions raced through his mind, staggering in their breadth and depth, and yet anger was not among them. Despite society's misgivings, she had as much right to a prior relationship as he.

It should have been obvious, elucidating everything and more. She was worried about how he would react. Sadly, her worries were not unfounded. Many men ended courtships over the exact same matters, even as they kept mistresses and visited brothels. The double standards for the fairer sex were indeed unfair. And while he preferred not to imagine her with another man, the past was the past.

What mattered now was the future. There would be no others in this relationship – not for *either* of them.

"It all makes sense."

She looked taken aback. "What makes sense?"

He rubbed the back of his neck. "I can't believe I didn't see it."

"Edmund?"

"Your secret." He looked up. "You no longer have to be afraid."

Her expression turned guarded. "I don't?"

"Of course not." He gave her a small smile. "You don't have to pretend anymore. I see who you truly are."

She let out a shaking breath, put her hand to her mouth. "Oh, Edmund, I– I hope you can forgive me. I never meant to deceive you."

He softly caressed her arm, not with passion, but with simple human comfort. "I know. And I understand."

"You do?" She took a deeper, longer breath. "I thought– I thought you'd be furious."

"I'm not angry. I'm frustrated," he admitted. "Not by the secret, but that you couldn't trust me. Did you truly believe it would change the way I feel?"

She lifted her shoulders. "After all the subterfuge…" Her voice trailed off.

He smiled sadly. "It's a sad state of society that ladies must hide such things. You should be able to live life as you choose, without anyone judging."

She looked taken aback. "I must admit – I'm surprised at how well you are taking this." She hesitated. "Would you be all right with your wife continuing such activities after marriage?"

He froze. "You want to continue?"

She notched up her chin and nodded.

He needed to stay calm. Perhaps counting would help. *One, two, three…* "Of course I would not be all right with such activities after we wed!" he exploded. "How could you even ask?"

She paled. "You just said you understood!"

"I understand you not wanting to wait until marriage to enjoy relations. That doesn't mean I'd be all right with my wife visiting other men! You will stay away from–"

"What!?" she screeched.

Her yell was so loud, he stopped, looked to the door.

Priscilla flushed, pinkness spreading all over. "You think I'm not a virgin?" she hissed. "That I've been with a man?"

"You said you weren't innocent. You used that exact word!"

"That's not what I meant! I'm not– I mean I've never…" The pinkness deepened. She took a deep breath, brought her emerald gaze to his. "That's not my secret."

He released a breath. It had seemed so obvious. "I'm sorry."

She looked at him a moment more, then softened. "No, I'm sorry. I did say I was not innocent, although I meant it in different terms."

His attention sharpened. "What terms?"

A hundred emotions flashed in her expression. "Before I tell you, you must promise not to share my secret with anyone. No matter what, you must keep it to yourself."

He hesitated. Instincts demanded he agree simply to gain her acquiescence, yet further evaluation urged prudence. What if she truly was in danger? He could not promise away his ability to help her.

"I will have every discretion." They locked gazes. "Unless it is something that risks your safety."

She tensed. Even now she appeared to waver, as her eyes darted to the hidden exit, searching for escape.

He would not grant it.

"Tell me, Priscilla." He deepened his voice, used a tone that worked with the most powerful lords of the *ton*. "I can share your burden."

She stared at him. Slowly nodded. "But first, there's something I have to do."

She pressed her lips to his.

Passion flared, instincts roaring. He immediately took control, bringing her flush against him. She was so soft, so beautiful. He ran his hands along her back, down her flank to cup her tender backside. They moved in perfect harmony.

The kiss continued for moments and then minutes, every sense urging him to claim her under the stars in their secret garden. Yet a tiny part of him held back, cautioning against risking the truth for which he'd waited so long. With his last bit of self-control, he ended the kiss, promising himself, and silently her, they would soon finish what she started.

She held on to him like a shipwrecked sailor to a raft, wind-lashed in a sea of uncertainty. He heaved in a deep breath, cradling her in his arms, showing without words he would provide all the strength she ever needed. "It's time, Priscilla." He tightened his hold. "What is your secret?"

She breathed slowly. "I... I–"

"Bradenton!"

They froze.

"I saw you come this way! Show yourself!"

Priscilla's paled to the hue of the moon above them. The light Scottish burr was unmistakable. "It's Lady Drummond's nephew!"

He swore under his breath. Once more they were in danger of discovery.

Exposure. Scandal. Betrothal.

"Do you think he knows about the garden?"

He shook his head, even as uncertainty hit. "He would have already entered if he did."

A new voice pieced the air, "Stay away from my brother!"

He froze. It couldn't be–

"Lady Sophia, what are you doing here?" Foxworth roared. "Whoever permitted you to wander the gardens alone needs a throttling. Better yet, someone else should take over the job of watching you!"

"I don't need anyone to watch me!" Sophia snapped, sounding every bit like her duchess mother. "I take care of myself and my family. I command you cease chasing my brother!"

"You command it?" Incredulity flared in Foxworth's voice, tinged with amusement. "I do not follow orders, lass. You, however, will stop this behavior before someone takes advantage of your misbegotten ways!"

Every protective instinct flared at once. Frustration at his sister who put herself in danger. Anger at the man whose behavior had inspired it. Most of all, fury at himself for allowing it to happen. Now Foxworth and his sister were seemingly alone. If someone came upon them, it wouldn't matter that Sophia had not yet launched, or that he was hiding with Priscilla behind a wall.

There could be two proposals tonight.

Chaperoning Sophia was not his role tonight. Their mother was here, as were two aunts and a cousin, and they had specifically instructed him to focus on his own pursuit. Yet his sister was clever and bold. Mother probably thought she was in the retiring room.

Foxworth was right about one thing. He had been negligent in watching Sophia. Even if it wasn't his job, he should have kept a better eye on her. He would not make the same mistake again.

If he got the chance.

There was no time to waste. He strode to the hidden door, reached out.

A gasp sounded.

He turned to see Priscilla frozen, her gaze riveted on him.

What was he doing? He had been so focused on reaching Sophia, he hadn't considered what would happen if he suddenly appeared from a hidden space with Priscilla. There was a chance they wouldn't notice her.

There was a much greater chance they would.

"Priscilla–"

"Go." Her voice was low, yet the tone behind it glinted with steel. "She needs you."

Something tightened around his heart.

"I will take care of everything," he promised. "Hopefully they'll believe I was in here alone. Wait for a few minutes, then return to the party."

For a moment, they locked gazes, then Sophia proclaimed, "I will not allow you to harm my brother."

"You do not allow me to do anything," Foxworth countered. "As for your behavior, that is something I will very much address later. Now return to the party immediately."

"I will not leave you to ambush my brother. I'll find him myself. Edmund!"

"What are you doing?" Foxworth growled. "Do you seriously think to escape me, lass?"

Heavy footsteps broke the clearing.

Edmund didn't wait a second more. He burst through the door, somehow remembering to shut it as he left. "What do you think you are–" He stopped.

The clearing was empty.

"Sophia!" He took two steps, halted as his sister almost ran into him, followed closely by the gigantic Foxworth.

He thrust Sophia behind him. She struggled, but he did not allow her forward. "Don't move!" he commanded.

She gasped. "Where did you come from?"

"You must have just missed me."

He turned towards the Scotsman. Foxworth stood like a tightly coiled spring, ready to leap at any second.

Edmund fought to keep his emotions under control. "What do you think you are doing?" he demanded. "Explain why I shouldn't call you out for endangering my sister."

"Edmund, no!" His sister cried.

The man gave a sharp bark of laughter. "I could say the same to you, Bradenton. Where were you when your sister was roaming by herself, challenging men she doesn't know?"

Every muscle tightened. "So help me, Foxworth, if you touched her–"

"Of course I didn't touch her!" Foxworth growled. "Despite what you think, I am a gentleman. I wanted to return your sister to the ballroom, nothing more. If you do not care for her properly, someone else will!"

Pure fury raged. "Stay away from her." He stood to his full height. "I am happy to address any issues you have with me."

Foxworth stared. Then he glanced at Sophia, and his features softened. "Now is not the time." He strode forward, giving one last look to Sophia as he brushed past.

It took every ounce of restraint for Edmund to stay silent, to allow the man to leave with no explanation. He would not further risk Sophia's reputation.

When he was gone, the silence ended. "What were you thinking?"

"Edmund, I–"

"Do not say a word. Foxworth might be uncouth, but he was right. If you ever do something like this again, I will lock you in your room!"

She flushed bright red. "But Edmund, I had to protect you!"

"Ladies do not protect lords, especially from dangerous men with hidden agendas. I will take care of Foxworth. You will stay where you belong, do you understand?"

"But Edmund!"

"Not another word!" he thundered. He was being harsh, but he couldn't bear the thought of something happening to his little sister. A single unwise moment could ruin Sophia's entire life. "You will obey me. Now I will escort you back to the ballroom, and you will stay with Mother for the rest of the evening. Understand?"

Her eyes shone in the moonlight. "Yes, Edmund."

He kept his gaze severe, refused to show any softness that would embolden her to risk herself again. He took her arm firmly as they walked down the path to the ball, nodding calmly to people without betraying the turmoil still raging in him. He would do whatever it took to ensure Sophia's safety. And then, he would find Priscilla.

And this time, he would learn the truth.

SOPHIA HAD SAVED her.

Edmund's sister hadn't realized it when she followed Foxworth, not when she confronted him with equal parts bravery and foolishness. She hadn't known it when she protested her inability to make her own decisions.

Not when Edmund took complete and utter control.

In those minutes, Bradenton had shown himself for the man he truly was. He took control of the situation – and his sister. He didn't give her a chance to explain. Instead he threatened to lock her in her room.

No doubt he'd do the exact thing to his wife.

Thank goodness she hadn't told him the truth. Would he have forbidden her to investigate, with or without him? Confined her to her quarters? He had no true power over her – at least not yet – but he was not a man to accept failure. No doubt he would find a way to force her to his will.

He always triumphed.

She needed a new strategy, one that kept her secrets close and Edmund far. For tonight, she simply needed to escape.

She waited impatiently for the minutes to pass, allowing the silence to stretch before opening the door and slipping into the thankfully empty clearing. She stood up tall and took a deep breath. With her head held high, she started back to the ballroom.

If people spoke to her, she didn't hear them. If they smiled, she kept her gaze neutral. She entered the building, then walked straight to her parents.

Her mother frowned. "Is everything all right?"

If having her heart shattered like a broken vase was all right…

"Yes, but I have a megrim and would like to leave. If you want to stay, I am certain I can arrange transportation home."

Her mother's frown deepened, but she nodded. "Of course we will accompany you, my dear. We've been here for hours, and the party is a grand success. Just let us give our farewells."

They crawled their way to the front, her mother stopping for practically the entire guest list. Priscilla kept her face stretched until a true megrim threatened, knowing any minute Bradenton could appear and demand the secrets she promised. Yet he remained strangely absent, even as the front entrance finally came into view. She strode faster, stronger…

She almost made it.

Yet, of course, Edmund always managed to thwart her. He appeared as if out of nowhere, so large, so handsome, so powerful.

So suspicious.

Her mother's face lit up like a child on Christmas. "Bradenton. How nice of you to see us off. I'm afraid we must leave, but we will see you soon."

"Most definitely." His voice brooked no argument. "I was wondering if I may have a word with Lady Priscilla."

"Of course," her mother answered before Priscilla could even open her mouth.

Edmund grasped her hand, placing it in the crook of his arm as he led her to a semi-private alcove. Still in view of the *ton*, they were in no social danger, yet appearances were deceiving. He threatened everything.

"Priscilla, I must apologize."

"There is nothing to apologize for." She gazed downward, fighting the compulsion to look into his eyes. "You had to go to your sister. We weren't discovered, and no damage was done."

"I had thought so, too. Until I saw you trying to escape."

She shot her head up, and satisfaction lit his gaze. No doubt her guilt was evident. "I wasn't trying to escape. I was simply ready to go home."

"Without finishing our discussion?"

"We were finished. We *are* finished."

"I see." He leaned down, lowered his voice. "You are mistaken, my dear. We are not close to finished. Not now. Not ever."

Her heart slammed against her chest. "You do not get to decide that."

"I would dispute that." He reached out, stopped himself just before he touched her. "I'm sorry we were interrupted. I would give anything to go back and undo that moment. But I had no choice. I thought you understood."

"I do understand. I even encouraged you to go." Anger blazed through her, at society for its treatment of women, at herself for desiring this man and at fate that he could never be hers. The words tumbled out. "It wasn't what you did, but what you said. You took complete control of Sophia. You were dictatorial, ruthless and uncompromising. You threatened to lock her in her room!"

He ran a hand through his hair. "She's my little sister. It's my responsibility to care for her."

"Will you place the same restrictions on your wife? Lock her in her room when she doesn't behave?"

"Of course not! I knew it wouldn't come to that with Sophia. I just needed to keep her safe."

"I understand that. But she is her own woman and deserves to make her own choices."

"She will make them, but I will also care for her, whether she likes it or not."

"But not me." She stood taller. "You have no power over me."

Challenge fired in his eyes. "Are you so certain of that?"

Her heart stumbled.

"What were you going to share in the garden?"

His gaze compelled her to reveal everything, yet exposure could bring far greater consequences than secrecy. "I changed my mind. It is best if I keep the secret to myself."

His lips tightened. "I see."

"Thank you for underst–"

"I will discover it on my own."

She reeled back from the definitive statement, the steel-like voice of a man who always won.

"I have to go."

He held her gaze for a moment, but then nodded, watching as she fled to her parents, as they said farewell to a few final people. His attention burned into her, sending tingles across her back and ice down her spine. As they finally walked through the door, she couldn't stop herself form turning back one last time.

He was no longer alone.

Lady Drummond had cornered him in the

alcove, and they appeared in close conversation. The discussion shouldn't be cause for concern, not if it was about the party or Clara. Yet it wasn't about either of those things.

Because clutched in Lady Drummond's hand was one of Lord P's letters.

Her letter.

There could be only one reason Edmund had shown it to Lady Drummond. One goal. One result. He had enlisted her help in finding her. But how?

Edmund pointed to the letter, gesturing as if he was writing. She gasped. Was he trying to trace the handwriting? She had corresponded with Lady Drummond multiple times, and the woman was very astute. She may very well recognize it.

Which means she may be sharing the truth this very instant.

Was she already captured?

CHAPTER FIFTEEN

Dear Edmund,

Do not chase all who run. Sometimes there are good reasons behind inexplicable actions, circumstances you can never imagine.

I, too, am looking for a match, someone who is calm, mellow and biddable. They will go about their life while I will go about mine, and we will both accomplish what is important to us, while fulfilling our duty.

I highly suggest you do the same.

Yours,
P

HE WAS SO close.

So very close to discovering who his informant was.

At last week's ball, Lady Drummond could not remember who wrote the letter, but she was certain it would come to her. Now she was perusing past correspondence in the hopes of finding a match. Soon, she promised him, she would have an answer.

He had also commenced his own investigation into the handwriting. So far he hadn't found a match, but he had every confidence. He *would* discover the truth.

For now, he was focusing on his other pursuit:

Lady Priscilla.

He stood outside her fashionable London townhouse, preparing for the likely confrontation. It was a beautiful day, the sky a flawless blue, the sun shining, a gentle breeze cooling the world. Lords and ladies strolled over perfectly manicured walkways while others rode in fancy open carriages. It was the perfect setting to discuss secrets, and the future, with Priscilla.

She had managed to avoid him all week. It was not an easy task, with the connections he possessed and her family's fervent support of his suit. Yet she skipped balls she normally attended, came and left early to others. He saw her at several, yet she managed to fill her dance card each time, as well as arrange to sit far from him. Of course, he could have thwarted all these endeavors had he chosen, but he resisted the urge to take control, giving her the space that would ease how she felt towards him.

He'd been so close to discovering the truth!

Blast Foxworth for ruining everything. He still didn't know why the man hated him, a mystery that would remain since the new duke had temporarily returned to Scotland. While frustrating to have to wait for elucidation, at least it kept the untamed duke away from Sophia for a time.

He'd thought about his interaction with his sister again and again, each time with a little more remorse. He had been too harsh with her. He did not regret confronting Foxworth, of course, or demanding he stay away from her. Yet his threat of locking Sophia in her room was unnecessary. He had spoken with her and apologized. She asked if he had been clobbered in the head.

Yes. Not physically, but in every other way by the woman who would be his wife.

No longer would Priscilla avoid him. Without further hesitation, he ascended the steps and gave three brisk taps on the door. It opened within seconds, attesting to the efficiency of the well-run household.

He handed the servant his card. Yet before the footman could turn, the duchess came hurrying to the door.

He bowed. "Your Grace."

She nodded and gestured to the footman, who quickly departed. "Hello, Bradenton. I assume you are here to see Lady Priscilla."

"I am."

"I'm afraid she is experiencing another me-grim. They seem to come upon her with astounding *regularity*." The duchess enunciated the last word, as if it contained some sort of message.

"I see. Please convey my deepest wishes for a rapid recovery."

"I shall. Perhaps you would like to sit for a while. There is a lovely bench on the street behind ours, right under the lamp post."

How intriguing. If he guessed correctly, the bench would directly face the back of the Sherring property. "I shall take your advice. It is a fine day, and I have much reflecting to do."

"Excellent. Better hurry, though. And you'll need this." She disappeared into the house, returned with the latest news page and a garment. She handed him both. "Wouldn't hurt to read the paper while you are waiting. Very closely I suggest. And you may get cold."

Edmund frowned. The serviceable yet threadbare coat clearly belonged to a servant! If he didn't know the duchess, he'd have thought her addled. "Thank you."

She turned, stopped. "And so you don't think me a poor mother, I usually have a servant follow at a distance. And when the thought occurs, as it undoubtedly will, of whether I am happy or comfortable with this, the answer is no. Yet she is her own woman, and I accept that. You need to decide whether you do." With the final cryptic words, she pivoted and disappeared into the house.

There was no time to decipher the meaning behind the hidden message. He strode down the steps and around the block to the wrought iron bench, a sturdy seat with intricate swirls and a high back. Perching on the edge, he held up the paper, yet did not read. Instead he peeked at the back fence of the townhouse.

He did not have to wait long.

Priscilla.

He knew her by instinct alone, for she looked nothing like the prim duke's daughter in the worn brown dress, the austere cap hiding her silky tresses. Yet she had the grace he knew so well, the elegant movements and sure steps of his lithe quarry. She carefully slipped through a broken board in the fence, stuffed her hands into her coat and started down the street, in the direction away from any fashionable area.

He rose, quick enough to follow yet casually enough not to be obvious, donning the coat in one fluid movement. It was rough and long, but it fit. He wouldn't pass close scrutiny with his quality pants and shoes, but quick glances wouldn't reveal his true station.

His mood darkened as he delved deeper and deeper into an unfortunate neighborhood. He fought every protective instinct urging him to spirit her away, to lift her up and whisk her to where danger could never touch her. Instead he continued on, staying near in case trouble beckoned. The duchess' words returned with new meaning. This time he must make the right decision.

So he followed his instincts, and he followed Priscilla.

"WHO CAN TELL me how many apples I have if I have three in the basket and two in the crate?"

Priscilla smiled as a dozen tiny hands shot up at once. A few months ago such a query would have elicited blank stares. "Yes, Jane?"

"The answer is five. At least until I eat three. Then the answer is two."

The other children giggled. In the back of the room, Jane's mother beamed.

"Very good." Priscilla put down the chalk and dusted off her hands. "There are additional problems on the board. I'd like the mothers to come forward and help the children finish."

The little ones squealed in excitement. They were not accustomed to having their mothers so near. Young children of the poor were often sent to work, but not here, in the large townhome that housed more than three dozen families.

They were in the largest room of the home,

which served as a playroom at times, a dining room at others and sewing studio at yet others. The paint may be peeling, the floors cracked and the rugs threadbare, but handmade tapestries and children's artwork showed it was a true home, filled with love and hope.

Elizabeth Henley, proprietress of Miss Henley's Sanctuary for Mothers and Children, came forward. She wore a plain blue day dress, yet it didn't diminish the striking beauty of her heart shaped face, flaxen hair and sapphire eyes. She was as lovely as any diamond of the first water, both inside and out. Her kindness had changed dozens of lives.

She took Priscilla's hand. "You are doing wonderful, my dear. I cannot thank you enough for teaching our children."

Priscilla gave a genuine smile, tension seeping from her body. The moments she stole at the sanctuary soothed her like nothing else. "I only manage to sneak away once a week. You're the one providing them with a safe home, honest work and the chance to be mothers."

Right now the mothers were on a break to help the children, but most of the day they sewed. They earned far more than typical seamstresses, since Elizabeth took only what was necessary to run the home they shared. The women saved as they worked and could eventually accumulate enough to support themselves.

How Elizabeth purchased the home in the first place was a mystery, for even in a poor area, a place this large was costly. She already owned it when Priscilla met her, as they struck up a conversation at a local bookstore. Priscilla had been both impressed and moved by Elizabeth's work and offered to help. She did not tell Elizabeth who she was, and the woman did not ask. Priscilla could not risk word getting out about her activities, thus she kept her true position a secret. Likewise, there was much about the proprietress she did not know, including how someone in her lower-class position spoke and acted as well as any lady.

Elizabeth's smile wavered. She glanced around. "Unfortunately it is not enough. We had three new mothers arrive last week, and two came today. I'm afraid we're going to run out of food."

Priscilla frowned deeply. The *ton* gorged on five-course dinners every night, while poor children did not have enough to fill their tiny bellies. She gave them all she could from her pin money, but clearly it was not enough. "I'll find a way to get more."

"You've already done so much." Elizabeth wrung her hands. "I just don't know what to do. I can't turn anyone out. I have to find a way to get more funds."

"Miss Henley, we have a visitor."

Elizabeth turned towards Miss Evans, the Sanctuary's housekeeper, cook and all-around helper. She had grey hair, ruddy red cheeks and a serious demeanor. "He says he's here to see Miss Priscilla."

Priscilla swallowed. In her months trekking through bad areas, she often felt like someone was following her, yet she had never seen anyone and no one had ever confronted her. Today, the feeling was heightened a thousandfold. She'd assumed it was nerves taut with strain, but now…

"He says he's a friend of hers. There's something odd about him. He's wearing quality clothing under a threadbare jacket, and he spoke like he was some sort of lord."

It. Couldn't. Be.

"Does he have black hair and blue eyes?"

Miss Evans nodded.

"Is he tall, muscular and handsome?"

Miss Evans nodded again.

"Do you have a vase?"

Elizabeth stared at her. "Are you expecting someone?"

"No, I'm–"

Edmund walked into the room.

Everyone froze.

Powerful, intense, gorgeous. The low-quality coat did nothing to hide Edmund's authority as he marched into the room as if he ruled it, his sheer size and powerful build marking him as a man who commanded others. Everyone turned, silently watching, their expressions ranging from awe to admiration to wariness. They did not know him as the Duke of Bradenton, but it didn't matter. The title did not make this man.

The man made the title.

"I apologize for arriving without notice." His tone was deep and low, his stance tall with confidence.

He strode to Priscilla, taking in her working-class garments, the shabby attire she had borrowed from a servant, yet no surprise shone in his deep blue eyes. Clearly he already knew about her clandestine activities.

What else did he know?

"That is all right, Brad–"

"Mr. Jenkins." Edmund nodded to the other people in the room. "It is a pleasure to meet you."

They all murmured welcomes, their eyes riveted to his form.

"Mr. Jenkins is…"

A duke. Her suitor. Her greatest temptation.

Yet she could admit none of those things. The people waited for her answer…

"My servant!"

"Your what?" Miss Elizabeth exclaimed.

"Your what?" the women exclaimed.

"Your what?" Edmund growled.

Priscilla smiled. Widely. "That's right. Jenkins is my servant. Of course I am not of great means, so he is my only servant. Fortunately, he takes orders very well. He is also excellent at cleaning." She leaned in, said in an extremely loud whisper. "Especially chamber pots."

The ladies looked on in shock as the children giggled. Amusement danced in Edmund's eyes, and a promise for retribution. "I'm afraid Priscilla is joking. I work for her, but not as a servant. Her family employs me to keep her safe. You could say I am in charge of her person."

The heat started at her neck and traced its way down her entire body.

"I was wondering if I could talk to her for a moment."

"Of course," Elizabeth quickly replied. "You can use my office." She hesitated, turned to Priscilla. "Do you need the vase now or after?"

Edmund's lips twitched.

"I will let you know."

She led Edmund to the office, stiffening when he touched her back. She quickened her pace to escape his grasp, yet he kept up easily. He followed her into the room, closed the door and *locked* it.

"I thought we could use privacy."

She swallowed. The office was modest, but it seemed positively miniscule with the large man.

"I've missed you." His voice softened, and unknown emotion shone in his eyes.

She bit back the same words. She'd tried to avoid thinking about him, failed in a tremendous fashion. For a moment, they just stared at each other, as she fought to ignore the kiss she couldn't stop imagining. She could practically feel his hand tracing down her skin, as he'd done so many times before.

At least he hadn't mentioned his informant. Surely he would have acted differently if he knew the truth. The realization brought scant relief. He was still investigating her, and by all appearances had enlisted others in his cause. Sooner or later he would discover the truth.

But hopefully not today. "Why are you here?"

"Do you realize how dangerous it is for a lady to walk alone in this part of town?"

She tensed at the quiet question. "If you plan to lock me in a tower, forget it. You have no say in what I do. I'm sorry you wasted your time coming here. I'll lead you out–"

"Stop."

Her breath hitched at the firmly spoken word. She looked to the door, but he stepped in front of her.

"Let me out."

"I wasn't finished."

Desire and apprehension mixed, yet one

thing remained consistent. She wanted that kiss.

He leaned down. "You're unusually nervous."

"That's not true."

"What are you thinking about?"

Licking you.

"Nothing."

"You're staring at my lips."

Like ice cream.

"We're never going to get anything settled until we take care of this."

"Take care of wh–"

He swooped down.

His lips were pliant and firm, as they caressed her softness. Capturing her flush against him, he held her near for his administrations, coaxing her lips open and dipping his tongue to the pleasures that awaited. She moaned her surrender.

The kiss ignited fiery passion and unadulterated need. He tasted like pure temptation, like everything she wanted and couldn't have. Sensations streaked throughout her body, pooling in her most tender spots. Throbbing, aching, so close to the heated source of power, she wanted so much more. She pushed closer to him, clutching taut muscle. He rewarded her by tightening his hold. The world melted away, leaving only the two of them, their bodies so close, so needy.

Suddenly he pulled away, leaving her to

heave in deep breaths, fighting the sparks of passion threatening to burst into flames.

Collect yourself! She commanded, yet her body paid no heed. Flushed with fire, she fought for strength. "Now that that is settled, you can leave."

He stood taller. "I think not, Lady Priscilla. You will hear what I have to say."

She folded her arms across her chest. For a moment they stared at each other, each heaving in breaths, flushed twin shades of red. As the seconds ticked by, he made his stance clear:

He would not leave until she listened.

"Fine. I will listen, but I have no intention of going home."

"I have no intention of demanding you go home."

"How can you ask me to– wait, what?"

He stood taller, yet his expression eased. He put a hand on her shoulder. "Your work is a vital part of who you are. I have no intention of demanding you leave."

Had she just entered an alternate world? "But… but you just complained about it being a bad part of town."

"Precisely. It is completely unacceptable you planned to walk here alone. From now on, either I will accompany you or you will bring two footmen, who will remain directly next to you. If necessary, I will provide them. You only need tell me the days and times."

"But–"

"That is non-negotiable. If you do not agree, I shall immediately start searching for a suitable tower."

"And I shall start searching for a vase."

"Come on, Priscilla." He lowered his voice, stepped closer. "I know you want to be free, but you don't want to get accosted. Even you can't feel safe walking these streets."

No, she didn't. She'd accepted the risk for the all-important work, yet if there was a way she could avoid the danger… "You truly don't mind me coming as long as someone accompanies me?"

"I can't say I don't mind…"

Here it comes.

"But I understand."

She parted her lips. "Really?"

"Really." He drew in a deep breath. "I'm not the dictator you believe me to be. I'll admit I was uncomfortable at first, but then I overheard you with the children. You are fantastic with them. As long as you keep safe, I will keep your secret."

She parted her lips, both in shock and guilt. After all the secrets he did and did not know, he still sought to compromise.

"I also understand your reaction to my behavior toward my sister." He paused. "I was truly afraid for her safety that night. I will always protect her, but I shouldn't have threatened to lock her in her room. I never have, nor do I plan, to actually do so. I had a long talk with her and even apologized."

Who was this man? The authoritarian was gone, replaced by a strong, yet reasonable leader. It pierced her anger, the only defense shielding her heart. "What have you done with the real Bradenton and where did you hide the vase?"

He softly touched her cheek. She leaned into him.

"I am Bradenton," he murmured. "I am more than your assumptions. More than your fear. We all have hidden facets, a person the world does not see."

If only he knew... Drowning in those blue eyes, the urge to share everything fired. But the words wouldn't come. Just because he accepted her charity work didn't mean he would condone her sneaking through homes, or lying to him all this time. She couldn't take the chance.

Which meant he had to leave, because every minute risked her heart.

She stood back, ignoring the sharp pain piercing her heart. "Thank you for your honesty, Your Grace. It is most kind of you." She turned to the door.

He hesitated briefly, but then moved aside and allowed her to unlock and open it.

She turned, swallowed. "I had best return to

work. Thank you for stopping by." And with that, she stepped into the hallway, away from Bradenton, away from her heart's desire. Away from what she could never have.

The mothers and children were still working on the problems, but Elizabeth hurried over. "Is everything all right?"

"Of course." Priscilla gave a strained smile. "I just had something to work out with Br– Mr. Jenkins. Everything is fine now, and he's about to–"

"Help in any way I can."

"What?" Priscilla and Elizabeth exclaimed together.

He looked back and forth between the two of them. "I assume you could use another volunteer."

"That's not a good idea!"

"It's not necessary!"

Priscilla looked at Elizabeth. Usually the proprietress was desperate for volunteers, but now she looked distinctly ill at ease.

Edmund folded his arms across his chest. "I insist."

Just when she decided he wasn't an overbearing, authoritative bear. Perhaps there was another way to convince him to leave. "Since you've offered, we could use help. Little Wilbur is sorely in need of a bath. He can be a little precocious, though. I'm not sure you're up for it."

Elizabeth's eyes widened.

"That will be fine," Edmund replied. "Just give me a minute to jot down a quick note. Do you have someone who can deliver a message for me?"

With another worried look, Elizabeth led him to a small desk in the corner.

"Tell me about Mr. Jenkins."

Priscilla bit back a groan as a beautiful redhead materialized behind her. Mary Atkins was bold, brazen and gorgeous, and drew attention from every eligible man in town. Priscilla made no judgement, but the thought of her adding Edmund to her list of conquests left a sharp discomfort.

But what could detract her?

"He talks to rocks."

Mary's perfect forehead creased slightly. "You can't be serious."

Priscilla fought to keep a straight face. "I'm afraid I am."

"Well…" Mary bit her lip. "He's very handsome."

"He gives them names, too."

"Names?"

"And tucks them into bed at night."

"Come to think of it, there are many attractive men. I better go."

Priscilla managed a sympathetic expression

just as Edmund returned and handed Elizabeth the note.

He leaned down. "Not only am I your servant, but I talk to rocks, do I?"

"I'm afraid so."

"Anything else I should be aware of?"

"Depending on your behavior, word may get out that you also talk to plants and horses."

"Then I suppose I will have to be an utmost gentleman." He gazed at her speculatively. "Do you have more surprises for me?"

She choked back a laugh. "Would I do something so duplicitous?"

"Just remember, I will demand payback."

She couldn't wait.

A PIG.

Wilbur was a pig.

Literally.

It explained that mischievous glint in Priscilla's eyes, the grin she made no attempt to hide. The women smiled, and the children endlessly laughed, as he attempted to clean a squealing pink pig who obviously preferred being dirty. By the end, the pig was clean, the room was soaked and he looked like he had jumped in the River Thames.

He had never laughed more.

"Wilbur is clean," he announced, accepting a

towel from Miss Elizabeth, whose deep frown lines had changed to wry amusement. She also seemed vaguely familiar, yet he kept this to himself.

"Thank you." She cleared her throat, a poor attempt at hiding her laughter. "I can't imagine why we have difficulty finding volunteers."

"A true mystery, indeed."

Priscilla took a long look up and down his waterlogged form, then said in equal parts surprise and amusement, "You did well. I assume you wish to return home after the excitement."

"On the contrary, my clothing will dry. I am happy to provide additional assistance."

Priscilla's pursed those plump lips. He resisted the urge to nip one.

"Do you have another pig for me to wash?"

"I'm afraid not," she said regretfully.

"A lion then?"

"Not that either." Her lips turned up. "But if you really want to stay, I have a job. Some of the older boys decided to see how many frogs they could catch and–"

"Consider it done."

"I haven't even told you what we need."

He smiled. "You're not going to get rid of me."

She folded her arms. "We'll see about that."

Yet he held on, even after thirteen frogs, two mice and one very angry squirrel. Priscilla tried again and again to undermine him, yet he accepted it with good humor. Finally she gave up, and he aided with a variety of tasks. He never expected the satisfaction that came every time someone thanked him, the smiles when he changed someone's life for the better. His work in Parliament was vital, but there was something special about seeing the results of his efforts firsthand.

Watching Priscilla was also a joy. She taught the children with patience and delight, her passion obvious, her dedication unparalleled. She wasn't meant to be cloistered in a drawing room with embroidery in one hand and a cup of tea in the other. She was meant to change the world.

The hours melted away. They were working with Elizabeth to prepare for the evening's meal when brisk knocking sounded at the sanctuary's door.

"Another visitor?" Elizabeth looked up from the dishes she was distributing. A sense of familiarity surfaced once more, although he still couldn't place her.

"Do you want me to get it?" Priscilla asked.

"I'll do it." Elizabeth wiped her hands on her apron and walked out of the room.

The scream shook the entire house.

They rushed to Elizabeth. The proprietress stood in front of the open door, her hands on her cheeks, flushed pink.

It was a parade.

Dozens of sturdy footmen strode in, carrying baskets overstuffed with gifts piled three feet high. The first parcels were filled with food, a veritable feast of breads and cheeses and meats and desserts. There were fresh foods and colds ones, and staples that would last for weeks or more. After the food came essentials: blankets, clothing, shoes and household supplies, all new and of good quality. A supply of fat candles came last.

Drawn by the shout, women and children quickly filled the room, all staring at the men and their offerings. Shock gave way to broad smiles, then jumps of excitement and tears of joy.

Elizabeth looked like she was ready to faint. "I've never seen such a boon!" She put a hand on Mrs. Evans' shoulder, whose cheeks were as ruddy as a brick wall. "Who is it from?"

"I have no idea," Mrs. Evans breathed. "The men said our benefactor wanted to remain anonymous."

Priscilla cast Edmund a long assessing look. He didn't say a word.

"They said he expected nothing in return. They also claimed…" Mrs. Evans paused, her eyes becoming misty. "He said they would bring a new shipment every month."

"Oh heavens." Elizabeth shook her head. "This is a dream. To whoever did this, thank you."

Edmund forced himself to stay stoic, even as something moved within him.

"We shall have a feast tonight!" Elizabeth clapped her hands. "Mrs. Evans–"

"Don't worry. I already have plans!" Apparently recovered, Mrs. Evans eagerly beckoned the women into the kitchen.

Bradenton smiled. No doubt they would make good use of every item.

"I better assist them." Elizabeth turned towards the kitchen just as the wails of crying sounded. "Oh dear."

Priscilla looked to the backroom. "Do they need help in the nursery?"

Elizabeth wrung her hands. "Several of the mothers had to leave for work, and I promised I would help."

"We'll attend to the infants." Priscilla gently guided Elizabeth towards the kitchen. "I'm sure Mr. Jenkins knows how to handle a baby."

His experience handling babies: none.

"Of course."

"Thank you so much." Elizabeth rubbed her hands together. "There's just so much to do!" Without another word, she spun and hurried towards the kitchen.

Edmund followed Priscilla down a narrow hallway. Concern replaced joy as the crying grew louder, as they neared a task far more daunting than thirteen frogs, two mice and one very angry squirrel. He cleared his throat. "You do realize the only experience I've had with infants was the baby mouse I just fished out of Mrs. Evans' shoe."

"You'll be fine."

"No really. I thought they were simply short adults." He'd dealt with some of the most powerful men in England. Lords. Soldiers. Criminals.

The babies were more daunting.

They walked into a small room with pale walls and only a miniscule high window. There were eight babies in the tiny space, but only two flustered girls caring for them. The room was sparse but clean, with thin pallets, a few dolls and threadbare blankets.

Priscilla walked straight to a wailing infant. "Their mothers are working," she said sadly, gently touching the baby's stomach. Eyes clenched tightly, the baby turned desperately to the touch, his little lips pursed. "Elizabeth tries to get enough sewing for all of the women, but some seek additional employment in the hopes of gaining independence sooner. We assign several girls to watch the babies, but as you can see, it isn't enough."

No it wasn't. It was bitter unjustness, evidenced by the smallest victims of society's cruelty. He was working to change it, but it was never enough.

Maybe he could be enough here.

"They're so little."

A smile crooked the side of Priscilla's mouth. "They're new."

She picked up the baby, softly shushed him. Immediately he quieted down and sucked his thumb. She gestured towards an infant wrapped in a thin blanket. "Why don't you pick up little Lucy?"

The tiny thing was swaddled in white, but her face was bright red. She struggled, her little face scrunched up. "I don't think she likes me."

The side of Priscilla's lips quirked up. "Don't be silly. She doesn't yet know how difficult you are."

He approached the squirming infant. She was so tiny, so vulnerable. "I don't know how to hold her."

"Just make sure to support her head." She gently bounced the baby.

"Hello, little one," he rumbled. "I'm not sure either of us is ready, but here goes." Carefully he placed his hands under the tiny bundle. She was no larger than his palm, and so light he could barely feel her weight. He carefully brought her against his chest.

She was so soft, so warm. "Am I doing it right?"

Priscilla stared at him, her lips parted. For a moment she didn't say anything. "I… yes. That's right."

Lucy quieted, her cries softening as she burrowed into him.

She was *perfection.*

"I am Bradenton," he whispered. "I am a powerful duke, and everyone must do as I say. I hereby order you to have a happy and joyful life."

She made a little gurgling sound, and he chuckled.

The baby in his arms snuggled closer. And he wished for something he had never much considered before.

But he wasn't who this baby truly needed. "She wants her mother?"

Sadness entered Priscilla's gaze. "There is nothing that baby wants more than to be held by her mama." Her gaze hardened. "But she has to work. She dashes back to feed the baby, but most of the time, Lucy is alone."

It felt as if he'd been punched in the stomach. The tiny thing snuggled so close to him, as if desperate for human interaction. For love. *For her mama.* "If they got more money, could she, and the other mothers with such small babies, be together?"

Priscilla hesitated. "If it was enough, I suppose they could."

He would make arrangements the moment he returned home. He wouldn't wait for next month's delivery, but send a special courier with the funds. Soon, the tiny baby would be in her mother's arms, where she belonged.

"Thank you."

He looked up.

Priscilla's eyes shone brightly. "I know you're behind the delivery. You have no idea how much good it will do."

He hesitated. Yet there was no use denying the truth she already knew. "Providing food and supplies is little work. I have an excellent steward, and he arranged everything when he received my message."

"Before it came, they did not have enough food to last the month. It will change their lives."

He was beginning to see that. He'd focused so long on the big votes, but small things made large differences. "I would say the same to you, Priscilla. Your teaching means so much to them. I have a feeling this is just a part of your charitable work."

She colored slightly, looked down. "It's nothing."

He rocked the baby as he moved closer, until her sweet flowery scent enveloped him. "It isn't nothing. I love that you do this. I love how much you help people. I love–" He stopped.

You.

The unspoken word could no longer be denied. Not hidden away, not ignored. The emotion had been there for so long, stronger and more powerful with every single day.

He loved her.

CHAPTER SIXTEEN

Dear P,

I could not imagine my days with a calm, biddable wife. I wish for a true partner, a lady who is kind and brave, caring and loving, clever and witty. A lady with whom I can share my life's work and the family I am only now imagining. And if she sometimes frustrates me, I will accept it, because I accept her.

I have found someone who has everything I desire.

I wish you the same.

Yours,
Edmund

IT COULD NO longer be denied. No longer ignored. The emotion had been there for so long, stronger and more powerful with every single day.

She loved him.

It was so clear. The way her heart fluttered when they were together, how she longed to be with him, the kisses that made her body come alive.

Nothing had ever felt so right.

And now everything was so wrong.

She still couldn't be with him, not even with the realization that should change everything. Her life belonged to society's poor, the people who fought simply to exist. Without her efforts, more children would go hungry, more women would lose everything. She couldn't allow that.

Even if it destroyed her heart.

She had to somehow get over a relationship that never truly began. To mend the pieces of her shattered heart.

"The babies are asleep."

It took her a moment to realize who spoke the whispered words. Elizabeth stood in the doorway, gesturing to the slumbering children.

Priscilla gently placed the sleeping infant in his bed. Edmund gave his charge a tiny kiss before carefully lowering her down.

Priscilla's eyes watered.

With quiet goodbyes, they followed Elizabeth out of the room.

"You did wonderfully." The proprietress looked back and forth between the two of them. "Is everything well?"

"Of course," Priscilla said quietly.

Edmund paused, nodded.

Elizabeth turned to the duke. "Mr. Jenkins, could you help us with one more thing before you leave? We have a leak in the attic, but it's too difficult for me to repair. Perhaps you could take a look."

"Certainly." Edmund took the keys Elizabeth offered.

"Priscilla, can you show him where it is?"

Sure. Of course. Is it obvious I love him?

As the words threatened to emerge, she licked dry lips. "Certainly. Follow me."

They left the room and travelled down a narrow, dark hallway. The silence was deafening as they ascended a rickety staircase to the second floor, and the even more perilous ladder to the attic. He stayed close behind, and she could practically feel the heat emanating from him.

Suddenly her foot caught on a broken board. She gasped as she pitched backward, grasping for rungs she could never reach. Yet before she hit the ground, she landed against a hard chest. Iron bands wrapped tightly around her. To steady her…

Or to capture her?

"Are you all right?" The words were whispered, almost strained. He shifted yet did not let go.

She sucked in a breath laden with his scent.

"I– I just need a minute."

Even in the perilous situation, her body started to hum. Every inch pressed against him.

Do not ask if you can remain like this permanently.

It wouldn't work logistically.

Still, it might be worth a try.

"Do you think you can continue?"

"Yes." She forced herself forward, even as his arms tightened. He released her, and she climbed the rest of the way without incident, ignoring the urge to fall into him with every step.

This. Was. Very. Bad.

They reached the small ledge at the top, which led to a half-door. He looked back down. "Someone needs to repair this," he murmured. "Better yet, they should add stairs. Tomorrow, I think."

She gaped at him. No doubt a team of men would show up tomorrow ready to work.

"Are there other organizations like this?" He turned his bright blue gaze on her. "Charities that could use assistance?"

"I'm sure there are many," she breathed.

The man was literally trying to save the world. Her heart, now fully exposed, shuddered.

"The attic is through here."

He placed the key in the lock and turned. She stood back as he forced the door open to thick clouds of swirling dust. They waited until the worst of it thinned, then stepped in.

"You should lock the door."

He looked at her sharply.

Heat crept up her neck. "We always keep the door locked to avoid a child getting hurt."

"Of course." He did as she said, then pocketed the key.

She suppressed a shiver.

The attic was cluttered with decades-old clothing, dilapidated furniture and ragged household supplies. Elizabeth saved everything just in case they had a desperate need, and they often had such a need. With Edmund's contributions, hopefully they could switch to items a great-grandmother wouldn't find dated.

Dust surrounded and settled on them as they carefully tiptoed through the space. The space was narrow, pushing her almost into Edmund. She may have delved a little closer than necessary, accidentally of course. Twelve times.

She pointed to a patchy black spot on the ceiling. "That's where the wood is rotted. We have the supplies, but we couldn't reach far enough. I know this isn't your area of expertise, but–"

"I can do it." He easily hefted the heavy wood and supplies.

She stood back and watched. He worked with speed and efficiency, cutting out the rotted material and preparing the new piece. He measured everything as he made the replacement, taking care to make the patch seamless. He looked as at ease fixing a roof as he did speaking to the leaders of Parliament. In just a few minutes, he dusted his hands off and turned back to her.

"Is it acceptable?"

"Is there anything you're not good at?" She closed her eyes, opened them.

Amusement sparkled in his expression. "What do you think?"

"No one can possibly be good at everything."

Sudden desire sparked, charging the air between them. Then, because she simply couldn't stop herself, she said, "Perhaps we should test it."

Unspoken words played like a symphony in the dusty air. He moved closer, and all amusement fled. She couldn't move, could barely breathe.

He touched her cheek. "We would have to test it quite thoroughly."

"Quite," she murmured.

Their lips met.

Their other kisses had been glorious. Wondrous. Amazing.

And yet none compared to a kiss of true love.

Streaks of desire raced through her, sensitizing every area he touched, and he touched *everywhere*. He ran his hands over her, casting fiery heat through her clothing. He shaped her curves, tested her responses.

Pure pleasure.

She pushed deeper into the kiss, yet he would not relinquish control. They touched along their entire bodies as he plundered her mouth, exploring her as she explored him.

Something was happening to her. Aching need sensitized feminine parts, *moistened* them. She pressed further into the heat only he could provide, primitive instincts demanding she become one with this man.

She shouldn't.

She couldn't.

Could she?

A thousand emotions cast mind-shattering indecision. Wrought with risk, her choice would change everything.

It might be worth it.

She had sacrificed so much for her cause: her money, her time and now her very heart. She did not regret it, yet didn't she deserve something, a memory she could keep forever? She might not be able to build a life with the man she loved, but perhaps fate had granted her the opportunity to truly be with him.

Her mind spun, even as Edmund rained kisses down her vulnerable neck. It was the perfect moment to taste what she must soon sacrifice, while they were locked away with no chance of discovery. She would accept entering marriage without her virginity, for no doubt, any suitor would do the same. The time of month made conception of a child unlikely. This was her chance.

She would seize it.

She gasped as he brushed a breast. He circled its tip, kneaded, cupped, weighed. Though clothing separated them, her skin burned. He moved to its twin, then gave each straining peak a kiss. Sweat slicked under her stays, heat threatening to engulf her. What was he doing to her?

She needed to be closer to him. As close as two people could be. She leaned back, grasped her ribbons. Pulled.

He stilled.

She heaved in a deep breath, pushing further into the hands boldly possessing her breasts.

When he spoke, his voice was without its normal control. "What are you doing?"

"I want to be with you."

He gave a harsh intake of breath. "You don't know what you're saying. I don't have my usual control." Under her, powerful muscles tensed, so hard, so smooth. A warrior had replaced the gentleman duke. "I will not take advantage of you."

"I want this." She ran a hand along sculpted muscles. "I want you."

Storms raged in his eyes. "You are an innocent."

"I understand what happens between a man and a woman." She inhaled his woodsy scent. "I am ready."

His eyes dilated, turning darker, dangerous. Passion sparked in the air, its tendrils swirling around them. Still, doubts flashed in his expression. "Are you sure?"

"I've never been so sure of anything my entire life."

"So be it…" He leaned down. "You are mine."

He seized her lips, shattering reality into pure need. She fought to be closer, forgoing all control as he caressed her, as he fondled and touched her. But it was not enough.

They had to be closer.

With agonizing slowness he undressed her. She tried to assist, for the need was too great for it to be slow. He quickened his pace, and suddenly the rest of her clothing was gone, and she was naked before him, totally and utterly exposed. He moved back, viewed her in her purest form.

Heat crept everywhere.

"So beautiful," he murmured.

Then he grasped her once more.

Her vulnerable state brought even more excitement, more desire. The cool air caressed her bare skin, yet she was fiery warm under his heat. For a moment he moved back, and she gave a mewl of protest. Until she realized he was divesting his own clothing.

Oh. My. Goodness.

She gasped at her first look at the man, un-hidden, sculpted. He truly was a masterpiece, his body tanned and smooth, forged of pure muscle.

He placed his servant's coat on the floor, laying it on top of some soft bedding, before gently lowering her down. Now he took his time with her, teaching her the art of lovemaking. He was tender and kind, patient and understanding, as he took her to heights she never before imagined. He carefully joined with her, holding her tightly, ensuing she was all right before stretching her to accommodate him. Momentary discomfort was soon forgotten as he caressed tender limbs, gentling unaccustomed places. Before long, she was squirming under his administrations. The storm swirled higher and higher.

Then... surrender.

She softly cried out as he brought her to ecstasy for the first time. He held her tenderly, possessing her as if she was the most precious of gems. He brought her to the height of pleasure again and again, letting her dictate the pace, even as he led her. He was gracious and masterful, dominant and caring. She surrendered completely to him, as he cast pleasures she never knew possible. Finally, they moved in harmony one final time.

Then they soared.

AMAZING. UNBELIEVABLE. STUNNING.

Words couldn't truly describe the moments they shared, the lovemaking that far surpassed any of the past. It was so right, so perfect.

With the woman he loved.

Edmund gazed at the beauty beneath him. She was smiling softly, completely satiated, the uncertainty in her eyes for once absent.

"Is it always like this?" she murmured.

He leaned down for a kiss. "It is *never* like this."

She bit her lip. "In a good way?"

"In an extraordinary, amazing, wonderful way. You are..." He shook his head. "You, madam, have rendered me speechless."

She giggled. "I would imagine it is a first."

"Quite." He traced her bare arm. Her skin was still flushed from their lovemaking. She stretched, and desire reared once more.

Yet the sound of running came from downstairs, and she softly sighed. "We need to get back."

"Of course." He wished he could keep her sequestered forever, in a dusty attic filled with old clothing and memories, yet the real world beckoned. Soon he would no longer have to leave her. They would wed as soon as possible, with a special license if her family was willing. Then she would be securely ensconced in his world.

She belonged to him now.

He quickly donned his clothing, then aided her as well. The serviceable gown was less cumbersome than the delicate gowns of the *ton* and did not take long to arrange. It was delayed by the two long kisses he couldn't help but take.

Finally, their clothing was repaired, and Priscilla's hair was set right. She patted it. "How do I look?"

"Ravishing."

Her cheeks flushed more. She looked down, even as she smiled. "You need to stop doing that."

"Doing what?"

"Flattering me."

"You receive compliments from men all the time."

"Yes, but you're the only one I want to throw down and lick."

Heat flared. *He would be doing the licking.*

Yet right now she was as red as a freshly picked cherry. "Did I just say that out loud?"

"I'm afraid so."

She sighed. "Fine, I admit it. But we have to stop acting this way. There will be a scandal if we act like besotted love birds."

He took her hand. "I would never allow

that," he said seriously. "No one will learn of what happened today. As soon as we wed, no one will care anyway."

She froze. "What?"

"I would take you to Scotland this very minute if I could. Yet our families undoubtedly want a grand affair. My only requirement is that it's as soon as possible. My ball tomorrow evening will be the perfect place to make the announcement."

"The announcement?" Her voice was uncharacteristically soft, her pink complexion paled.

He narrowed his eyes. "The announcement of our betrothal, of course."

She visibly swallowed. Then, straightened.

If she thought to challenge him, she would find herself against an opponent as she had never met. He never had so much to lose. Never so much to gain.

"We are not getting married."

He folded his arms across his chest, stood to his full height. Yet instead of fear, she notched up her chin and looked him straight in the eye.

How he loved this woman.

Yet nothing would stand in the way of her becoming his. Not even her. "I thought you understood the consequences of our behavior."

She shook her head. "We always have a choice."

"You know the man I am, Priscilla. Did you really think I would take an innocent and not make her my bride?"

"I appreciate the chivalry, yet it is unnecessary." She stood taller. "I will not marry you."

The world disappeared under his feet, felled by emotional weapons: dismay, frustration, shock. Above all, determination. "You will marry me."

"I will not." She clenched her fists, jutted up that perfect little nose. It was all he could do not to kiss her.

He kept his voice calm, yet infused power behind it. "I will give you several options."

Warily she nodded.

"I can throw you over my shoulder and kidnap you to Gretna Green. That is my preferred option."

Her nostrils flared. "Don't. You. Dare."

"I could go to your father and make an arrangement you cannot escape."

She scowled.

"Or you can tell me the massive secret that is most certainly the cause of your uncertainty, so I can vanquish it."

She tensed, didn't say a word.

He lowered his voice, softened his stance. "Think about it, Priscilla. The match makes sense. We have the same goals, desires. Physically…"

She blushed.

"I do not need to tell you that part is extraordinary. We are both looking for matches this season. Most of all, I feel…" He hesitated. The words danced on his tongue, yet they wouldn't come, not when she was so steadfast in denying him. "I feel that we suit."

Disappointment flashed in her eyes, so fleeting he wasn't sure if he imagined it. For a moment she hesitated, but then her eyes shuttered. "I'm afraid none of those options are acceptable. I'm sorry if I led you to believe this would lead to something more. I simply wanted… this. But now we must move on. I will be announcing a betrothal soon, as I'm sure you will. Not to each other."

Whisking her to Gretna Green it was.

It truly was tempting. He could manage it, yet not without scandal. He would not start a marriage like that. "Tomorrow I will visit your father."

She gasped. "You wouldn't."

He raised his eyebrows.

"I will not accept the match." She said it forcefully, yet they both knew how society worked. The power her father wielded, the power he wielded.

She would have no choice.

"I–"

Banging startled them both.

He was the first to recover. "Yes?" he called.

"It's Elizabeth. I wanted to check if you

needed anything else for the repair."

"Nothing else is required. The leak is fixed." He looked squarely at Priscilla. "Everything is as it should be."

Priscilla clenched her fists. For a moment they just stared at each other, then without a word, she turned and stomped to the door. Edmund stayed close behind but said nothing as he helped her down the ladder, as Elizabeth watched warily. When he offered to walk Priscilla home, she scowled but accepted.

Yet she sped ahead as soon as they left the sanctuary. Clearly she wanted no more discussion, and he accepted it. Tensions were high – they would talk in the morning, when they both could think clearly. Of course he stayed close, not stopping until she slipped through the fence.

He quickly walked the short distance to his own home, then strode to his room, his steward close on his heels. He barely noticed the inviting furniture, the crackling fire or luxurious furnishings. He had a single focus.

He turned to his steward, forced the scowl away. Of course his excellent servant gave no reaction to his behavior, nor did he mention the threadbare coat.

Edmund whipped it off. "Have this sent to the Duchess of Sherring in a plain box."

"Of course, Your Grace."

The steward would, of course, have the

utmost discretion. No one would learn of the unusual exchange.

"A message arrived, Your Grace." He offered a thin letter, sealed with a "D."

Edmund took it and threw it on the sideboard. "Thank you. Tell my valet I will not be needing his services tonight. In fact, tell the entire household to stay away. I have a strategy to devise."

"Very good, Your Grace." With the upmost decorum, the steward left, closing the door softly behind him.

Edmund slammed the table.

He'd been so close! He assumed Priscilla understood the consequences of intimacy, that she finally accepted their match as inevitable. Only she was still denying the truth.

He growled, forcing himself to calm. Normally, logic and rationality ruled him, but his heart usurped all matters related to Priscilla. Why was she acting this way? Her excuses failed with every heated look she gave him. The secret he almost learned was stopping her; he was sure of it! What secret was so powerful, it stopped her from taking what she so clearly wanted?

He went to the sideboard and poured himself a glass of something stronger than the early evening dictated. Yet it was not nearly as strong as what he needed.

He looked down at the letter his steward left,

tore it open with ruthless efficiency. Scanned its contents, stopped.

And smiled.

It was a request for an audience. Urgent it said, requesting his presence as soon as possible the next morning. It did not say why, only that its writer possessed vital information.

He folded the paper, rubbed the textured surface across his finger. Lady Drummond's summons could mean only one thing. Tomorrow he would learn the identity of the mysterious Lord. P.

Then he would claim his duchess.

CHAPTER SEVENTEEN

Dear Edmund,

The truth. It has the power to illuminate, to build, to destroy. It is a difficult thing to admit, especially when it forges the very path lives will take. Yet it is time you learn my truth.

I am your best friend.
Your colleague.
Your informant.
I am Priscilla.

I beg you to understand, this ruse was for good cause. It was never antagonistic, no poorly made jest to fool, ridicule or hurt. Its purpose was solely of survival. As a lady, I can never have the sway of a lord, and I feared no lord would ever welcome my aid. So I created the fictitious Lord P.

I have prowled the lairs of dastardly lords, cajoled them into giving up their se-

crets. I knew you would never approve, and without your power, my life's work would be halted. I would be relegated to ballrooms and drawing rooms, and I simply cannot accept that.

I know you have tried, and I appreciate that. Yet you simply cannot change your powerful nature, the need to protect and possess those you care for. It is why you must let me go.

Why I must let you go.

Why have I shared this in a letter? Because this letter will never reach you.

How I wish it would be so easy to write a simple letter of truth, and have you accept and understand. Yet even as you delve closer and closer to the truth, I fear the consequences should you ever discover it. Thus I must continue to hide from you, for as long as I have the power to do so.

There is one more secret I hold, yet I cannot bear to say it, not even in a letter I will never send. Yet it changes everything. Although I cannot say it, please know that I hold you in the highest esteem. If only…

Yours,
Priscilla (Lord P)

P.S. I never believed the ladies' retiring room was near Lord Roxbury's garden.

THE WARM SUN caressed Priscilla's cheek. She leaned into it, stretching muscles sore from her first glorious taste of lovemaking. In the gentle first moments of waking, she pushed aside uncertainties of the future, fears of the past. She reveled in the memory of joining with Edmund, becoming part of something amazing. He had been so masterful, so powerful, yet gentle and kind. It had been more beautiful than she ever imagined.

"Wake up, my lady. The sun has long since risen, and your mama wishes for your presence."

Priscilla opened her eyes. Sunlight streamed through open curtains, illuminating the luxurious room. It was the same, and yet somehow everything was different.

Including her.

Ellen, her maid, chattered cheerfully. "You have a lot to do today. The Bradenton ball is tonight!"

For most, the premier event of the season heralded a night of enchantment. Everyone would be there, dressed in their finest, dancing, dining and enjoying the best delights in the world. Among the glittering ton, it was a night of splendor.

For her, it held untold danger.

Uncertainties crashed down on her like an ocean wave, threatening to drown her. Edmund acted as if she were already his, and there was no telling the lengths to which he would go to make it true. His declaration to see her father today was no threat. If her father agreed…

The worst part was how much she truly wanted the match. How much she wanted him. Last night had been everything she dreamed of and more. *He* was everything she dreamed of, and the thought of giving him up broke her heart. Yet there was too much uncertainty, too much at stake.

Perhaps if there was more behind his pursuit, something stronger, something rarer. Something from the heart, then just maybe the risk would be worth taking.

She was out of time. Her only hope was to immediately accept another offer, giving Edmund no choice but to drop his suit. Even if he discovered the truth, he wouldn't have power over her. Their relationship would stay in the past.

The very thought broke her heart.

"You have mail, Lady Priscilla."

Priscilla accepted the stark white letter from her maid. "Thank you."

She swiftly tore through the seal. Her smile widened as she read her Greatest Admirer's missive, chock full of details about several naughty lords. Thank goodness, for she had been less than productive due to one very infuriating duke. This information would go a long way to changing votes.

As typical the letter held more than facts. This time, it was two simple sentences:

Do not forget to care for yourself. For you are loved.

"Priscilla, may I speak with you?"

Priscilla started, and the letter slipped from her grasp. As her mother leaned down, she dove for the paper.

"Priscilla!" her mother admonished as she tucked the paper into a hidden pocket.

"Sorry, Mother." She smoothed down her dress. "It was a personal letter."

The duchess' eyes darted to the pocket. "I saw the word loved. Was the letter from a suitor?"

"No!"

The duchess folded her arms across her chest.

Priscilla cringed. Why had she been so emphatic in her denial? Plenty of suitors wrote letters professing love, even to women they had just met. Yet now she couldn't deny it. "It's from a friend."

Her mom cocked her head to the side. "I am certain I saw the word loved."

Priscilla grimaced. Her mother noticed every little detail. "It was simply advice. My friend said I should take care of myself because I am loved. It is trivial."

Her mother's stance softened, and she held

out her hand. "Come with me."

The duchess led Priscilla to the settee, where they both sat down. She touched her arm. "There is nothing trivial about such advice. It is both wise and factual."

"Of course, Mother."

The duchess squeezed her arm. "Do not *of course* me child. You are indeed loved."

Priscilla stiffened. Of course her parents loved her, and she loved them. It was natural.

Her mother sighed. "Priscilla, do you know what love is?"

She started at the unexpected question. "Of cour – I mean yes."

Her mother gave a small smile. "Love can be a difficult thing to understand, much less admit, in today's strict society. It is not considered the fashionable thing, yet I believe it is as vital as the air we breathe. Do you want to know what love means to me, Priscilla?"

She hesitated, shook her head.

"You."

She stared.

"Do you know how I felt when you were born?" The duchess looked into the air, yet her eyes gazed into the past. "You were so beautiful, so perfect. You stole a piece of my heart that day. Your laugh lit up my world, and your father's, too. Suddenly life takes on new meaning.

"It is difficult to explain, but you change

when you become a mother. You see the world through new eyes, with possibilities you never before imagined. It's like nothing you've ever felt before, or could ever imagine. A child is hope, a promise, a bridge to the future. You will always be the baby who giggled so sweetly, the toddler who delighted me with her first steps and the little girl who set out to change the world. You have grown into a kind and beautiful woman, a strong woman, and I could not be more proud. So when life seems impossible, or when you do not know which way to turn, remember I am here for you. Forever."

Priscilla didn't move. Couldn't even respond.

Yet she felt it.

She was indeed loved.

"I better go." Her mother gave a small smile. "I will see you at breakfast."

Priscilla simply nodded.

She didn't know how long she sat there, contemplating her mother's words. Despite all the problems, she felt calmer, more at peace. She was not alone.

The maid came closer then, her secret smile indicating she had heard. "It's a lovely day, isn't it?"

Priscilla nodded, shook her head to clear it. There was much to ponder about her mother's elucidations, yet she would do so another time. Today would already be life-changing.

"Thank you for bringing the mail."

"Of course," the girl nodded. "It was convenient the messenger came so early, since I could give him the outgoing mail."

"Outgoing mail?" Priscilla repeated absently. "That's good." She froze. Slowly, carefully turned to her nightstand. Her *empty* nightstand.

"Ellen–" Somehow she managed to keep her voice calm. "What happened to the letter?"

"The letter?"

"The one on the nightstand."

"Oh." Her maid smiled. "The one addressed to The Duke of Bradenton?"

Priscilla nodded. The letter she had written simply because she had to express the words. The letter she never intended to send. The letter that *exposed* her.

"I sent it out with the rest of the mail." Ellen's smile faded. "I assumed that's what you wanted."

Do not panic.

Do not panic.

Do not panic.

Priscilla took a deep breath. "I'm not mad at you, but it wasn't ready to go." She hopped onto the hard floor. "Help me get dressed, so I can intercept it before the courier leaves."

"Actually–" Ellen wrung her hands. "I sent it out at first light. It's probably already been delivered."

Panic.

Panic.

Panic.

"I saw it when I was tidying up early this morning." The maid cringed. "You've left letters there in the past, so I assumed you wanted it sent. It's been hours."

Hours since the letter had been delivered to Edmund.

Hours since he probably read it.

Hours since he may have learned the truth.

"I WILL SOON depart for an appointment with Lady Drummond, and then the Duke of Sherring. I expect success from both."

"Very good, Your Grace. I will ensure all is ready." His steward placed a thick pile on the table. "I brought your letters."

Edmund rubbed the back of his neck. Today had the power to bring great victory, or disaster. Priscilla was cunning and unpredictable, brave and fiercely intelligent. It was part of what he loved about her, yet it threatened even the most carefully crafted plans. He must move quickly and with strategy, convince Sherring to approve the match without sharing anything scandalous. Yet he would do whatever was necessary to secure Priscilla as his bride.

He hated using such draconian tactics, yet what choice did he have? Cornered, Priscilla may do something drastic. She may accept an offer from a man who speaks to rocks, horses or plants. She may run away. She may even put herself in danger. He would prove that her rightful place was by his side.

He looked out the window, at the sun still low in the horizon. It was too early to visit Lady Drummond. His gaze centered on the letters. Perhaps a little work would make the time pass quickly.

He reached for the first letter.

A LADY VISITING a duke should calmly announce her presence.

A lady should serenely wait to be admitted.

A lady should not duck under the footman's arm, scurry past the housekeeper and run up the stairs like a runaway monkey.

Yet that was exactly what Priscilla did. Muffled shrieks followed her as she negotiated the stairs in a fashion most assuredly similar to a monkey. Fortunately, the servants were too startled, or horrified, to give chase, giving her time to try room after room. Finally, she spotted a door at the end of the corridor, larger and more ornate than the rest. She raced down the hall and opened it.

She shot into a dark, masculine room decorated in shades of deep green and blue. A cracking fireplace illuminated luxurious mahogany furniture set next to plush, overstuffed settees. Edmund sat at a massive, gilded desk, surrounded by piles of papers and priceless antiques.

He stood up in shock. "What in blazes?"

The servants must have finally regained their senses, or their courage, because half a dozen of them piled up behind her. Everyone spoke at once, a cacophony of apologies, explanations and bewilderment.

"Silence!" With Edmund's single word, the servants ceased all movement. It was that simple for him.

What did that mean for her?

"What is going on? Priscilla, are you all right?"

She smoothed her dress and stood serenely, as if she had glided in like a proper lady and not scurried in like a proper monkey. "I was wondering if you could give me a moment of your time, Your Grace."

He looked behind her. The servants seemed to have lost their ability to speak, and most were staring with open mouths. Several bobbed like fish.

"Of course." The words were mild, yet his tone held curiosity and suspicion. Of course her wild escapade would concern him, but what else could she do? She had to stop him from opening the letter.

If he hadn't already.

There was no way to know from his neutral expression. He addressed the servants, "I have matters to discuss with Lady Priscilla. You may return to your duties."

The servants looked no less shocked, even as they rushed to obey their master's bidding. As the door softly clicked shut, she realized why. "I am alone with you in your bedroom."

"You are indeed."

She closed her eyes. This was very, very bad. Bradenton's employees were discreet, yet even the most disciplined servants would have difficulty containing so tantalizing a story. When word got out, scandal would come immediately. Unless…

"Do not worry. No one will care about a little meeting when we announce our betrothal tonight."

"No." Somehow she would find a way to neutralize the latest danger. "That's not why I'm here."

He moved closer. He was dressed in a suit of pure black, his hair neatly combed and his cravat intricate and perfect. "Why are you here?"

"I… I…" She tried again, yet the words wouldn't come. The truth was impossible, no excuse plausible. Her gaze fell on the desk. Letters in various stages of opening were arranged in neat piles.

Including hers.

The letter was unopened. She let out a breath of relief, then froze as his eyes narrowed. He may not have yet seen it, but it was in his possession. How could she possibly steal it without him seeing?

He followed her gaze.

"I want to talk about us!" She shouted the words, and he whipped his head back.

The suspicion in his eyes deepened. "Have you decided to accept my offer?"

If only… "I'm afraid not. I've come to explain why I cannot marry you."

"We've already settled this." His voice was firm, his stance hard. "You can and you will."

She stood taller. "You are not the only one with a say."

"You're right." He smoothed out his sleeves. "In a few hours I have an appointment with your father."

She suppressed a gasp. She hadn't realized he'd move so quickly.

"I would have gone first thing this morning, but I have another appointment."

Something tilted in her stomach. "Another appointment?"

"This one does not concern you. I have a matter to discuss with Lady Drummond."

This time she did gasp.

His eyes darkened. "Are you all right?"

Not in the slightest. For him to delay speaking

to her father, the matter with Lady Drummond would have to be vital. Urgent.

Something like finding out the identity of his informant.

Unwittingly her eyes once again fell on the letter.

He noticed.

"What are you looki–"

She kissed him.

It was an act of desperation, of every emotion that couldn't be contained. He immediately seized control of it and her, pulling her flush against the body she knew so well. Her softness pressed against his hardness as he ran his hands up and down her sides, smoothing her.

Her body grew ripe for his touch.

She fought not to get lost to the sensations, the touches. She reeled as he spun a sensual web, as her body responded the only way it knew how. She opened her eyes to stare directly at the letter. It was so close, yet so far. Only perhaps…

She pushed a little more into him, and he took a step back.

An impossible plan formed, one with little chance of success, yet any chance was better than the certainty of capture. She urged him back again. Closer, closer, and then almost within reach. If she could grab it, hide it somewhere within her skirts, then just maybe she could accomplish the unthinkable. She reached out, touched its smooth, cool surface. Just a little closer…

An iron hand clamped around her wrist.

"What are you doing?" The voice in her ear held full control. Edmund pulled back, even as he kept her in his firm grip. His deep blue eyes shone with clarity. "What are you about, Priscilla?" He followed her gaze, and this time did not stop.

Her breath hitched.

He carefully set her back, even as he kept a hand on her, to contain her as much as steady her. He used his other to paw through the letters. He uncovered hers, with a single word in flowing script. "Bradenton."

She couldn't help but still when he uncovered it. His looked at her, then down at the letter and then back at her. And then his eyes widened.

That was the moment he knew.

Her heart thundered against her ribs, her lungs struggling to gasp enough air. Fear, horror and panic tangled in her chest, casting tremors that shook her body and heated her face. She stared at the man she loved, the man whom she had undoubtedly already lost, as he finally discovered the truth.

The man who now held all control.

"It can't be." He shook his head, even as the dawn of realization shone. He let out a long heavy breath, at stark contrast to her rapid pants. "Priscilla." The voice was questioning and answering at the same time, disbelieving and yet utterly certain. "Explain yourself."

She shook her head wildly, even as she tugged at the arm he still hadn't released. His features hardened.

He released her, but his expression commanded she stay. It did not matter. There was nowhere she could escape.

He picked up her letter, turned it over in his hands.

"Please."

Yet he paid her no heed as he undid the seal, opened the letter.

And read.

It did not take long. His eyes darted back and forth as he consumed the truth that exposed all. Her heart thundered so loud it was a miracle he could not hear. Finally, he finished.

The intensity in his eyes was unnerving. Once more he had shed his gentlemanly façade, and now a warrior stood before her, challenging, uncompromising, all-powerful. She reached for the letter, but he folded it crisply, slipping it into his jacket pocket. It was all the evidence he ever needed to control her.

Her life was now in his hands.

He did not say a word as he brushed past her to the door. He opened it a sliver. "Send Lady Drummond my regrets and my gratitude. Tell her I solved the mystery on my own. I will be getting all the answers right now."

He closed the door, locked it. Priscilla edged back, grasping the table behind her. Edmund did not stop until he towered above her. His heat surrounded her, his power threatened to consume her.

"You are Lord P."

A statement, not a question. And no way to deny it.

"I should have realized..." He stopped, brought his bright blue gaze to her. "Explain. The truth this time."

She touched her lips, where he had kissed mere seconds ago. "I meant everything I said in the letter. My subterfuge was never intended to hurt you. It was the only way I could make a difference."

She took a deep breath. "We were told to ignore it. The poor. The suffering. The pain. Yet I never could. I pledged to do something to stop it as soon as I could. I researched Parliament, learned about the members for and against social causes. That's when I first heard about you."

She remembered back. "My first investigation happened by accident. I was at a ball when I overheard a lord and lady speaking about politics. The lord always voted against social actions causes, and the lady was a friend of mine. I wondered if she may be able to convince him to change his mind."

"She did." She smiled, remembering her first success. "From then on my investigations flourished. I soon realized I could do so much more if I actually had some sway in Parliament, which of course I didn't. So I decided to find someone to whom I could pass information."

"Me."

Her smile faded at the harshly spoken word. "There was no other choice."

His eyes turned incredulous, and she continued, "You were the logical choice by far. You were already a fervent supporter of social causes, and no one held as much power as you. When you want something..." She swallowed. "You *usually* get it. I was hoping you'd be open to using my information, but I knew you would never accept it from a woman. If I told you who I was–"

"I would have said it was far too dangerous." He ran a hand through his hair. "The investigations, the sleuthing. You were not hopelessly lost at Lord Roxbury's – you were investigating. I also assume it was you who hid behind the tapestry?"

She nodded miserably. "I'm sorry for deceiving you. Once we got to know each other in real life, things became more complicated. Feelings got..." She stopped, looked down. "I enjoyed our time together. Very much."

"What were you thinking?" He clenched his fists. "When I think of the danger you put yourself in! These men make powerful enemies.

Do you have any idea what could have happened to you?" His voice grew louder with every word.

"Yes!" She gathered all her strength, the anger and power that propelled her. "I know every single risk. Yet I choose to continue, because the danger I face pales in comparison to a poor woman alone on the streets or a tiny orphan with no one to care for him. That is who I am fighting for, and why I will never stop trying to change the world, no matter the risk!"

His fury filled the air. "You may be willing to risk it, but I'm not. You will cease your investigations immediately!"

It felt like a knife in her belly. "No!"

"I will not have you risking your life. I forbid it!"

She jabbed him with a finger. She might be smaller than him, but her will was just as strong as his. "You have no right to forbid me to do anything! I was hoping you would continue our working relationship, but if you won't, I will find someone else."

"You will not find anyone else," he growled. "Do not underestimate my power, Priscilla. Whatever I have to do, I will ensure you do not put yourself in danger again."

Fear flashed through her, not for herself physically, but for her life's work. While he technically had no control over her, his power was wide and far. If he wanted to stop her... he would.

"This is why you refused the match." Edmund breathed out. "Why you only pursued suitors who were occupied. You wanted someone who would be so distracted he wouldn't notice you traipsing through dangerous men's homes."

"Yes," she admitted. "I hoped… hope to find someone who wouldn't notice my activities."

"Who wouldn't stop you, you mean."

She hesitated, nodded.

"It's too late for that."

This was not going well. As everything she feared came to life, she searched for a way to undo it. "Please, Edmund. Nothing has to change. You said so in your letters. We can still work together, just like before. Think of all we accomplished."

"Nothing can continue." His harsh tone bore no contradiction. "I never would have accepted your help if I understood the risk."

"You knew the risk!" she cried. "It makes no difference that I'm a woman."

"It makes all the difference. What would *happen* to you is very different." His voice was deep and low. "This cannot continue. That relationship has ended. Forever."

Tears threatened as she lost what was never truly hers, gave up a future that could never be. "You truly want to never see me again?"

"*We* are not over."

She froze. "What?"

"You and I are not over." He stalked toward her. "Not even close."

"But you said our relationship has ended."

"Our working relationship." His eyes flashed. "I will not allow you to put yourself in danger again. But you and I, we are just getting started." He stood up tall, folded his arms across his chest. "Tonight, I will announce our betrothal."

Chapter Eighteen

The Duke of Bradenton formally invites
The Duke and Duchess of Sherring and their
family
To attend an evening ball
For a night of dancing, dining and
A most important announcement

Reality shattered.

The woman he'd courted, pursued and *loved* was his informant. He'd sent her on perilous quests to unearth information about the most dangerous lords in the *ton*. He'd put her in danger, again and again. That he didn't know it was no excuse. He was furious, most of all, at himself.

How could he have missed it?

The signs were so obvious. Both Priscilla and Lord P kept secrets. They shared similar goals and interests. They were clever and witty and cared greatly about the cause. Blazes, the letter P!

The illumination had a million consequences, yet one thing would never change:

She was his.

The truth had not made him want her any less. If anything he was even more awed by her courage, her sacrifice, her pure goodness. He had known she was amazing, yet this showed just how incredible she was.

He could not give up Priscilla. *Would not.* Yet emotions were raw. She would respond better if he were calm, yet thoughts of the danger upended him. Even if he had to act the powerful autocrat, he could not allow her to risk herself.

"You still want to marry me?" Priscilla stared at him. "But I thought–"

"This doesn't change my desire to marry you." He tried to soften his voice, yet it came out hard, cold. He was doing it wrong, but he couldn't stop. "I bedded you last night."

She swallowed, looked down. Her eyes sheened.

Curse it.

"Priscilla–"

"No!" Her eyes lit with stubbornness and strength. "We will not marry because I did what every man does on a regular basis. Not because it is logical and most certainly not because of scandal. I will not allow you to sacrifice yourself for duty. Despite what you claim, you want a woman who will sit at home while you save the world. I'm sorry, Your Grace, but I'm going to save the world myself."

She was glorious. He should tell her it was far more than duty that drove him, yet he stood in stoic silence as she walked towards the door. She turned, and for just a moment, something flickered in her eyes, anguish, vulnerability, something stronger he couldn't identify.

He moved forward, but she quickly opened the door, her features disappearing into a hardened glare. "I will continue my work. No matter what you do, or who you tell, I *will* find a way. You can't stop me." Her voice choked. Then she turned and fled, slamming the door behind her.

It took every ounce of restraint to not follow her, sling her over his shoulder and whisk her to Gretna Green as he had earlier threatened. Even if it nearly killed him, he would bide his time, formulate a plan. That he had handled this wrong was without a doubt, yet what else could he have done? Told her to risk her life? Given his blessing? If something happened, it would be his fault.

She was wrong about one thing. This was not over, not even close. He strode to the door, opened it. Time to win this battle.

The future depended on it.

"IT'S GOOD TO see you again, Bradenton."

Sherring offered a warm smile and a hearty handshake. It was a positive sign, yet Edmund could not return it. He gave a serious nod. "Your Grace."

"Come in, come in." The duke shut the door and gestured to an overstuffed chair.

Edmund shook his head, then a second time when the duke offered spirits. He would need all his facilities to conduct the detailed and logical strategy he'd formed for the most important fight of his life.

"I would like to marry your daughter, Your Grace."

He had not meant to blurt it out, yet the words came of their violation. So much for strategy and planning. Hopefully, they would be enough.

He did not want to expose Priscilla's secrets.

Or his.

Sherring leaned against the desk, his eyes narrowing. He said nothing for a moment. "It was my hope you would offer, yet based on my daughter's behavior, I assume matters have not progressed as smoothly as all that."

If there had been a vase in the room earlier, he may have needed a surgeon. "I'm afraid Priscilla is resistant to the match," he admitted. "She has misconceptions about what type of suitor would be best."

"It would appear so." Sherring folded his arms across his chest. "It would seem my daughter prefers men who talk to rocks."

So much for a man's confidence... "She prefers a man who talks to rocks so he doesn't talk to her." He would not share all her secrets, yet some explanation might be of use. "She does not truly want a match."

Sherring sighed. "I suspected as much. An obsession was the defining character of her suitors." He eyed him closely. "Except for you."

Edmund stepped forward. "I may not be what she thinks she wants, but I can provide what she needs. A true match between equals, two people with similar positions, social standing and goals." He launched into the speech he prepared. "I am a man of power and means, from a reputable family and excellent social standing. I can provide her with all she requires, a secure and comfortable life."

"My boy, if you think Priscilla wants a secure and comfortable life, then you do not know her at all."

Edmund stopped short. It was not what Priscilla wanted, yet he assumed it was what her father would want to hear. Had he miscalculated?

"I love my children."

Bradenton looked up.

"It may not be the fashionable thing, or the most common, but I care deeply about Priscilla and my boys. Of course I want a suitable match, but above all, I want her to be happy. I would never approve a match that didn't make her happy, no matter how advantageous."

Sherring turned towards a painting on the wall. It showed the duke as a young man, with his duchess and four young children. Even as a child Priscilla had that spark in her eyes. "Of course I wish for my daughter's safety and well-being. It's the reason I demanded a match in the first place. Yet she can attain the same benefits with the suitors she claims to prefer. Tell me, Bradenton, why you?" The duke's expression turned serious. Although older, he was still a powerful man, a father defending his daughter. "I told Priscilla I would give her a choice, yet you are asking me to overrule it. Why should I grant your request?"

Edmund opened his mouth to tell him about the logic of it all. His position. His wealth. His power. And yet it was not what the duke wanted to hear. So he looked straight at the man who would be his bride's father and...

Admitted what he had not been able to tell Priscilla.

And when he had finished, the duke patted him on the back. "Now that's what a father wants to hear." He lifted his glass. "Welcome to the family, son."

"We're looking for Priscilla Livingston."

"Clearly, she isn't here. Our Priscilla is barely out of the nursery."

"She can't be this beautiful woman."

Priscilla stared, open mouthed.

"Well, poppet, aren't you going to greet your loving brothers?"

She shouldn't be happy. Shouldn't be relieved her brothers had returned, en masse, their power magnified by their numbers. The protective men would most certainly side against her when it came to Bradenton. Yet when her oldest brother, Alexander, opened his arms, she couldn't stop herself.

She ran to him.

They took turns hugging her. All were well-built and handsome men, with the trademark emerald eyes of the Livingstons. Striking, yet different, they would soon be the talk of London. Alexander, the duke's heir and an earl, already had the regal bearing of his inheritance with his black hair and tanned skin. Richard was all about power, a lightning-fast swordsman with an astounding mind for numbers. Then there was Nicholas, once the baby, now the largest of the group at well over six feet and three inches. His light blond hair and angel-like charm hid steel-like strength.

They were powerful men, yet to her, they were simply three boys who loved to tease and care for her. Now they patted her back, ruffled her hair and giant Nicholas even lifted her up for a big bear hug. She complained and grimaced and made a fuss.

How she had missed them.

Finally, they let her go, with broad smiles so similar yet different. "Let us look at you then," Alexander stood back. "I must say, my dear, you are beautiful. It's only been months, but you seem different."

"I am the same," she protested. Yet the words tasted strange, even to her. Nothing was the same, nor would it ever be.

They couldn't know what happened between her and Bradenton. "You three are looking well. I am certain the eligible misses will think so."

The triple looks of horror were so comical, she couldn't help but giggle.

"It's been strange going through so much of the season without you. You spent longer with our cousins than I expected."

The men exchanged glances.

Priscilla narrowed her eyes. "That's where you were, right? With James, helping him with his estate while he recovered from the fever?"

Their cousin, a duke himself, had taken a bad illness a few months before. The entire family had visited for what they assumed would be a funeral, yet James had made an astounding recovery. While Priscilla and her parents returned to London to prepare for the season, her brothers had stayed to help run the estate. Yet the trip seemed excessively long…

"Of course we were helping." Something flashed in Alexander's eyes. "A few... issues arose that needed to be dealt with."

No doubt there was a story behind that.

No doubt they would not tell her.

"Enough about us. We're here now, and there is much to discuss." Alexander's gaze hardened as he instantly transformed from playful older brother to the second father he deemed himself. Her other brothers followed, until she felt the full weight of their scrutiny.

Not good.

She stood up tall. "I'm fine. Tell me more about your trip."

Alexander folded his arms across his chest. "We are far more concerned about your adventures."

She kept a light smile upon her lips. "This season has been like any other. You need only read the sheets to keep abreast of all the happenings."

"At the moment, we are solely interested in the happenings of one lady." Richard's expression turned as hard as Alexander's. "And that lady has been in the papers an awful lot."

Priscilla straightened. "It's not my fault."

Triple looks of incredulity pierced her.

"It isn't." She smoothed down her dress. "You know how gossip spreads. Everything is embellished."

"This time, there's truth beneath the stories." Alexander pursed his lips into a tight slash. "To be honest, we take some responsibility. As your brothers, it is our duty to help you navigate society."

Richard nodded his agreement. "If we had been here, matters never would have progressed this far."

"We will do whatever it takes to resolve matters," Nicholas added.

Priscilla took a deep breath. She had forgotten how powerful her brothers were all on their own.

The man who would one day be Duke of Sherring glared at her. "We are here now."

The others nodded.

Even as they showed their power, something fired within her. She was as much the child of a duke as they were. "I'm glad for your company, yet I require no assistance. I can handle my own affairs."

"Did you leap from a moving carriage?"

"To be fair, it wasn't actually moving."

"Get in a fight with a shopkeeper four times your size?"

"He certainly wasn't more than three times my size."

"What about Bradenton?"

"Edmund is none of your business."

It had been the wrong thing to say as her

brothers' expressions turned from dismayed to thunderous.

"I would very much dispute that." Alexander's words were quiet, yet held controlled strength. He studied her carefully. "Is there anything else we should know about?"

Well…

She spent her days investigating criminal lords.

She ran a secret society for social action.

She ventured into the slums weekly.

She visited a gaming hall while pretending to be a man.

Oh, and she made love to Edmund.

"Absolutely not."

"I very much doubt that."

She clenched her skirts. "Everything is fine. It is no concern of yours."

Their expressions darkened further.

She forged on, "I am no longer a child. I am an adult woman who makes my own decisions."

Alexander stepped forward. "You may be grown, but we are your brothers. It's our job to ensure your safety."

They sounded a lot like someone else she knew.

"I am perfectly fine on my own."

"Really?" Nicholas countered. "Even in the country, rumors of your antics reached us. Do you know what it's like to not be able to defend you? No doubt there's far more you aren't telling us."

She stared at her brothers and they glared at her, like duelists meeting at dawn, neither backing down, and neither giving up.

"No matter how old you are, we will protect you." Richard said. "You are our little sister."

She sighed. "I'll admit there were a few minor issues, but nothing to cause scandal. Your reputations are safe."

"Our reputations?" Alexander held up his hands. "The last thing we are worried about is our matches! We care about you, Priscilla. We love *you*."

Her breath caught in her throat. It was easy to fight against their anger, their overbearing nature, their stubborn authoritarianism. But their love?

That was a far greater challenge.

Yet though she loved her brothers, she couldn't let them live her life.

"We are only trying to care for you, poppet." Richard stepped forward.

"We want your safety and happiness," Nicolas added.

"We will always stand by you," Alexander promised. "Scandal or not."

She stared at them for a moment, fighting to stay strong. It would be so easy to accept their rule, to stand down and let everyone dictate her life, yet she simply couldn't. Not if she wanted to live the life she chose.

"I understand. And I truly appreciate your dedication," she said quietly. "Yet as I said, all is well."

"It will be as long as you accept."

She stiffened.

Bradenton.

They man they hadn't mentioned was the center of everything. Like her parents, friends and the entire ton, they believed she would soon be betrothed. How would they take it when she told them the truth?

It might be safer to flee to America and send them a letter.

"Father has already given the order that I must accept an offer this season, and I agreed. I simply have not yet decided whom that man will be."

All three brothers stood taller. Flexed their muscles. And stared.

She put her hands on her hips. "It's my choice."

"You made your choice!" Alexander held up his hands. "The man with whom you danced a hundred waltzes. The man who saved you when you jumped from a carriage. The man whose bedroom you were in. Alone!" He stopped, took a deep breath. When he spoke again, his voice was quieter, yet no less powerful. "Bradenton is a good man. We've known him since we were children, and I consider him a friend. That's the only reason I'm not calling him out right now. Still, I have half a mind to–"

Priscilla's breath hitched.

Alexander paused again, breathed out. "You will accept his offer."

"I cannot." She meant to speak firmly, yet the words came out quiet, whispered.

Her brothers' anger faded, and they came closer.

Nicholas took a hand, Richard the other. "Can you tell us why?"

She looked down, shook her head.

"Has he done something?" Richard's words were casual, yet backed by steel. "Is there something we should know about?"

"Do we need to talk to him?"

"Throttle him?"

"End him?"

"No!" She breathed in, freed her hands and wrapped them around herself. "He's offered. In fact, he essentially dictated we'll wed as soon as possible!" She shut her eyes. She hadn't meant to admit that.

They should have been horrified.

Instead they nodded their approval.

Alexander seemed far calmer. "Bradenton is a good man. The match will be a favorable one."

"But I don't want it. Doesn't that matter?"

The men looked between each other. Richard sighed. "Can you explain?"

Not without them locking her in her tower.

"I simply prefer other suitors. I will soon accept one of the offers I've received."

"Please tell me it's not the one who talks to rocks."

Despite herself, she smiled. "Has everyone heard of him?"

They nodded simultaneously.

"No, it's not the one who talks to rocks. I'm not nearly that desperate."

"I do not understand, Priscilla." Alexander shook his head, "Any other woman would be thrilled to catch Bradenton. While other lords may be suitable, he is exemplary. It simply makes sense that it's him."

"Perhaps for you, but not for me. Yet Father has gotten it in his mind that he's my only choice. Please, will you help me?"

Her brothers exchanged silent glances. Then Alexander spoke for them all, "I'm sorry, Priscilla. I may not have been here, but I've heard enough. You will accept Bradenton's offer."

She held back tears as she looked to the others. Yet their gazes remained stoic.

Just like in the story, she would need to rescue herself.

"Hello, children."

Priscilla spun.

Her mother stood in the doorway, her expression as somber as the bitterness churning in her stomach. The duchess should be ecstatic at her brothers' return, yet instead her eyes were guarded, shuttered.

What had happened?

"Boys, I must talk with your sister."

Her brothers must have sensed the serious mood, for not a single one complained about being called a boy. Each gave their own farewell, a hug from Nicholas, a hand on the shoulder from Richard and a kiss on the forehead from Alexander. They filed out.

Her mother wasted no time.

"Your father spoke with Bradenton."

Priscilla felt the blood drain from her face. "Edmund was here?"

Her mother gave a small smile. "Yes, *Edmund* was here. He just left."

Priscilla closed her eyes. Thank goodness he hadn't asked to see her. She needed at least a little time to prepare for their inevitable encounter tonight. "What did he want?"

"I think you know," her mother said softly.

He had asked for her hand. The words could have been yelled for how blatant they were, yet he had not exposed her ruse. Had he done so, her father would have climbed to the roof and read the banns without notice or church.

"What did Father say?" Priscilla spoke without emotion, at complete contrast to the storm raging inside.

"I think you know the answer to that as well."

Her throat dried. He had accepted on her behalf. She could fight, but in the end it wouldn't matter.

When the duke wanted something…

She shook her head without even realizing it. "No."

Her mother strode to the gorgeous gown hanging on the bed, the ethereal masterpiece Edmund gifted her. "You will go tonight. You will wear this dress and the diamond necklace. And when he announces your betrothal, you will agree."

No.

Yes.

Emotions swirled, upending reality and distorting desires, wishes, and needs. She fought for anger, the only feeling she could handle. "He said he wouldn't force me. You said you wouldn't!"

"I would never force you to marry a man you did not love."

She froze. "What?"

The duchess came closer. "I will not allow you to give up something precious because of duty or fear. Tell me, Priscilla, do you love him?"

She blanched. "I… I…"

She tried to force out the denial, willed herself to say it.

She said nothing.

"That's what I thought," her mother said, not unkindly. "Priscilla, I am far more aware of you than you realize."

Priscilla grimaced, but did not respond. Her mother could never understand.

"I fight for the same causes as you."

"Of course, Mother."

Her mother sighed, gave her a pointed look. "Social action."

The world halted.

Her mother looked up. "You may think I fill my days with gossip and parties, but there is far more. Even married to a powerful duke, I fight for the causes important to me. Perhaps I should have been honest with you from the beginning." She sighed. "I didn't want you to feel like an outsider."

Priscilla stared. Her mother was one of the most respected duchesses in the *ton*. Could she possibly have a secret life?

The duchess smiled softly. "Things change when you become a duchess. Your father fell in love with me because of who I was, not in spite of it. And he has allowed me to continue my work."

"Your work? I don't understand."

"It is much like your efforts, the Distinguished Ladies of Purpose." She gave a secretive smile. "The purpose of social action."

Priscilla gasped.

Her mother pierced her with a shrewd look. "You didn't think I knew about your clandestine activities? You hate to sew, and yet you suddenly start a sewing guild. You suffer once-a-week megrims, yet you are fine the rest of the time. Your pin money disappears, yet you rarely buy anything. I know all that you do, and why."

"You know about all that?" Priscilla whispered. "But how?"

"Because I am your mother," the duchess said. "Because I am so very proud when you change the world. But most of all, because I love you. Your happiness means everything to me. Do not forget, I have always been your *greatest admirer*."

Priscilla gasped. Her greatest admirer? "You're the one who's been sending anonymous messages to my guild?"

Her mother smiled. "As I said, you do not know everything about me. But never doubt how very proud I am of you. Exactly as you are."

Priscilla sniffed, looked down. Her mother opened her arms wide…

And embraced her.

And in her mother's arms, everything was just a little better. Whatever the future brought, she had gained an ally. Her greatest admirer.

Tonight, she would need her more than ever.

CHAPTER NINETEEN

THE WORLD SPARKLED with enchantment.

Priscilla had attended countless balls, night after night, week after week, yet never had she seen such brilliance, such pure, unrestrained luxury as Bradenton's affair. Hundreds of candles illuminated gilded furnishings, set in massive chandeliers above a seemingly endless expanse. The ballroom was massive, with doors leading to hallways, flanked by dozens of rooms. A large band played in the corner, their excellence apparent in the flawless music. And the people…

While every event was a reason to impress, the *ton* had taken grandness to a new extent. Ladies danced in ball gowns threaded with genuine stones, their tresses arranged in silky curls. The men wore suits in the latest styles, their cravats intricate and crisp, as they led their partners with bold moves. The couples twirled on the gleaming dance floor, graceful, elegant and beautiful.

Priscilla's gown floated around her like an ethereal cloud, sparkling under the candlelight. It felt even more magical than in the shop, with matching jewels and her hair twisted into an intricate creation of curls. She truly looked like a princess ready to meet her prince.

Yet the perfect façade hid a broken heart.

Not broken, but shattered, as she fought to give up her true love. Yet she had no other choice, not if she wanted to change the world. And from that moment with her grandmother so long ago, she had wanted nothing else.

So she would ignore that it was a night of magic, a night of *matches*. Many had come to make their own, and to watch others do the same. Most of all, they marveled at the announcement an updated invitation promised. Most thought they already knew.

Bradenton's match.

Their betrothal.

Her surrender.

There had to be a way to stop it! When her father told her of his agreement with Edmund, she pleaded for him to change his mind. She tried every strategy that had ever worked, charm, anger and demands, and yet he would not alter his decision. She would marry Bradenton, and if she did not she would be removed to the country until she agreed.

She could do no good from the country. If she left London during the height of the season, all her hard work would be lost. She couldn't allow herself to be whisked away, but if he commanded it, she would have no choice. For now, her father owned her.

If she didn't stop this, Bradenton would be next.

She had to do something. Her only thought was to announce her own betrothal with someone else before Bradenton's announcement. At this point, it didn't matter who it was, or if he spoke to rocks, only that he allowed her to continue her all-important work. Bradenton would be furious, and would likely try to interfere, yet if the suitor was well-positioned it just may work. Her father would not want scandal when he still had her brothers to match.

Tonight she would choose her own husband. Someone who wasn't Bradenton.

Her heart cracked.

It was the right thing to do. It was the *only* thing to do. No matter how much she loved him, she couldn't surrender. He had already forbidden her to work, and they weren't even betrothed!

Where was he? Edmund was one of the few people who could get away with being late to his own ball. His family was here, greeting the people who arrived, but the master of the house was nowhere to be seen. Instead of getting annoyed, the ton lauded their leader even more, speculating on the vital business that kept him from their presence. Of course, many glanced her way, no doubt wondering about her role. The announcement simply had to be about her, said a thousand hushed whispers. They were likely right.

From the corner, she stood watching. She should be out there dancing, deciding which man to pursue. She only had this one night, and not even its entirety, for once Bradenton made the announcement, no lord would dare go against him. Yet she didn't leave her perch, not even to sign up for a dance. She had to see Edmund first, at least from afar. Somehow convince herself this was the right thing to do.

A hearty laugh distracted her, and she turned. She cringed. Lord Roxbury.

Her stomach soured even more as he made a crude gesture. He was talking to Lord Snarvelle, another who cared only for his riches and the mistresses he mistreated. Their wide smiles indicated laughter, but she was too far away to hear their conversation. Snarvelle said something, and Roxbury put his hands to his lips, as if to shush him. Roxbury looked left and right, then gestured for Snarvelle to follow.

She straightened. Where were they going?

Anything Roxbury and Snarvelle discussed was no doubt unsavory, possibly criminal. Most importantly, it may be something she could use to sway their votes.

She didn't hesitate. Soon she may have to give up her work, but tonight she made her own choices. As the two men disappeared down a corridor, she hurried after them.

Fifteen minutes later she was thoroughly disgusted.

For long, long minutes she listened to Roxbury and Snarvelle discuss women, and not in a way any person, much less lady, should ever hear. It was disgusting, but nothing she could use. Everyone knew of the men's liaisons, including their wives. She would have left a while ago, yet they had moved too close to her hiding spot. She would have to wait until they returned to the ball to escape.

Finally, Snarvelle said, "We better get back. I'm curious about Bradenton's announcement."

Roxbury humphed. "It's obvious he's going to offer for the Sherring chit. I heard they were alone in his…"

Heat flooded her, even as the voices faded out of hearing distance. If people were talking about their illicit behavior, would another man even offer for her?

She waited another minute. but no more sounds came from the hallway. She stepped out.

And stared at the large man before her.

His grin was pure evil. "What do we have here?"

WHERE WAS PRISCILLA? According to his friends, she had arrived an hour ago, when he had still been crafting his plan for the night. Her brothers had not yet arrived, and her parents were happily chatting with the rest of the *ton* while their daughter was missing. When she belonged to him–

Stop.

He fought instincts demanding possessiveness, protectiveness. If he could ever have a true relationship with Priscilla, he had to allow her freedom. Which meant no whisking to Gretna Green and no locking her in a tower. He had formulated a plan, one he hoped would secure him a willing bride.

He still planned on announcing their betrothal tonight.

Yet now she was nowhere to be found. Perhaps she was in the retiring room or some corner chatting with friends. Eventually she would have to appear.

He interacted with guests, greeted countless people in conversations he couldn't remember. Yet as the minutes passed, his apprehension grew. What if she was in trouble? What if she had decided to go sleuthing? The last thought made his blood run cold.

Now he actively looked for her, threading in and out of groups, looking over the sea of people. He was about to make his way towards the ladies' retiring room when a gruff voice exclaimed, "What is taking Roxbury so long?"

He halted, turned, walked slowly toward Snarvelle. The thin, balding lord was as crooked as Roxbury, yet not nearly as sly. Edmund hated inviting either to his event, yet he didn't want to give a blatant insult they would remember at voting time.

"He should be back by now."

"Roxbury is missing somewhere in my home?"

Snarvelle started. He gulped. "We didn't touch anything, Your Grace. We simply wanted a private space for a conversation. About ladies, you see."

Bradenton glared.

"Yes, well..." Sweat formed on Snarvelle's brow. "We spoke for a few minutes and headed back. Roxbury realized he dropped his watch and went to retrieve it. I was just wondering what was taking him so long."

What... or who. Sudden fear iced his veins, as every protective and possessive instinct he'd been restraining fired. "Where were you?" he growled.

"Down the corridor," Snarvelle squeaked. "There was an open door at the end, a guest room. It was decorated blue."

Bradenton didn't wait to hear more. He pivoted, moving as fast as he could without breaking into a run. He was likely mistaken, but he couldn't ignore the possibility that Priscilla was investigating Roxbury. The first time, she had almost been caught. What if this time, she had?

A woman screamed.

She'd miscalculated so much.

The danger of her investigations.

The consequences of her actions.

Edmund.

The first two were painfully obvious, literally and figuratively. Roxbury had taken her by such surprise, she'd barely screamed when he grabbed her arm and dragged her into the guest room. She had flung herself forward then, but he was too strong. He pushed her back, closed the door. *Locked it.*

Now as he stared at her with a lecherous grin, all she could think of was Edmund. How she never told him she loved him. How she had not fought for them. How she gave him up.

From now on, she would fight.

"Were you waiting for me, sweet thing?"

"Of course not!" An involuntary shiver wracked her, even as she stood taller and said in her most haughty voice, "I don't know what you're thinking, Lord Roxbury, but this is completely inappropriate. Let me out."

"Come on now, sweet thing." His grin widened as he stalked forward. "I know how you are. Everyone does."

She scooted back, just out of his reach. The stench of male sweat reached her. "Excuse me?"

"Don't play coy, love. I know all about you and Bradenton. How you went to his bedroom the other day."

She blanched.

"Oh yes, everyone knows about that. Course they don't care too much, since they figure you're about to get betrothed. But Bradenton has been a pain for a while now. Why don't you share some of your favors?"

"I will never share anything with you!" she hissed. "This has gone far enough, Lord Roxbury. I don't know what you think you know, but I am a lady. I am also the daughter of the Duke of Sherring and a good friend of the Duke of Bradenton. What do you think will happen when they find out what transpired?"

His toothy grin was filled with malice. "I assume they'll marry you off as soon as possible and pretend it never happened. Wouldn't want scandal and all that. Now come here, sweeting. You look delectable in that dress. I wonder how you look without it."

Then… he lunged.

"Edmund!" she screamed as she jumped back. Her back hit the wall hard, stealing her breath and sending stars dancing before her eyes. Her stomach lurched with fear. She spun, but there was nowhere to escape. As Roxbury's meaty hands grabbed at her, she clenched her eyes shut.

Then... a roar.

Crashing. Banging. Yelling.

She opened her eyes to a fight between giants. Once more Edmund had turned into her warrior. Roxbury already sported a swollen eye, but Edmund deflected every blow, his swift reflexes far superior to the lecherous man. They parried back and forth, Roxbury huffing and puffing amidst Edmund's knife-sharp focus. Priscilla gasped when the soft man got a lucky shot in Edmund's shoulder, yet the duke barely reacted. The brute was simply no match for Bradenton.

The fight was over almost as quickly as it began. As Edmund reached his hand back to prepare for another blow, Roxbury whimpered, "I didn't mean anything. She was asking for it!"

With a growl, Edmund pushed him against the wall. "Didn't mean anything?" His voice was deadly. "I know exactly what you were about to do. Never again, Roxbury, do you hear me?"

"But I–"

"Never again, or you will see the power I

truly wield. You think I'm a gentleman? If you ever touch an unwilling woman again, from the loftiest lady to a flower girl on the street, you will answer to me. I will come for you, and this time I will not be nice."

The color drained from Roxbury's face.

"I'm also sick of you doing everything in your power to hurt society. From now on, you will support all measures to aid those in need. If you don't, I will tell everyone what happened today."

"You can't. You won't. Lady Priscilla–"

"Will be just fine," Edmund finished. "I can protect her from scandal. Can you say the same about yourself? Do you think your friends, business associates, wife will support you?"

Roxbury paled. "I agree!" His words meant nothing, but the fear in his eyes said he would think twice before crossing Edmund.

"Leave my home, and never return. From now on, you are a changed man." Edmund let go of Roxbury.

Roxbury fell to the floor and… attacked.

Priscilla jumped back as the two large men fought once more. Roxbury fought dirty, yet Edmund was far stronger. Her heart thundered as Roxbury just missed connecting. Fear infused her. Edmund was by far the better fighter, but what if Roxbury got a lucky shot? She had to do something!

She spun around. There had to be something

she could use as a weapon.

She spied a vase…

With all her might she launched herself at the large blue and gold piece, picked it up by its smooth curved sides. She stumbled towards the fighting men, waited for just the right moment…

And clobbered Lord Roxbury.

"What in the world?" Lord Roxbury screamed. He lunged for her, but Edmund drew his fist back and gave one mighty swing.

And giant, evil Lord Roxbury went down.

Edmund opened his arms.

She dropped the vase and flew into them.

"Oh Edmund… I… I…" Emotions raged now that the danger was past. She choked back a cry.

"You're all right. I've got you."

He held her like he'd never let go, and she never wanted him to. She melted into him, accepting his strength and his warmth, his care and concern. Love surrounded her as she held the man who had infiltrated her heart.

The man she would never let go.

Somewhere in the background men came. Edmund ordered them to take Roxbury away. The ruffian was already stirring, apologizing profusely and agreeing to all of Edmund's demands. Then they were alone again.

Finally, the tears slowed and then stopped, and she sniffed. He handed her a soft cloth. She wanted to stay like this forever, but things needed to be said. No longer was she determined to sacrifice their love. Somehow she would find a way to keep both her dreams.

He softly caressed her back. "Are you all right?"

"Yes, thanks to you. Did he hurt you?"

He shook his head, even as she continued to examine him. If he wanted the right to watch over her, she would care for him as well. Thankfully, he was unharmed. Large but slow Roxbury had barely connected, and Edmund was more disheveled than hurt.

"Edmund, I don't know what to say. I never imagined this would happen. Thank you for coming after me." She smiled through misty tears. "For always being there."

He smiled at her, but not with his typical mask. Brilliant emotion shone in his eyes.

Her breath hitched. It was almost as if he…

He straightened his suit, ran a hand through his hair. Then…

He handed her a letter.

CHAPTER TWENTY

Dear P,

It began with a letter.

A whisper of information, ink and paper and a quest to change the world. I chose you because of your tireless work to help the poor, yet something else formed: a connection, a kindred spirit, a familiar soul.

The letters were forged to make a difference, yet far more emerged. We shared stories of the past and present. Dreams for the future. Joys and heartbreaks, delight and pain. And as I came to know the mysterious Lord P, you went from informant to friend, from friend to best friend.

Without seeing your face, your letters told me who you are. You are kind and caring, clever and witty, heartfelt and sincere. We grew closer and closer, beyond the many secrets.

And then I found Lady Priscilla hiding behind a hedge.

In the letters it took months, yet some-

thing sparked within an instant of your true presence. A future filled solely with duty changed into something far more. And suddenly my emotion had a name.

Love.

I love you. Lord P. Lady Priscilla. It does not matter what I call you. It does not matter if it is through a letter or face to face. You bring joy I never imagined, a bright future I never dreamed possible.

I do not wish to stop you from the work that defines you. We will find a way to further the cause we both love. I have always said we could do more together. I truly believe that.

And so now I have a single question. One I am ASKING.

Priscilla, will you do me the honor of becoming my wife?

Yours,
Edmund

ALL ALONG SHE had been wrong. She had used her quest as an excuse, but the truth was she was scared. Scared Edmund did not love her as she loved him, scared to surrender herself, scared to receive such a precious love in return.

She feared no more.

"I love you, Priscilla. Since the moment I saw you hiding in the hedges, defiantly claiming innocence, I knew there was something extraordinary about you."

"Yes, and that statue–" She blushed deeply. "Never mind."

He smiled. "I apologize for my harshness when I discovered the truth, but I was horrified I had sent you into danger. I am protective, but I believe we can find a way for you to fulfill your calling, one that involves not a single drawing room, tea room, or–" He lifted an eyebrow. "Behind-the-hedges retiring room."

She laughed softly.

"Your work at the sanctuary changes lives. I'm certain there are many such places in need of help. I would like to find them and offer my assistance, yet I cannot do it alone. Perhaps you could aid me in this endeavor, identify where help is most needed, create sanctuaries and run them. It would be grueling, difficult work, but..."

"It would change lives," she breathed. Excitement grew in her. It was an opportunity to make a difference to so many people.

"As for your investigations, they can be continued."

Her breath hitched.

"In a way."

She gazed at him carefully. "What do you mean?"

"Am I correct that most of your information comes simply from conversations?"

She nodded. Much of her sleuthing did not involve anything more dangerous than a probing talk with the target lord, or his lady.

"If you promise to be subtle, I do not see harm in such efforts." He gazed at her earnestly. "Do you think it could be enough? Could you give up sneaking through the homes of criminal lords?"

After tonight, she never wanted to search a lord's house ever again. With his plan of researching and creating homes for those in need, she could help as many or more children than by endangering herself. When she needed a taste of action, she could continue her conversations. She could have everything.

Including the man she loved.

She stood up tall, kept her voice businesslike. "I need to write a letter."

"Now?"

She nodded.

He narrowed his eyes, but went to a desk, where he retrieved the necessary instruments. She took them and quickly sprawled a note.

He read it out loud.

Dear Edmund.

I will marry you.

Yours,
Lord P

P.S. I love you with all my heart.

He smiled widely and wickedly, a roughish

grin of pure happiness. He opened his arms.

And without a care as to who could see them…

She jumped into them.

"I love you, Priscilla. No matter who you are or what name you call yourself, you are my greatest gift."

She smiled with all the joy in her heart. "I love you, too."

He gave her one last lingering kiss. "Why don't we tell the world the good news, before the scandal we've been tempting finally arrives?"

"It's a miracle we're not the talk of London."

"Oh we are," he assured her. "But everyone knew we would wed."

"Oh they did?"

"Of course," he said in mock seriousness. "After all, it is what I commanded. And I am accustomed to winning."

She shook her head, yet could not stop the beaming smile.

"Are you ready for our announcement?"

Their betrothal. Instead of fear, pure joy flourished at the thought of being with this man forever. "Are you quite certain the announcement wasn't a banishment of all of the vases in London?"

He laughed. "I fear no vases. I am the Duke of Bradenton."

"Do not forget how powerful future duchesses can be. I have decided to extend an invitation for your sister to join the guild after all."

"Your sewing guild?"

She smiled. "My *social action* guild."

He laughed. "I should have known. But what of her guardian? I hear he is extremely strict."

"That's all right," she purred. "I have ways of accomplishing my goals when it comes to the Duke of Bradenton."

"I suppose he may be persuaded – at a cost."

"What cost is that?"

"You." He turned serious. "I will always love you," he promised. "And you will always be free."

She smiled through unshed tears. "And I will love you forever."

He held her close, her powerful warrior. "We will build a beautiful life together, forged in love and lasting into eternity."

And as usual…

The duke got his way.

The Duke of Bradenton and Lady Priscilla Livingston

Cordially invite you to their nuptials

Two will become one in a

Celebration of love, life and goodness

Note from the duke: If you choose to give a gift, I kindly request

No Vases

About the Author

Melanie Rose Clarke has wanted to be a writer since she was a little girl. Sixteen years ago, she married her own hero, and now she creates compelling stories with strong heroines, powerful males and, of course, happily every afters. She writes historical (regency) romance, contemporary romance, paranormal romance, romantic suspense and women's fiction.

Melanie is a three-time Golden Heart® finalist. Her manuscripts have earned numerous awards in writing competitions, including several first place showings. With over two decades of professional writing experience, Melanie has written thousands of pieces for businesses and individual clients. She has worked in advertising and markcting, and her freelance articles on the web have garnered hundreds of thousands of views.

She writes amidst her five beautiful children, her dream come true. Besides writing, she loves to read, exercise and spend time outdoors. She is a member of Mensa.

I love to connect with readers! For exclusive news and goodies, sign up for my newsletter at www.MelanieRoseClarke.com.

You can also find me on social media:
Facebook – facebook.com/MelanieRoseClarke
Twitter – twitter.com/MelanieS_Clarke
Bookbub – bookbub.com/profile/melanie-rose-clarke
Instagram – instagram.com/melanieroseclarke

www.ingramcontent.com/pod-product-compliance
Lightning Source LLC
Chambersburg PA
CBHW060756210726
48292CB00013B/190